Texas John
Slaughter

Texas John Slaughter

William W. Johnstone
with J. A. Johnstone

PINNACLE BOOKS
Kensington Publishing Corp.

www.kensingtonbooks.com

PINNACLE BOOKS are published by

Kensington Publishing Corp.
119 West 40th Street
New York, NY 10018

PUBLISHER'S NOTE
Following the death of William W. Johnstone, the Johnstone family is working with a carefully selected writer to organize and complete Mr. Johnstone's outlines and many unfinished manuscripts to create additional novels in all of his series like The Last Gunfighter, Mountain Man, and Eagles, among others. This novel was inspired by Mr. Johnstone's superb storytelling.

All Kensington titles, imprints, and distributed lines are available at special quantity discounts for bulk purchases for sales promotions, premiums, fund-raising, educational, or institutional use. Special book excerpts or customized printings can also be created to fit specific needs. For details, write or phone the office of the Kensington special sales manager: Kensington Publishing Corp., 119 West 40th Street, New York, NY 10018, attn: Special Sales Department; phone 1-800-221-2647.

ISBN-13: 978-0-7860-3366-9
ISBN-10: 0-7860-3366-5

First printing: April 2014

10 9 8 7 6 5 4 3 2 1

Printed in the United States of America

Authors' Note

This novel is loosely based on the life and times of legendary Old West lawman, rancher, and gambler John Horton "Texas John" Slaughter. The plot is entirely fictional and is not intended to represent actual historical events. The actions, thoughts, and dialogue of the historical characters featured in this story are fictional, as well, and not meant to reflect their actual personalities and behavior, although the authors have attempted to maintain a reasonable degree of accuracy.

In other words, none of what you're about to read really happened . . . but maybe it could have.

Chapter 1

John Horton Slaughter wore a grim, determined expression on his goateed face as he strode along the boardwalk toward the sounds of violence. People in his way hurriedly stepped aside.

They got out of Slaughter's way for two reasons: he was the sheriff of Cochise County, Arizona Territory, with the tin star pinned to his vest to prove it, and he carried a sawed-off, double-barreled shotgun with a familiar case that indicated he knew how to use it.

The shouted curses and crashes of furniture being thrown around came from Upton's Top-Notch Saloon and Gambling Establishment, a place that had been a thorn in Slaughter's side ever since he'd been elected sheriff a year or so earlier. The owner, Morris Upton, had come from back east somewhere and was a shady character as far as Slaughter was concerned.

Of course, at times he had also been considered a shady character—a rustler, even—by some folks, Slaughter reminded himself as he approached the saloon's bat-winged entrance. But that didn't make him feel any more sympathetic toward Morris Upton or the Easterner's rowdy saloon.

Today of all days, Slaughter thought angrily as he slapped the batwings aside and stepped into the saloon.

Peace didn't suddenly occur because of the sheriff's entrance. The brawl was too far advanced. At least two dozen men were wrestling, slugging, and trying to bash each other's brains out with broken table and chair legs.

Fortunately, no guns, knives, or broken bottles had come into play . . . yet.

Slaughter stood just inside the door and solemnly regarded the melee in front of him. He wasn't a big man, but power seemed to radiate from his compactly built frame, anyway. He was in his forties, a time when many men began to slow down as the years caught up to them, but not John Slaughter. He was still a vital, energetic man.

He had Viola to thank for that, he had thought many times. A beautiful, passionate wife would keep any man young.

As Slaughter looked across the room, his gaze locked with that of Morris Upton, who stood behind the bar with both hands resting on the hardwood. Upton's lean, saturnine face, topped with a shock of iron-gray hair, was creased in a frown, but Slaughter thought he didn't really look that unhappy about the brawl.

In the saloon business, a bad reputation could actually be good for business. The cowboys from the big cattle spreads came into Tombstone looking for excitement, and the Top-Notch certainly gave them that.

Slaughter recognized cowboys from several different crews among the combatants. When the other hands on those ranches heard about what had happened, they would be eager to come to town and settle the score.

Before they got around to that, though, they would guzzle down gallons of Upton's liquor and lose plenty of money to his house gamblers. Then, after any ruckus that broke out, he would collect damages, too.

It was a good setup, as long as you didn't care whether anybody got hurt.

Slaughter lifted the sawed-off and pointed the weapon toward the ceiling, then decided not to play into Upton's hands by blowing a hole in it. He waited until one of the battling cowboys reeled within reach and slapped the twin barrels against the side of his head, knocking him to the floor. The cowboy lay there, momentarily stunned.

The cowboy's friend saw what had happened and charged Slaughter, either not noticing or not caring that the newcomer was a lawman. Slaughter rammed the shotgun's barrels into the man's belly. When the man doubled over in pain, Slaughter brought the weapon's stock around in a sharp blow that cracked against the man's jaw and put him on the floor, too.

Wading into the brawl, Slaughter knocked down men right and left, sometimes with the shotgun and sometimes with a well-placed fist. As he cut a path through the battling cowboys, some of them began to realize what was happening and drew back. They didn't want to wind up being tossed into Slaughter's jail.

As Slaughter neared the bar, he grabbed an over-turned chair, dragged it with him, and used it to step up onto the bar. From that commanding position, he bellowed, "Hold it! The next man who throws a punch will do thirty days in the hoosegow!" His powerful voice cut across the hubbub in the big room.

Cowboys stopped fighting to turn and look up at the man standing on the bar.

Slaughter was an impressive sight, from his broad-brimmed, cream-colored hat to his expensive boots. He was a rich man, something many peace officers weren't, and always dressed well. He wore a gray tweed suit over a darker gray vest and white shirt, with a string tie around his neck. The suit went well with his dark hair and salt-and-pepper goatee.

In addition to the sawed-off shotgun, he carried a pearl-handled, Single Action Colt Army revolver holstered on his right hip. He was known to be fast on the draw, but he had even more of a reputation for deadly accuracy. When he fired his gun, he seldom missed, and everybody in Cochise County knew it.

"I'm glad you're here, Sheriff," Upton said. "Things were about to get out of hand."

Slaughter surveyed the damage in the saloon. "If they'd got any more out of hand, Upton, they would have pulled this place down around your ears."

"Oh, I doubt that would ever happen. Not with the sterling law enforcement we have here in Tombstone."

Slaughter managed not to snort in disgust, but it wasn't easy. Tombstone had a city marshal, but Slaughter and his deputies were the ones who really kept the peace most of the time. Upton knew that.

"I won't waste my time asking who started this," Slaughter told the sheepish cowboys who filled the saloon. "And I'm too busy today to drag anybody off to jail unless I have to. So clean up this mess and throw some money on the bar to pay for the damages. Then get out."

"What?" Upton exclaimed. "What do you mean by telling my customers to get out, Sheriff?"

Slaughter used the chair to climb down from the bar, then turned to Upton. "I mean just what I said. The Top-Notch is closed for the rest of the day . . . pending an investigation of this disturbance."

"You . . . you can't do that," Upton blustered.

"I'm the sheriff. I reckon I can."

"But that'll cost me ten times what the damages were!"

"That can't be helped. I'm sick and tired of having to come down here and break up these fights, especially when I have better things to do."

And today was a day when he had much better things to do, he thought.

"All right, Sheriff," Upton said, his voice curt.

Slaughter knew he had made an enemy out of the saloonkeeper, but he didn't care. He and Upton hadn't been friends to start with, and that would never change.

Slaughter stood there while the cowboys shuffled

around, set up the overturned chairs and tables, and coughed up the damage money. Then they all filed out of the saloon with gloomy expressions on their faces.

Upton wasn't the only one who seemed sorry to see them go. The frock-coated house gamblers and the girls in spangled dresses who served drinks and took customers upstairs glared at Slaughter, too.

When the saloon was empty of patrons, Slaughter told Upton, "This place will be closed down again every time a brawl breaks out in here."

"You can't hold me responsible for what my customers do," Upton insisted. "It's just not fair."

"Fair or not, that's the way things are going to be from now on." Slaughter tucked the scattergun under his arm and stalked out of the saloon before Upton could argue more.

He paused on the boardwalk outside and took his watch from his pocket. When he flipped it open, he saw that the time was almost three o'clock. Dealing with this trouble had caused him to cut it a little close, but he wasn't too late.

He walked toward the hotel where he lived when he was in town, which was most of the time, rather than on his ranch in the San Bernardino valley some sixty miles east of Tombstone. As he approached the hotel he saw a buggy rolling along the street from the opposite direction, trailed by half a dozen cowboys on horseback. A riderless saddle horse was tied on the back of the vehicle.

The buggy's driver, a young man with a shock of fair

hair under his pushed-back hat, brought it to a stop in front of the hotel. He hopped down and turned back to help his female passenger climb out of the buggy.

She wore a dark blue gown that managed to look elegant despite the thin, unavoidable layer of trail dust on it. Her figure was elegant as well, slender but curved in all the right places.

Her thick raven hair was piled atop her head in an elaborate arrangement of waves and curls, but several strands of it had escaped from their confinement and hung on the sides of her exotically attractive, olive-skinned face. As she turned to face Slaughter, he thought those loose strands of hair made her even more lovely.

Slaughter tossed the shotgun to the grinning youngster who had driven the buggy into town. The young man caught it deftly. A deputy's badge gleamed on the breast of his bib-front shirt.

As he held out his hands to the woman, Slaughter said, "Viola, I swear you look more beautiful every time I see you."

"Don't waste your time with flattery, Texas John," she told him as she took his hands. "I think you can put that silver-tongued mouth of yours to better use."

"I never argue with a lady." Slaughter drew her closer to him and kissed her. He drew back just long enough to add, "Especially my wife," then brought his lips down on hers again.

Chapter 2

John Slaughter was born in Louisiana, but raised in Texas. As he drifted west following the war and his first wife's death, first to New Mexico then on to Arizona, somewhere along the way he had picked up the nickname Texas John.

His personality was a bit reserved by nature, but he tolerated the name. However, he generally took offense if anybody called him "Tex."

His dear wife, however, could call him anything she wanted. Considerably younger than him, vibrant, beautiful, able to ride and shoot as well as most men and better than some, Viola Howell Slaughter was a true daughter of the West.

He had met her in New Mexico Territory while her father was driving a herd of cattle to Arizona. Their courtship had been a fiery, volatile one that met with some disapproval from her family because of their difference in age, but when it became obvious that John and Viola were madly in love with each other, their marriage was inevitable.

In the years since, they had worked side by side to establish Slaughter Ranch in the sage-covered San Bernardino Valley, and it was one of the most prosperous spreads in the territory. Viola loved the ranch so much she had been unwilling to move to Tombstone with Slaughter when he was elected sheriff, but she visited often.

The two of them sat in the hotel dining room, drinking coffee. The young, fair-haired deputy, who happened to be Viola's younger brother Stonewall Jackson Howell, came into the room, looked around, spotted the couple, and weaved his way around the tables toward them.

"Got the buggy put up, Sheriff," Stonewall reported as he took off his hat and held it in front of him. Despite the fact that Slaughter was his brother-in-law, Stonewall always treated him with respect. Slaughter was also his boss, and Stonewall wasn't likely to forget that.

"I appreciate it," Slaughter said. "And I appreciate you going out to the ranch to fetch Viola in, too. Such errands don't really fall within the scope of your duties as a deputy, after all."

"Shoot, I don't mind." Stonewall grinned. "It was a pretty day. I was glad for the excuse to get out of town." His expression sobered as he continued. "Heard that I missed another dustup in the Top-Notch, though."

"Morris Upton's place?" Viola asked with a frown. "He's been causing trouble for you ever since he came to Tombstone, hasn't he? You didn't tell me about the problem today, John."

Slaughter waved a hand. "There was nothing to tell, really. Just a bunch of cowboys beating on each other. I reasoned with them."

Stonewall said, "Reasoned with 'em by bendin' your shotgun barrels over a few heads, the way I hear it."

"Idle gossip always makes events sound more sensational than they really were," Slaughter snapped.

"Sure, Sheriff," Stonewall said. "Reckon I best get back over to the courthouse and see if Burt's got anything for me to do."

"That would be a good idea," Slaughter said dryly. "Your sister is staying for several days, so you won't have to take her back to the ranch for a while."

Stonewall put his hat on. "So long, Viola." He turned and left the dining room.

Viola sipped her coffee, then carefully placed the cup on its saucer. "Really, John, I don't know why you waste Stonewall's time sending him out to the ranch for me like that. I'm perfectly capable of coming into town on my own. I'd bring some of the hands with me like we did today, just in case of trouble."

"I know that. But I also know you're capable of getting it into your head that you could slap a saddle on a horse and ride all that way on your own."

"I'd be perfectly fine if I did. Or have you forgotten how well I can shoot?"

Slaughter wasn't likely to forget that. He had seen plenty of evidence of her gun-handling skills in the past.

"I know you can take care of yourself," he said gruffly, "but this part of the territory is still too wild for a woman to be traipsing around by herself, even one as competent as you, my dear. There are still renegade Apaches up in the mountains and gangs of rustlers roaming around, not to mention road agents who would be on the lookout for such a tempting target as yourself. No, I'll feel much better about your visits if you continue letting Stonewall or me fetch you whenever you want to come to town."

"What if he's gone sometime and you need all your deputies here?"

"I'll just have to make do."

"There's no point in arguing with you, is there?"

Slaughter smiled. "On this issue, very little."

They put that aside and talked for a while about what was going on at the ranch. So far, they hadn't been blessed with any children of their own, and he suspected that they wouldn't be.

However, they had taken in numerous foster children— white, Mexican, and Indian—and that meant the big adobe ranch house usually rang with laughter and young voices. Slaughter missed that pleasant hullabaloo as much as anything else about ranch life when he was in town.

Well . . . almost as much as anything else, he mused as he looked across the table at his young wife.

He was about to suggest that they adjourn to his suite upstairs when he heard a commotion out in the street.

Someone rode past the hotel shouting something, but he couldn't make out what it was.

Viola heard the racket, too. "Do you need to go see what that's about?"

"If it's trouble that I need to tend to, someone will come looking for me." He decided that it might be wise to postpone his plans for a few minutes, just in case.

Sure enough, less than ten minutes had gone by when Burt Alvord appeared in the arched entrance to the dining room.

Only twenty years old, which made him a few years younger than Stonewall, Burt was nevertheless Slaughter's chief deputy because of his tracking ability and his utter fearlessness in the face of danger. He was already half bald and wore a neatly trimmed mustache, which made him look older than he really was.

Slaughter could tell from the concerned expression on Burt's face that the deputy was looking for him. He stood up and picked up his hat from the table. "I'll see you later, my dear."

Viola got to her feet as well. "If you think I'm going to let you run off without finding out what this is about, Texas John, you'd better think again."

Slaughter didn't want to take the time to argue with her, so he just crossed the dining room with her in tow. "Is it safe out there, Burt?"

"Oh, yeah. There's no trouble, Sheriff, just some big news I thought you ought to know about."

"Then by all means, let's go hear the news."

Slaughter took Viola's arm, and they followed Burt

out of the hotel. A large crowd had gathered down the street in front of the assay office.

In recent years that office hadn't gotten as much work as it once had, back in the boomtown days of the Earps and the Clantons, roughly half a decade earlier. The silver deposits in the mountain ranges around Tombstone had begun to play out. If all the mines ever shut down, Tombstone could well wind up a ghost town, although there were enough ranches in the area that it might hang on to existence as a supply center for those spreads.

At the moment, some of the old excitement seemed to be back. Many of the townspeople and some cowboys who happened to be in the settlement listened avidly as a man unknown to Slaughter stood on the boardwalk in front of the assay office talking. "It's one of the biggest veins I've ever seen, I tell you. High-grade silver ore, too, enough of it to make everybody in this corner of Arizona rich!"

One of the listeners was a little skeptical. "If there was a vein like that anywhere in the Dragoons, it would've been found before now. Somebody's either salted a claim, or they're playing some other sort of trick on you, mister."

"Believe what you want, friend," the stranger said. "The fella in the assay office is running his tests right now on the ore I brought in. If you don't believe me, maybe you'll believe him."

As far as Slaughter could recall, he'd never seen the fellow who had brought the news of the silver strike into town. That made him a little leery of accepting the story at face value, although there was nothing unusual about strangers passing through Tombstone. With all the prospectors and drifting cowhands in the area, it happened all the time.

The uproar continued as some people eagerly believed the story while others dissented. Slaughter allowed it to continue. As long as people were just talking, the law had no need to step in.

A few minutes later, the assayer appeared in the office doorway and set off a new outburst of shouted questions. People wouldn't quiet down, even when the assayer tried to talk.

Slaughter told Viola, "Stay here." He added over his shoulder to his chief deputy, "Keep an eye on her, Burt."

Slaughter was smaller than many of the townspeople in front of him, but that didn't slow him down as he shouldered his way through the crowd. When the citizens realized who he was, they made room for him, and a moment later he stepped up onto the boardwalk with the assayer and the stranger who had brought in the ore.

When Slaughter faced the crowd and held up his hands, everyone quieted down almost immediately. He turned to the assayer and asked, "What about it, Tom? What's your opinion of the ore you just tested?"

"It assays out at just over eighty dollars per ton, Sheriff," the man replied. "Definitely high-grade ore."

That verdict brought excited shouts from the crowd. The naysayers were completely drowned out. The man who had brought in the ore whooped and shouted, "I told you! I told you so, didn't I?"

Almost instantly, the assembled townspeople began to scatter. Word of the new strike would spread like wildfire. Even though it was fairly late in the day, a lot of people would take off for the Dragoons right away, bent on beating everybody else to the mountains and filing claims on the new strike. The lure of getting rich quickly never wore off.

In fact, Slaughter saw it on the face of his chief deputy. Burt looked like the proverbial cat on a porch full of rocking chairs. He wanted to jump, but didn't know which way.

Slaughter looked around for the stranger. He intended to question the man more about the discovery. The assayer was the only one still standing on the boardwalk with him.

"Where'd that other *hombre* go?" Slaughter asked.

"I didn't notice him leaving, but he probably went to the general store to pick up some supplies and then head back to the mountains. That silver really is high-grade, Sheriff. If I had any desire to chip ore out of the rocks, I'd be right there with him. But I'm not really cut out for the mining life."

"Neither am I, not at my age," Slaughter growled. He looked at Burt Alvord again. "I have a hunch that all the young fellows in Tombstone won't agree with me, though."

Chapter 3

True to Slaughter's prediction, less than an hour later Tombstone had an empty look about it. The only men on the streets were grizzled old-timers, and fewer of them than usual. Many of the veteran prospectors had taken off for the Dragoons to make one more stab at hitting it rich.

Some of the storekeepers and clerks had stayed behind in town, along with the handful of doctors, lawyers, and other professional men. It would have been difficult to round up a dozen able-bodied men between the ages of twenty and fifty.

Including Sheriff John Slaughter's deputies.

By the time he'd gotten to the courthouse after escorting Viola back to the hotel and seeing her safely ensconced in his suite, Burt and Stonewall were out in front of the courthouse putting the finishing touches on the packs they had loaded on a couple mules.

Slaughter groaned. "Not you two. You're not gallivanting off to the mountains in search of a silver bonanza, are you?"

"I'm sorry, Sheriff," Burt replied, "but you heard what Tom said. Eighty dollars a ton!"

"Do you know how much work it is to mine a ton of ore?"

Stonewall said, "We're young and strong. We can handle it. And this might be our only chance to ever get rich, Sheriff!"

"I could forbid it, you know. You work for me. I could tell you to get rid of those pack mules and go on about your jobs."

"Yeah, but you won't. You remember what it was like to be young and a real go-getter."

Burt frowned, thinking that maybe Stonewall wasn't taking the best tack in the argument.

Slaughter had to chuckle at his young brother-in-law. "So I'm old and slothful, eh?"

"Well, no, that ain't exactly what I meant, John . . . I mean, Sheriff. It's just that only so many chances come along in a fella's life, and if he don't try to grab as many of 'em as he can, he winds up lookin' back someday and wishin' that he'd done things differently."

Slaughter could understand that. He had always done his best to seize the opportunities that came his way. Few things were worse than for a man to live a life of regret.

Besides, other than occasional brawls like the one

earlier in the Top-Notch, Tombstone and all of Cochise County had been pretty peaceful lately. No Indian raids, no rustlers driving wide-looped herds toward the border, no gunfights or murders.

"All right, The town will muddle along without you for a few days. But I'm still not convinced that strike is genuine. You're liable to wind up very disappointed."

"But you heard the assay report," Stonewall insisted. "Eighty dollars a ton! Isn't that what you told me, Burt?"

"It sure is," Burt agreed.

The optimism of youth, Slaughter thought. He waved a hand in the air. "Go ahead. But if you see that it's not going to pan out, I expect you to get back here without wasting any time."

"You can count on us, Sheriff," Stonewall said.

If that was true, they wouldn't be running off to the mountains to look for silver. But maybe he really was getting old, Slaughter told himself. And a man was only young once.

With Stonewall and Burt gone, he made the evening rounds himself. Tombstone was about as quiet as he had ever seen it. With the Top-Notch closed and the other saloons in town practically empty, the potential for trouble was almost nonexistent. Finished, he locked up the sheriff's office in the courthouse and went back to the hotel.

He might be too old to go running off to the mountains at the first wild rumor of a silver strike . . . but he wasn't too old to enjoy spending some time in the

company of the hot-blooded young woman he happened
to be married to.

The next day, from the top of a shallow rise just south
of town, a man peered through a pair of field glasses at
the streets of Tombstone. He lay there utterly still for
long moments as he studied the settlement. Morning
sunlight washed over it, revealing little movement.

Finally satisfied with what he saw, he lowered the
glasses and slid back down the slope. When he could
stand up in a crouch without the possibility of being
spotted from town, he did so and hurried toward a
nearby draw where several dozen men waited on horseback.

The man with the field glasses was about thirty years
old, lean, and darkly handsome. Stubble covered his
cheeks and jaw. He wore high-topped boots, whipcord
trousers, and a tan cotton shirt. A steeple-crowned sombrero hung on the back of his neck by its chin strap.

He carried a revolver holstered on his right hip, a
sheathed bowie knife on his left side, and had the in-
definable look of a man who knew how to use those
weapons.

As he went down the bank into the draw, one of the
riders edged his mount forward and asked in Spanish,
"How does the town look, Chaco?"

"Empty. Well, not totally, of course. A few people are
moving around. Women and old men, mostly."

The rider, who was as burly as Chaco was wolfishly

lean, threw back his head and laughed. "We have come to visit on a good day, eh, *amigo*?"

"You're right, Gabriel. We'll probably find little opposition." Chaco raised his voice. "That means it will be that much easier to ensure that no one is killed, eh, compadres?"

Despite his name, Gabriel appeared decidedly unangelic. He scowled. The other men looked as much like hard-bitten *bandidos* from south of the border as Chaco and Gabriel did, but mutters of agreement with Chaco's statement came from several of them. From the time they had crossed into Arizona, Chaco had made it clear that there would be no loss of life in Tombstone if at all possible. He had led them successfully so far in their campaign, so they weren't inclined to go against his orders.

Gabriel held the reins of Chaco's horse. He took them and swung up lithely into the saddle. After settling his sombrero on his head, tightening the chin strap, and checking to make sure that his Colt slid freely in its holster, he nudged the horse into motion and led the way toward Tombstone.

It was a little after nine o'clock. The bank had just opened.

Slaughter was in the habit of rising before sunup, but sometimes that habit was put aside, especially after a night spent in passionate reunion with his wife, whom he hadn't seen for several months.

As a result, the blazing red orb was well up in the sky before he sat down to breakfast in the hotel dining room. Viola was still upstairs asleep; he would take some coffee to her when he finished his meal.

He wondered how things were going with Stonewall and Burt and the other silver-seekers in the Dragoons. It was too soon for them to be discouraged, he thought with a faint smile. Dreams of a bonanza died hard.

But after a few long days of backbreaking labor with pick and shovel without finding any of that rich, high-grade ore—which was the outcome Slaughter fully expected—his two young deputies might start looking at things in a different light. They might decide that steady wages held more appeal than a lot of hard work for nothing.

When he had finished his steak and eggs and hotcakes, a buxom blond waitress in a starched white apron came over and asked with a sweet smile, "Would you like some more coffee, Sheriff?"

"No, thanks, Hannah, but if you'd pour a cup I can take upstairs to Mrs. Slaughter, I'd surely appreciate it."

"Of course. Is Mrs. Slaughter enjoying her stay in town?"

"Well, she only got here late yesterday afternoon . . . but I certainly hope so."

Slaughter stood up and walked over to the big front window while the waitress went to fetch the coffee. Only a few other people were in the dining room this late, and they didn't pay any attention to him as he looked out at the street.

His eyes narrowed slightly as he noticed a large group of riders drawing rein in front of the bank. The fact that they were all Mexicans didn't bother him; the number of them, about a dozen, did. His squint deepened as he looked along the street and saw two more groups of strangers, each about the same size, loitering on horseback at opposite ends of the street.

He hadn't been a lawman all that long, but he'd always had an instinct for trouble. Alarm bells ringing in his brain, he turned and strode back to the table where he had left his shotgun and snatched it up, then turned toward the door.

Hannah came out of the kitchen carrying a cup and saucer. "Sheriff? Your wife's coffee?"

"No time for it now," Slaughter snapped.

He was right about that. He had just stepped out of the hotel lobby onto the boardwalk when he heard gun thunder erupt from inside the bank.

Chapter 4

Viola Slaughter stretched in the bed. The sheets were smooth and luxurious as they slid against her bare skin and prompted a little sigh of contentment deep in her throat.

Of course, she had nice sheets on her bed in the ranch house, too, but that was different. With John in Tombstone nearly all the time, that bed was just for sleeping. Viola didn't take any particular pleasure in that.

She reached out, but his side of the bed was empty. She had expected that, so she wasn't actually disappointed. John was an early riser, usually up well before her. He had said something the night before about bringing coffee to her this morning, so she figured he was down in the dining room getting his breakfast. She would see him soon.

In the meantime, she got up, found the nightgown she had discarded in the throes of passion, and pulled it over her head.

Sitting down at the dressing table, she picked up her brush and started running it through her hair, which was loose and hung in thick dark waves below her shoulders. She wanted to look good when John came back upstairs.

The sound of gunshots somewhere outside made her eyes widen as she looked at herself in the dressing table mirror.

It wasn't that uncommon for guns to go off in Tombstone. The place had settled down some since its boomtown days, but drunken cowboys still had to let off steam and many arguments were still settled with lead.

But so early in the morning?

That seemed more sinister. She set the brush down, stood up, and moved to the open window, where a yellow curtain billowed slightly in the morning breeze. She pushed it aside and looked out.

The first thing she saw was her husband striding across the street at an angle toward the bank with his shotgun in his hands. As more shots blasted, she realized they came from the two-story, redbrick building that was John's destination.

As usual whenever trouble broke out, John Slaughter was headed straight for the middle of it.

Everything would have been all right if one stupid teller hadn't decided to be brave. The foolish *hombre* probably wanted to make a good impression on his boss, Chaco thought, and figured reaching for a gun was a good way to do it . . . even though he was outnumbered more than ten to one.

As for Gabriel, well, Chaco couldn't blame his old friend too much for what happened next. After all, the teller shot at him first, and Gabriel had reacted as any man would when he heard the whisper of a bullet passing close beside his ear.

He returned the fire. His shot was more accurate, smashing the teller's shoulder. At least Gabriel hadn't killed the man.

Emboldened by the teller's action and perhaps spooked by the slugs flying around, the bank president and two of the male customers produced pistols and started to blaze away at the robbers.

Chaco and a couple men had already cleaned out the tellers' drawers and the vault. They carried large canvas express pouches full of bills and gold pieces. Since the money was their only objective, Chaco shouted, "Let's go, let's go!" as he backed toward the bank's double front doors, a gun in his hand.

A bullet from the bank president's pistol whined near his head. Chaco triggered two swift shots in return. The bullets came close enough to the banker's head that they almost parted his pomaded hair. The man yelped and dived for shelter behind a desk, just as Chaco intended.

The two gun-wielding customers had scrambled for cover, but they continued throwing wild shots after Chaco and his men as the bank robbers fled. Gabriel roared a curse as a slug burned across his upper left arm. A man called Ricardo stumbled as he was hit in the leg.

Close by, Chaco holstered his gun and reached out quickly to grab Ricardo's arm and steady him. With Chaco's help, Ricardo was able to stay on his feet and get outside onto the boardwalk.

More shots exploded from both directions as the groups at the ends of the settlement began firing to provide a distraction and keep people off the street. Chaco and his men headed for their horses tied at the hitch rails in front of the bank.

A man shouted in a deep, powerful voice, "I say, I say! Hold it right there, you *hombres*!"

Chaco's head snapped around, and he saw a man with a sawed-off shotgun stalking straight toward them. The morning sun reflected off the sheriff's badge pinned to the man's vest.

Slaughter had recognized the signs of an impending bank robbery as soon as he spotted the three groups of men. The shots from inside the bank confirmed his hunch. A moment later, the bunch of Mexicans he had seen going in earlier came boiling out of the bank's front doors.

Shots roared from the ends of the street. Slaughter figured those for the rest of the gang clearing a path for a getaway.

He couldn't deal with that. He had plenty of trouble right in front of him. He shouted for the bandits to stop and leveled the scattergun at them.

One of the men yelled, "*Policía!*" and fired at

Slaughter. The bullet kicked up dust a couple feet to his right. Slaughter fired one of the shotgun's barrels.

The buckshot smashed into the man's chest and drove him backward off his feet. He fell under the hooves of one of the horses, spooking the animal. The other mounts danced around skittishly as their owners grabbed at them.

Several more bandits opened fire on Slaughter. He heard another man shouting in Spanish, but couldn't make out the words over the roaring guns. The bullets whistling around Slaughter's head forced him to throw himself down behind a water trough. It wasn't much cover, but it was better than nothing.

Rushing a dozen men by himself probably wasn't the best idea he'd ever had, he told himself. If his deputies had been where they were supposed to be, instead of off in the Dragoons trying to get rich, it would have been a different story.

Slaughter raised up quickly and let loose with the shotgun's other barrel. At least half of the bandits were mounted, but one fell off his horse as the animal reared up, stung by Slaughter's buckshot. Slaughter had to duck again as more bullets thudded into the trough, causing little splashes in the murky water.

He was pinned down. In a minute, as soon as all the robbers were mounted, they would sweep past him on their way out of town and probably fill him full of lead.

The sharp crack of a rifle suddenly split the morning air. Three rounds sizzled across the street toward the bandits. A woman's high, clear voice cried, "John, move! Get behind that wagon! I'll cover you!"

Startled, Slaughter turned his head to stare toward the hotel. Viola stood on the boardwalk, barefoot and beautiful in a long white nightgown with her thick dark hair falling around her shoulders. The Henry rifle in her hands spouted flame as she fired again at the robbers.

Viola didn't hesitate when she saw her husband about to confront the bank robbers. She knew he kept an extra rifle in the room's wardrobe. She jerked open the door, grabbed the Henry, and headed downstairs.

She knew anybody in the lobby and the dining room would stare at her as she ran past in her nightclothes, but it was not the time to worry about modesty. She dashed out onto the boardwalk and levered a round into the rifle's chamber.

As she lifted the Henry to her shoulder, she spotted John lying on the ground behind a water trough across the street, not far from where the bandits were trying to bring their milling horses under control. That was a bad spot for him to be.

Several yards in the other direction, someone had parked a wagon. John would be safer behind it, Viola decided. She cranked off three rounds from the Henry as fast as she could work the rifle's lever, then shouted to her husband and told him to move. She resumed firing.

All the confusion prevented her from being able to

tell if she had hit any of the robbers. They were all in the saddle except for the man who lay on his back with his arms outflung and his chest a bloody ruin where he had caught a charge of buckshot from John's sawed-off.

Viola was ready to duck back into the hotel if they returned her fire, but that wasn't what happened.

One of the bandits yanked his horse around and charged straight across the street at her. Viola's eyes widened in surprise as he rushed her. She tried to draw a bead on him, but he leaned forward over the neck of his straining mount as she squeezed the trigger. The shot missed.

She cried out as the man left his saddle in a diving tackle that carried him into her with a breathtaking crash.

Chaco couldn't have explained why he charged the woman with the rifle. He was upset to start with because so much had gone wrong. They had gotten the money, which was why they had come to Tombstone in the first place, but his hope had been that they could accomplish the goal without a lot of violence.

That ideal was ruined. Juan Segura lay dead in the street with his life blasted out of him by that lawman. Too many bullets were still flying around. Someone else was bound to get killed or hurt.

The woman with the rifle appeared and added to the chaos. Under different circumstances, Chaco would have been shocked at the way she displayed herself in public in a nightdress, but he was more worried about the .44-40 rounds she sprayed around his compadres. He had to stop her before she killed one of his *amigos*.

He took the simplest, most direct way of doing so.

Almost before he knew what was happening, he found himself lying on top of her on the boardwalk. She writhed and twisted underneath him as she reached for the rifle she had dropped as they fell. Chaco grabbed her wrist and stopped her from retrieving the Henry.

As she spat angry words at him that he barely heard, he surged to his feet and hauled her with him. Several of his men pounded up alongside the boardwalk.

"*Amigo!*" Gabriel shouted. "Bring her! They won't shoot if we have the señorita with us!"

Steal a young woman? Chaco's mind rebelled at the very thought.

And yet he knew Gabriel was right. A hostage would put a stop to the melee and save lives in the long run. He would make sure the young woman wasn't hurt, and they could release her as soon as they were well clear of Tombstone. The townspeople would find her in short order.

Even though doing so went against everything he considered moral and proper, Chaco pulled the young woman with him as he headed for his horse. Gabriel had caught the animal's reins and held them out to him.

"No!" the woman cried. Realizing what was about to happen, she swung a fist at his head.

She was a fighter, Chaco thought as he avoided the blow and took the reins from Gabriel.

His big, ugly friend leaned down from the saddle, looped a long arm around the woman, and hauled her up in front of him on the horse's back. "I will take care of her, *amigo*!" Gabriel declared with a leering grin.

That was better in a way, Chaco thought. He had already felt how soft and warm the woman's flesh was under the nightdress, and he didn't need a distraction of that sort as he tried to lead his men to safety.

Besides, despite the leer, Gabriel wouldn't harm her. He was a gentleman at heart.

Chaco leaped into the saddle and spurred for the edge of town. With his men surrounding him, Gabriel, and the beautiful hostage, they all galloped out of Tombstone and headed south.

Chapter 5

Slaughter lunged to his feet and broke for the parked wagon as Viola opened fire again, but he hadn't made it that far when he saw one of the bandits racing hell-bent for leather toward her. He hadn't had a chance to reload the shotgun, so he dropped it and jerked his pearl-handled Colt from its holster.

Before he could draw a bead on the bandit's back, several more mounted outlaws surged between him and the man. Slaughter heard Viola cry out. He started across the street, but a hail of bullets all around him forced him to throw himself behind the wagon, anyway.

He crouched there and snapped several shots at the gang, pretty sure he winged a couple men, but none of them toppled off their horses. Except for the man he had downed with the first blast from the shotgun, all the bank robbers were still in the saddle as they swept away from the front of the hotel like a whirlwind.

In the middle of that whirlwind, Slaughter saw to his horror, was his wife.

He caught only a glimpse of Viola perched on the back of a horse in front of one of the bandits, but the flash of white nightgown and the thick, wavy black hair flying in the wind told him without any doubt that it was her. He shouted her name, but had no way of knowing if she heard him.

Several townspeople came out onto the boardwalks holding guns. As they pointed the weapons at the fleeing bandits, Slaughter bellowed, "Hold your fire! Hold your fire, I say!"

With Viola in the midst of the outlaws, there was too great a risk that a stray slug might hit her. Even though he was outraged that they would carry her off, her safety was the most important thing to consider.

Slaughter looked around wildly for a saddled horse at one of the hitch rails. His only thought was to go after the men and rescue his wife.

He didn't see any horses nearby, and even if there had been, he couldn't chase down several dozen outlaws on his own. Even if he caught up to them, they would riddle him with bullets and Viola wouldn't be any better off than she had been.

Worse, really, because with Slaughter dead there wouldn't be anybody left in Tombstone to put together a posse and go after the bandits.

The fleeing riders had reached the edge of town. As they started out into the semi-desert landscape that surrounded the settlement, their horses kicked up a huge cloud of dust that rose behind them and screened them from view.

Bitter anger filled Slaughter's heart as he stared after the men who had kidnapped his wife.

"Sheriff Slaughter! Sheriff, they cleaned us out! They took everything!"

The frantic voice made him turn to see Cyrus Stockard, the president of the bank, coming toward him. Stockard was always neatly groomed, but he looked disheveled and half-panicked. He held a Smith & Wesson .38 in his hand, probably the gun that he kept in a desk drawer in case of robberies.

Not that it had done much good.

Despite the fear he felt for Viola, Slaughter forced his mind back to his job. "Anybody hurt at the bank, Mr. Stockard?"

"They shot Tim Gaines, one of my tellers. I don't know how badly he's wounded. I've already sent for the doctor."

"What about you?"

Stockard shook his head. "I'm fine, just cleaned out. They looted the tellers' cages and the vault and took every dime, Sheriff. Every dime!"

"We'll get the money back," Slaughter vowed, although he knew good and well that if it ever came down to a choice between his wife and the bank's money, he would pick Viola without a second's hesitation. He intended to bring both her and the money back safely.

"How can you get it back?" Stockard demanded. "You can't organize a posse and go after them. Most of the men in town are gone!"

Stockard was right about that, Slaughter thought grimly. It wasn't only his deputies who had run off to the Dragoons to look for silver. Nearly all the men he normally would have recruited for a posse had been bitten by the fortune-seeking bug, too.

"We'll worry about that a little later," he said with another glance at the dwindling cloud of dust south of town. "Right now, I need to see if anyone else was hurt in the raid."

For the next few minutes Slaughter hurried up and down the street, checking with the merchants, even though every moment that passed meant Viola and her captors were getting farther away from him.

Several stores had been robbed during the chaos, as well as the bank. But surprisingly, considering the hundreds of bullets that had flown back and forth during the fracas, none of the townspeople had been killed and only a few citizens were wounded. Tim Gaines's bullet-shattered shoulder seemed to be the worst injury.

All the outlaws had gotten away except one, and that man was a job for the undertaker. Slaughter stood over the man and looked down at his unfamiliar, beard-stubbled face.

"Ever seen him before, Sheriff?"

The question made Slaughter look around. He recognized Luther Gentry, an elderly beanpole of a man who owned one of the livery stables in town. In overalls, a flannel shirt, and a shapeless old hat, he was an unimpressive figure.

"No, he's a stranger," Slaughter said in answer to the liveryman's question. "From the looks of him, though, I'd say he was a *bandido* from below the border."

"That's what they all looked like to me," Gentry said. "I seen 'em gallop past my barn on their way outta town. I would've taken a shot at the varmints with my old muzzle-loader, but I, uh, saw that they had a lady with 'em. Looked like your missus, Sheriff."

"That was Mrs. Slaughter, all right."

"Reckon you'll be goin' after 'em?"

"Of course I will."

"Then I want to come with you."

Slaughter frowned. "I appreciate that, Luther, but—"

"You think I'm too old," Gentry broke in. "Could be I am, but I can keep up better'n you think I can, Sheriff. Miz Slaughter's always been mighty nice to me. She always comes by the stable when she's in town to check on her buggy team, but I got the feelin' she mainly just wants to say howdy."

Slaughter didn't doubt that. Raised as the daughter of a frontier cattleman, Viola had never been one to put on airs or consider herself better than other folks. She was just as comfortable talking to a liveryman or a chuckwagon cook as she was conversing with the territorial governor.

He didn't have much to choose from when it came to a posse, either, Slaughter reminded himself.

"Thank you, Luther," he told the old-timer. "You say you've got a rifle?"

"Yeah, and an old cap-and-ball hogleg, too."

"Bring them both, and all the ammunition you can carry. Pick out a good horse from your stock and meet me in front of the courthouse in half an hour."

"I'll be there," Gentry said with an eager nod. "We'll get them varmints, you'll see, Sheriff."

"I hope you're right," Slaughter said.

For the sake of all that bank money and the other loot the outlaws had carried off . . . but mostly for Viola.

Slaughter spent the next half hour gathering his posse, for want of a better word, and supplies for the chase after the bandits. He couldn't afford to wait any longer. The border was less than fifty miles away, and his jurisdiction ended there.

Not that a matter of jurisdiction was going to stop him where Viola's safety was concerned. But he couldn't ask the men who were going with him to break the law by following the bandits into Mexico.

The only good thing was that the Mule Mountains lay directly between Tombstone and the border. The raiders would have to go around the mountains or through them, and either way would slow them down some.

Slaughter was stalking along the boardwalk like a caged panther when a redheaded kid about twelve years old stopped him and asked, "Can I come with you, Sheriff?"

"What's your name, son?" Slaughter replied with a frown.

"Sammy Shay, sir."

"How old are you, Sammy?"

"I'm fourteen," the youngster declared. Slaughter thought he was probably fudging by a couple years.

"Well, that's too young to ride with a posse." Slaughter held up a hand to forestall Sammy's argument. "But I've got a job for you if you want it. Can you ride fast?"

Sammy's head bobbed up and down eagerly. "I sure can!"

"Got a good horse?"

"Yes, sir, a sweet little mare."

"Then saddle her up and light a shuck for the Dragoons, Sammy. You know my deputies Stonewall Jackson Howell and Burt Alvord?"

"Sure I do." Sammy looked down at the ground for a second. "They, uh, chased me when I was shootin' off firecrackers on the Fourth of July."

Even under the grim circumstances, Slaughter almost chuckled. "All right. You find my deputies and tell them what happened here today. Tell them I said to rattle their hocks back to town and pick up the posse's trail. Pass that word to every other man from Tombstone you see up there in the mountains. Can you do that?"

"You bet I can! You want me to go now?"

"Just as fast as you can," Slaughter said.

Sammy turned and sprinted for home and that mare of his, while Slaughter continued on down the street till he reached the courthouse.

Fewer than ten men had gathered in answer to his summons. The bank robbers would outnumber them by a margin of more than three to one.

It was a pretty motley group of posse men, too. Slaughter saw the other two bank tellers, Ross Murdock and Joseph Cleaver. He wondered if the young men were volunteering because they wanted to or because their boss Cyrus Stockard had ordered them to.

Diego Herrara, the cook at one of the local hash houses, was there, as was the saddle maker, Grover Harmon. Herrara was too fond of his own cooking and was almost as wide as he was tall, while the stocky, walrus-mustached Harmon was as old as Luther Gentry. The two old-timers were friends, too, Slaughter recalled.

Pete Yardley owned a general store and was one of the merchants who'd been robbed by the bandits. With his spectacles, thinning brown hair, bushy mustache, and prominent Adam's apple, he looked about as dangerous as a buttermilk pie.

Jack Doyle was a professional gambler who worked most often in Upton's Top-Notch. His presence surprised Slaughter. Evidently he didn't hold a grudge against the sheriff just because his boss did.

A sweating, red-faced, heavyset man in a brown tweed suit and a derby was a stranger to Slaughter. He introduced himself as Chester Carlton and explained that he was a drummer who'd been staying at the hotel. "I'd like to come along with you if that's all right, Sheriff. I've been traveling around out here in the West for quite a while, but never had the chance to take part in any real excitement."

"You may get more *excitement* than you bargain for, Mr. Carlton," Slaughter warned him. "But if you can stay in the saddle and pull the trigger on a gun, I won't refuse your offer of help." He looked around at the others. "Anybody need a gun? There are rifles in the sheriff's office if you do."

Murdock, Cleaver, and Carlton all spoke up. Slaughter took them inside the courthouse and armed them with fairly new Winchesters and boxes of ammunition. The other men all had weapons of their own, and the armament was as wide an assortment as they were, including single-shot rifles, repeaters, pistols, and shotguns.

Better than nothing, Slaughter thought.

He hoped fervently that he wasn't going to get all these men killed.

Chapter 6

Viola was scared, but knew better than to let her fear take control of her. If she allowed that to happen, she would be paralyzed with terror and wouldn't be able to escape, even if the opportunity arose.

The big bandit holding her in front of him on the horse was a bit free with his hands, but he didn't grope her too shamelessly. She tried a couple times to twist out of his grip, but couldn't budge his arm. She gave up when she realized that if she jumped off while they were galloping, she would probably break her leg . . . or her neck.

Like it or not, she told herself, she might be better off biding her time and waiting for a better chance.

The outlaws didn't slow down until Tombstone fell several miles behind them. When they finally pulled their mounts back to a walk, Viola tried to turn and look behind them, but she couldn't see over her captor's shoulder.

He laughed. "Ha, little one, you look for your *novio*, eh? You think he's coming after you?"

"I know he will," Viola said. "He's—" She stopped herself before she said *Sheriff of Cochise County*. If the bandits knew she was married to a lawman, they might consider her an even more valuable hostage and hang on to her longer. She hoped they would release her once they were well clear of the settlement.

"Don't get your hopes up, *chiquita*," the big man told her. "I already looked. There's nobody back there."

Despite her determination to be strong, Viola's heart sank. She knew John would come after her, of course, but she would have felt better if he was already on the trail with a posse.

A posse, she thought. Where was he going to get a posse with most of the able-bodied men in Tombstone off looking for silver in the Dragoon Mountains?

A groan of despair welled up her throat. She forced it back down for two reasons.

First of all, she wasn't the sort to give up. She never had been and never would be. For another thing, she didn't want to give the brute holding her the satisfaction of knowing that she was scared.

The man who had tackled her on the boardwalk and knocked the Henry out of her hands had been riding a little ahead of her and the big outlaw. He let his horse drop back until he was alongside them.

Viola noticed he was younger and slimmer. When he looked over at her, she thought she saw something . . . haunted . . . in his dark eyes.

He asked, "Are you all right, señorita?"

She didn't correct him and tell him that she was a señora. The less they knew about her, the better. Unobtrusively, she slipped off her wedding band and closed her hand around it.

"How do you think I am?" she asked tensely. "Attacked, dragged off the street, kidnapped! If you have any decency, sir, you'll release me right now!"

He tried to look her in the eyes, but his gaze dropped to her body and then jerked away as guilt flashed in his eyes. Even though the white nightgown was very plain, not provocative, and covered her from neck to feet, he suspected there was nothing underneath it except her. Clearly that bothered him.

"Releasing you was exactly what I intended, señorita, but now that I have had time to think about what happened in Tombstone, I believe things have changed."

"What are you talking about?" she snapped.

"You came to the aid of the sheriff. I heard you call out to him. The two of you know each other."

She put a disdainful tone in her voice as she said, "Everyone in Tombstone knows Sheriff John Slaughter."

"*Sí*, the famous Texas John. I have heard that in addition to being a lawman, he owns a large rancho east of here in the San Bernardino Valley. Everyone in Arizona Territory knows of John Slaughter."

"Then you know you don't want him on your trail," Viola said. "You'll be better off if you leave me right here and head for the border as fast as you can."

The young man seemed to be the leader of the bank

robbers. "I would if I had not seen Sheriff Slaughter's face as we rode out of Tombstone with you as our prisoner. It was the face of a man losing a loved one."

Viola frowned, but didn't say anything. The bandit had made some big assumptions, but he had drawn the right conclusions.

"I think in the long run we may be safer, as long as we have the daughter of Sheriff John Slaughter as our prisoner."

Well, maybe not *all* the right conclusions, Viola thought.

Luther Gentry furnished horses for the members of the posse who didn't own one, along with a couple pack animals. With the border as close as it was, the chances of them needing as many supplies as they were taking were small. It didn't seem likely the posse would be gone from Tombstone for that long.

But there was no guarantee the outlaws would cross the border into Mexico. They could always turn and head in another direction, and Slaughter thought it was possible they might do just that in hopes of eluding pursuit. It was better to be prepared for anything.

Slaughter was a man of strict habits, and he credited that discipline for much of his success in life. But he was also a man who played hunches from time to time, relying on his instincts to tell him when to do so. He had learned to be ready to take action when such a hunch came to him.

Luther Gentry and Grover Harmon moved their horses up alongside Slaughter's. Harmon was as short and squat as Gentry was tall and skinny. The wide-brimmed brown hat Harmon wore had an unusually tall crown, as if to make up for his lack of stature. A magnificent mustache stuck out on either side of his face and curled down to frame his mouth.

"We tried to get some more members of the Spit 'n' Whittle Club to come along with us, Sheriff," Harmon said.

Slaughter recognized the reference to the group of old-timers who got together almost every day on the benches near the public well.

"The rest of 'em begged off on account of rheumatiz and the like. Those old men are a bunch of complainers, I tell you what."

"It ain't like we don't do our fair share of complainin', Grover," Gentry pointed out. "Wasn't it you who was just talkin' this mornin' about his piles?"

"Well, yeah, but that's a legitimate complaint. Sheriff, did you ever have that terrible itch—"

Thankfully, the sound of swift hoofbeats coming up from behind them interrupted Harmon's question.

Slaughter reined in and turned in the saddle to see who was following them. He didn't recognize the rider, who wore tan pants, suspenders, and a patched, faded work shirt. A battered old bowler hat was pulled down low over his ears. The newcomer held an old Springfield rifle across the saddle in front of him. Evidently he intended to join the posse.

"Who's that?" Slaughter muttered.

The other men had reined in to look back, too. Gentry shaded his eyes with a hand and squinted for a moment. "Appears to be Mose Tadrack."

The name was vaguely familiar to Slaughter, but he couldn't place it. "Who's Mose Tadrack?"

"Swamper down to the Oriental Saloon," Harmon answered.

"He can't figure on throwin' in with us," Gentry said. "I don't think I've ever seen the fella when he wasn't at least half drunk. Most of the time he'd fall down if he wasn't hangin' on to a broom or a mop."

That didn't sound like a promising recruit to Slaughter. He was already saddled with a posse that might have trouble bringing in a band of marauding pie thieves. He didn't need a drunkard, to boot.

Tadrack rode up to where Slaughter sat on horseback. Up close, he was even less impressive, with a receding chin that made his Adam's apple look like it stuck out more than normal. But he was sitting fairly straight in the saddle, and his eyes, although a little watery, were clear. "Sheriff, if you're going after those skunks who carried off Mrs. Slaughter, I'd like to come with you."

Slaughter was a little impressed that Tadrack mentioned Viola being kidnapped, but didn't say anything about the bank money. "It's liable to be dangerous, Tadrack."

"Yes, sir, I know," the swamper said with a nod. "But as soon as I heard what happened, I . . . I knew I wanted to help. It just took me a little while to get ready."

"To sober up, you mean," Harmon said.

A flush crept over Tadrack's face. "Yes sir, Mr. Harmon. That's what I mean."

Gentry asked, "How many gallons of coffee did you pour down your throat, Mose?"

"Enough," Tadrack replied curtly. Then Slaughter heard him mutter under his breath, "I hope."

Slaughter didn't appreciate the two old-timers horning in with their questions when he was in charge of the posse. "Why do you want to come with us, Tadrack? What's Mrs. Slaughter to you?"

"Why, I doubt if she even knows I exist, Sheriff. I'm sure she doesn't know my name. But one night when I was . . . under the weather . . . she helped me get back to my shack. She even came in and fixed me something to eat. I . . . I couldn't believe it . . . a lady like her giving a hand to the likes of me. . . ."

"I believe it," Slaughter said quietly. It sounded exactly like something Viola might do, even though he would have fussed at her for taking such a chance if he had known about it. He lifted his reins. "If you want to come with us, you're welcome."

Then he turned his horse and rode south again, with the rest of the posse trailing behind him.

Chapter 7

The blue-gray peaks of the Mule Mountains loomed in front of the outlaws as they continued southward. Clumps of manzanita and juniper covered the steep slopes that were cut by deep canyons. Viola had been in the Mules before, but was not overly familiar with them.

"Are you going through the mountains?" she asked Chaco.

He still would hardly look at her. With his gaze facing ahead, he replied, "To go around them would take an extra two days to reach our destination."

"And what's that? The border?"

Chaco didn't say anything. He had the extremely annoying habit of ignoring questions he didn't want to answer.

It always made Viola angry when she said something to someone and they acted like they hadn't even heard her when she knew good and well they had.

"You're wrong about me, you know," she said sharply.

"I'm not Sheriff Slaughter's daughter. My family is just acquainted with his, that's all."

That wasn't exactly a lie. John had met her father and brothers on the trail during a cattle drive over in New Mexico Territory, even before the two of them were introduced,

Again Chaco didn't reply, but the big man, whose name Viola had learned was Gabriel, chuckled. "Even if you're just a family friend, señorita, you are very valuable to us. A young, beautiful hostage is the best kind to have!" Laughter boomed out from him.

Viola restrained the impulse to drive an elbow back into his gut. It wouldn't do any good. He was built like a barrel, and his stomach was hard as one.

Now that some time had passed since the raid on Tombstone and her kidnapping, her fear had subsided somewhat. She didn't trust the hardened outlaws not to harm her, of course, but she didn't seem to be in any immediate danger. At the moment, she was more angry than anything else, but she knew it wouldn't do any good to give in to that feeling.

They reached the foothills by early afternoon and climbed into them. At the top of a hill that would give them a good view back to the north, Chaco reined in and lifted a hand in a signal for the others to halt.

He slid down from his saddle, pushed his sombrero back off his head, and raised a pair of field glasses to his eyes as he peered back in the direction they had come from.

Gabriel dismounted as well. He stood beside the horse

and held up his arms. "Come on, little one. I'll help you down so you can walk around a little."

"What if I don't want down?" she snapped.

"We've been riding for quite a while," Gabriel said with a shrug. "And you're not exactly dressed for it, señorita."

That was certainly true. As a matter of fact, Viola very badly wanted to get off the horse for a few minutes. But she didn't want to admit it to the big bandit.

Discomfort won out over pride and stubbornness. "Oh, all right."

She reached down to take hold of his arms as he lifted her off the animal's back. Having solid ground under her again felt good, even though the sandy surface was hot on the soles of her bare feet.

Chaco lowered the field glasses. "I don't see anyone, but they're back there. I can feel them coming after us."

"Of course they're back there. Sheriff Slaughter isn't going to let you get away with robbing the bank or with kidnapping me. You'd still be better off to release me before he catches up to you."

Gabriel waved a hand at their rugged surroundings. "Leave a beautiful señorita stranded in a place like this full of cactus and scorpions and rattlesnakes? That would be a terrible thing to do!"

Viola had to admit, at least to herself, that she wouldn't enjoy spending much time in these mountains on her own, especially in her state of undress. She didn't want to continue as the outlaws' captive, but she had started to wonder if she wouldn't be safer in their company for the time being.

Something had to be done about certain situations, though. She stepped in front of Chaco and forced him to look at her. When he tried to turn his eyes away, she moved so that he couldn't help but see her. "I need some clothes and some privacy in which to put them on."

He frowned and shook his head. "I'm sorry. We don't have any clothes suitable for a lady."

"I don't care if they're suitable. A spare shirt and a pair of trousers will be better than what I have on. A hat and a pair of boots or some moccasins would be good, too. Honestly, you can't expect me to ride all the way to Mexico dressed only in a nightgown!"

Stubbornly, he looked away from her again, but not before his eyes flicked down to her body, followed by the same flash of guilt she had seen in them earlier.

"I will see what I can do," he muttered. "Gabriel, watch her."

"*Sí*," Gabriel said, grinning again. "Never have you given me a more pleasant job, *amigo*."

The other men had dismounted to rest their horses. Chaco walked over to them, "Ortiz!"

A small man with a mustache that looked like a fuzzy caterpillar crawling across his upper lip stepped up. Chaco spoke to him in rapid Spanish. Viola followed the exchange with no trouble as Ortiz replied. After spending a number of years in Arizona Territory, she spoke Spanish like a native.

Chaco asked the man if he had any spare clothes.

Ortiz answered that he had an extra shirt but only the trousers he wore. Chaco told him to fetch the shirt, then asked among the other men for a pair of trousers. He had to check with several of them before someone finally agreed to supply the garment.

Several minutes later, Chaco came back to Viola with a faded red shirt and a pair of denim trousers draped over his right arm. He had a pair of moccasins and a flat-crowned hat in his left hand. "This is the best I can do. The pants will be too long, I am sure, but we can cut some off the legs once you have them on."

"Thank you," she replied stiffly. "Now there's a matter of privacy . . ."

"Of course. You can go behind those manzanita bushes over there."

He pointed to a clump of several bushes that were tall enough and thick enough to provide at least a semblance of decency, Viola thought, although it was possible a few flashes of skin might be seen through them as she changed.

Not by Chaco, however, since she was sure he would keep his eyes averted the whole time. She didn't expect such consideration from the rest of the outlaws.

Chaco handed the clothes to her and then surprised her by following her over to the manzanitas. "You go behind the bushes. I'll turn my back, but keep talking to me so I'll know you're there."

"Such a gentleman," she said dryly. To tell the truth, she was grateful to him for getting her the clothes, but she didn't want him to know that. Her gratitude only went so far. After all, he was the one who had kidnapped her in the first place.

"You haven't told me your name," he said when the manzanita bushes were between them.

"It's Viola," she said without thinking, then wished she had lied about it. Since he had heard of Sheriff John Slaughter, there was a chance he had heard of the sheriff's wife Viola, too. Since he already suspected there was a connection between her and John, that might be enough to confirm it.

Chaco didn't seem to think anything about it. "Viola. That's a lovely name. My name is Chaco Romero."

"All right." She wasn't about to compliment him on his name. Since he wanted her to keep talking, she asked, "What made you become an outlaw, Señor Romero?"

That question drew the most animated response she had gotten from him so far. "I am not an outlaw!"

Viola lifted the nightgown to her waist and stepped into the trousers. "You certainly looked like one to me when you were robbing the bank in Tombstone." She heard him sigh.

"That was regrettable but necessary to further our cause."

She lifted the nightgown to her neck, draped it in front of her, and put her arms in the shirt sleeves, buttoning it quickly. "You're a revolutionary!" she guessed.

"That is correct. My men and I are dedicated to over-throwing the dictator Díaz and the restoration of the rightful rule of law to Mexico."

Viola knew that one revolution or another was always

brewing in Mexico and had been ever since General Porfirio Díaz had taken over as president a little more than a decade earlier. She had no doubt that some of the revolutionaries were sincere in their desire to improve the lot of their countrymen, but she also knew that many of them used the political upheaval as an excuse for looting, raping, and killing. It remained to be seen which sort of "revolutionaries" these men really were.

So far, other than Chaco's stiff-necked prudery, she hadn't seen any indications that they were anything other than bandits.

As Chaco had told her, the trousers were too long, but she rolled the legs up at the bottom and saw no need to cut them off. She pulled the nightgown over her head then slipped her feet into the soft leather moccasins, grateful for their protection. Walking around barefoot in the desert was asking for trouble.

The moccasins were a little loose, but fit fairly well. One of the outlaws must have small feet, she thought. She had hung the hat on a branch. She picked it up, settled it on her head, and drew the strap taut under her chin.

"Señorita Viola?" Chaco said.

"I'm here," she replied. He had told her to keep talking so he would know she wasn't trying to sneak off, but she had forgotten.

She stepped out from behind the bushes. The shirt was a little tight across the bosom, so she had been forced to leave the top button unfastened. She had also rolled the sleeves up over her forearms. Strictly speaking, more skin was exposed than there had been while she was wearing the nightshirt, but she felt more decently dressed.

Gabriel let out a low whistle of admiration. "You look like a little revolutionary yourself, *chiquita*. I'd say you should give her a gun, Chaco, but she would probably shoot us all!"

"Until I ran out of bullets," Viola said.

Gabriel threw back his head and bellowed with laughter.

Chaco just shook his head. "The horses have rested long enough. Everyone mount up. I want to be deep in the mountains by nightfall."

Chapter 8

Slaughter scanned the horizon ahead of the posse in search of a dust cloud kicked up by the gang's horses, but he didn't see anything. If the bandits had pushed their mounts hard for the first few miles after fleeing Tombstone, they could have a good long lead.

At least he knew he was still on the right trail. It didn't take much of a tracker to follow the wide swath of hoofprints left behind by the horses. The bandits didn't seem to be going to any trouble to conceal their tracks. Evidently, speed was more important than anything else.

Pete Yardley pushed his horse alongside Slaughter's. "Sheriff, I hope you're not holding back on account of me and the other fellas. We can handle a faster pace if you want."

Slaughter glanced over at him, a weedy gent in his late forties. "I'm trying to keep from wearing out the horses too soon, Pete. We may have to make a dash later, and I want them to be as fresh as possible."

"Oh. Well, that makes sense, I reckon." Yardley hesitated, then went on. "It's just that we know you probably don't have a whole heap of confidence in us. We're not the sort of fighting men you're used to having at your back when you're riding into trouble. But we won't let you down, Sheriff. You have my word on that."

"Thanks, Pete. I'm mighty glad to have you fellows along with me."

As a matter of fact, Yardley was right. Slaughter *had* been holding back a little. He knew if they caught up to the outlaws, his inexperienced posse would have to take on a far superior force. There was a good chance all of them would be shot to ribbons, and then Viola wouldn't be any better off than she was before.

Possibly less, because she wouldn't have any value as a hostage if the pursuit was eliminated.

Slaughter's real hope was that redheaded Sammy Shay, the kid he had sent galloping to the Dragoons, would find Stonewall and Burt and send them racing back to Tombstone with a lot of the other men who had gone to the mountains to look for silver. They would be a real posse, and it might be enough to tip the odds in their favor.

Strategically, that was the best course of action, and Slaughter knew it.

At the same time, the knowledge that his wife was the helpless prisoner of a gang of vicious outlaws gnawed at his guts like a starving coyote. There was no telling what they might be doing to her, but chances were it wouldn't be anything good.

The hours on the trail dragged past, but the day seemed to rush by. The Mules loomed in front of them, maddeningly close to all appearances, but still out of reach. Slaughter's original estimate of how long it would take to reach the border faded to insignificance. The posse would be spending at least one night on the trail.

Late in the afternoon, they came to a small creek that twisted through a wider, shallow streambed. It would be a good place to camp, Slaughter decided, because in Arizona Territory a traveler didn't ignore the presence of water. It was a commodity sometimes difficult to come by.

"We'll stop here for the night," he announced, even though part of him cried out to go on. He had to put aside his personal feelings and be a smart lawman. They couldn't risk losing the trail in the darkness.

The men dismounted, glad to be out of the saddle for the night.

Scrubby junipers and oaks grew along the banks of the streambed, which probably ran full only during times of flash flood. Slaughter set Murdock and Cleaver, the two bank tellers, to gathering enough wood for a small fire. He looked at Herrara. "You won't mind cooking for us, will you, Diego?"

"Of course not, Señor Slaughter," the squat Mexican said. "I brought along some tortillas and frijoles and some cabrito and chiles for stew."

Slaughter clapped him on the shoulder. "Good man. We'll eat well tonight, anyway."

As a stableman, Gentry naturally took over tending to the horses, with his friend Grover Harmon to help him. The two old-timers let the animals drink from the creek, then picketed them where there was some graze.

"We'll set up guard shifts," Slaughter told the group. "Two men at a time, five shifts. No one should miss out on too much sleep that way."

Figuring that it would be a good idea not to have the two oldest members of the posse standing watch at the same time, he split up Gentry and Harmon, pairing the stableman with Ross Murdock and the saddle maker with Joseph Cleaver. Slaughter didn't want the two inexperienced bank tellers on duty at the same time, either, so that worked out.

As for the others, he put Herrara with Pete Yardley and Jack Doyle with Chester Carlton.

That left Mose Tadrack for Slaughter to pair up with. He went over to the swamper. "How are you doing, Tadrack?"

"I . . . I reckon I'm fine, Sheriff," Tadrack said. His Adam's apple bobbed up and down as he swallowed. He held out his right hand in front of him. In the fading light, Slaughter saw how it trembled. "I won't lie, I'm a little shaky. Could use a drink. But I didn't bring any with me, and the sun burned all the booze outta me today. So I'll be all right as soon as my nerves settle down."

"I hope so. You'll be standing guard with me tonight. Think you can handle it?"

"Sure." Tadrack smiled faintly. "I don't sleep much, anymore. Too many nightmares when I do."

Slaughter nodded, but he thought that maybe it had been a mistake to bring a drunk along. He had no doubt that Tadrack meant well and wanted to help. Viola had done nothing more than treat him decently, the same way she would have treated a dog.

But when trouble came, as it inevitably would, could any of them depend on him? Or would his whiskey-starved nerves cause him to fall apart?

There was no way of answering that ahead of time. Slaughter could only hope.

"We'll take the middle shift," he told Tadrack. "I'll wake you when it's time."

"Thanks, Sheriff." As if he'd been reading Slaughter's mind, he said, "I won't let you down."

The sheriff just grunted and moved off to see how Murdock and Cleaver were coming along with the fire.

He had them dig out a pit in the dry streambed where the bank, even though it was shallow, would shield the fire from the view of anyone watching from the mountains. It was probably an unnecessary precaution— the outlaws would have to be complete fools not to know that a posse would be on their trail—but Slaughter believed in being careful. It never hurt, and most of the time it helped.

Once the fire was burning, Herrara got busy with his work, and soon the air was filled with delicious aromas. Slaughter had always enjoyed being out on the range, and the evening wouldn't have been bad if not for the fear that lurked inside him, fear for Viola's honor and her very life.

After they had eaten, Gentry and Murdock took up their posts as guards and the rest of the men spread their bedrolls on the bank and turned in. Slaughter pillowed his head on his folded coat and saddle, wondering where Viola was and what she was doing. With that on his mind, he didn't expect to sleep right away, but dozed off.

His slumber was fairly deep, but he woke with the true frontiersman's knack of knowing when it was time to rise. The night was quiet. A quarter moon hung low in the sky.

Slaughter had removed his hat, coat, boots, and gunbelt when he lay down to sleep. He picked up his boots first and shook them out to make sure no scorpions had crawled into them. He pulled them on, stomped his feet down into them, and buckled on the pearl-handled Colt. His Henry rifle lay beside his bedroll. He picked it up, and clapped his hat on his head.

Fairly raucous snoring came from the two old-timers, disturbing the night's tranquility. Slaughter thought wryly that the outlaws might be able to hear that racket all the way up in the mountains. He went over to Tadrack's bedroll, hunkered on his heels, and nudged the swamper's shoulder.

Tadrack came awake with a quiet cry, almost a gasp of terror.

Slaughter gripped his shoulder. "Take it easy, Mose. It's just me."

"Sheriff." Tadrack was breathless. "I-I'm sorry. I was dreaming."

"Yeah, I figured. Come on. It's our time to stand guard."

Herrara and Yardley had the shift that was coming to an end. Slaughter and Tadrack walked over to where they stood beside some junipers on the creek bank.

"Anything going on?" Slaughter asked.

"Nothing, señor," Herrara said.

"Everything's quiet," Yardley added.

Slaughter nodded. "Good. You boys get some sleep now."

"I won't mind that a bit," Yardley said.

Once the other two men were gone, Slaughter told Tadrack, "Why don't you stay here? I think I'm going to take a *pasear* along the creek and scout around a bit."

"All right, Sheriff. What do I do if I see anything unusual?"

"Let out a holler for me. Hold your fire unless you're attacked. We don't want any wild shooting."

"I understand."

With the Henry tucked under his arm, Slaughter walked along the ragged creek bank. He intended to go a few hundred yards, then swing in a half-circle around the camp and come back to the creek a few hundred yards in the other direction. That way he could be sure no one was trying to slip up on the others while they slept.

He was just about to turn away from the creek when he heard a faint scuffing sound behind him. He recognized it as the sound boot leather makes on sandy, gravelly ground and started to wheel around. He figured that

Tadrack had followed him for some reason, although why the swamper hadn't called out to him, he didn't know.

Slaughter had turned only halfway when orange flame erupted from the muzzle of a gun and split the darkness, practically right in his face.

Chapter 9

Now that she was at least somewhat properly dressed again, Viola would have liked to have a horse of her own to ride, as long as she had to stay with these self-styled revolutionaries.

They didn't have any extra mounts, however. They had lost a man back in Tombstone, but his horse had run off. So she was forced to continue riding double with Gabriel. She might have asked Chaco to let her ride with one of the other men, but Gabriel was the devil she knew. He was big and crude and from time to time his hand "accidentally" strayed where it shouldn't have, but at least he didn't blatantly paw her.

As they rode higher into the Mules, she asked him, "What's your last name?"

"Why do you care, a fine lady like you?"

"You should have realized by now that I'm not exactly the sort of lady who swoons at the first sign of trouble."

That brought a laugh from him. "*Es verdad*. Most *ladies* wouldn't run out into the street in their nightclothes and start blazing away at a bunch of bank robbers with a rifle."

"So you admit that you're nothing but outlaws," Viola said.

"I admit nothing." Gabriel's voice became harsher. "Someday, my enemies may hang me or put me up in front of a firing squad, but still I will admit nothing." His tone softened as he nodded toward the man riding ahead of them. "Never doubt what is in Chaco's heart, though, señorita. Whether you choose to believe it or not, he is a good man. Sometimes to achieve their goals, good men have to make use of . . . not so good men. Like me."

Viola left it at that for a few minutes, then said, "You still didn't tell me your last name."

"It is Hernandez. Gabriel Hernandez."

"Whatever prompted your poor mother to name you after an angel?"

"I know. It's not exactly fitting, is it?" He guffawed again.

The canyons that led through the mountains were deep and steep-sided. Scrubby vegetation grew on the lower slopes, while the upper ones were mostly bare and rocky. The canyons twisted so sharply and so often that the riders seldom moved more than twenty or thirty yards in a straight line before they had to go around another bend.

It was perfect country for an ambush, Viola thought.

In the past, only large, well-armed bands of travelers dared to venture into such areas because the Chiricahuas would lie in wait for pilgrims in smaller groups.

A year earlier, the largest band of Chiricahua holdouts under Geronimo and Naiche had surrendered to the army and effectively put an end to the Apache wars. There were still isolated bands of bronco Apaches that raided along the border, however. It would be a long time before the settlers in southeastern Arizona Territory forgot the fear they had lived with for so long. The renegades kept that fear alive.

No matter what her ultimate fate might be, at that moment, Viola was glad that she was with the outlaws. Not even those stubborn bronco Apaches would attack a party so large.

The canyons climbed gradually toward a pass that would take them through the mountains, but they wouldn't reach that pass before nightfall. The light was already dwindling. They would need to make camp soon.

Chaco called a halt when the canyon twisted again and they came upon a spring that formed a small pool where it bubbled out of a rock wall. Junipers surrounded the pool. It was a pretty place.

Viola wondered if the outlaws had known it was there, then thought it was pretty likely they had. She swung a leg over the saddle and dropped to the ground as soon as Gabriel reined in.

He swung down beside her and rumbled, "Don't try to run off."

"Where would I go? We're in the middle of nowhere."

"Maybe . . . but from what I've seen of you so far, señorita, I wouldn't put it past you to think that you could survive out here on your own, at least until that posse catches up."

That was exactly what Viola had been thinking, but she wasn't going to admit it to him. She went over and knelt down beside the pool. Scooping up water in her hand, she drank. The spring water was crisp and cool and tasted good.

Chaco didn't have to give orders. The men went about setting up the camp as if they had done it many time before, which they had.

Viola stayed out of the way, sitting on a little slab of rock she found. She was aware that Gabriel watched her and did nothing to help with the camp, which told her that Chaco had probably given the big man the responsibility of making sure she didn't escape.

Deep in the canyon, night fell quickly, a sudden gathering of shadows once the sun was gone. Several of the men built a fairly large fire, however, and it cast its reddish glow from one side of the canyon to the other, including the pool.

Chaco went over to her. "How are you doing, señorita?"

When he called her that, she thought about her wedding band she had slipped into one of the trouser pockets. It was the first time she'd had it off her finger since her marriage to John. Although not wearing it bothered her, she still didn't want the men to know she was married to the sheriff. She would just have to put up with that odd feeling of not having a ring on her finger.

"Well, I'm still the prisoner of a gang of ruthless *bandidos*," she answered curtly. "You can draw your own conclusions from that, Señor Romero."

"I told you—"

"Yes, I know. You're revolutionaries, not outlaws. That doesn't change the fact that you robbed the bank and shot up Tombstone."

"No one was killed in Tombstone," Chaco said. "No one except one of my men." His voice caught a little. "A good man. Shotgunned to death by the sheriff like an animal."

"You can't blame Sheriff Slaughter for that." Viola's voice was cold. She knew she was probably treading on dangerous ground, but she couldn't stop herself from adding, "That man would still be alive if you hadn't ordered him to help you rob the bank."

Chaco turned his head away, and as he did Viola saw the pain flash across his face. Obviously, the same thought had occurred to him during their flight toward the border.

"We all knew the risks," Chaco said without looking at her. "The fact remains, I gave orders that no innocent people were to die in Tombstone, and my men followed those orders. They always shot high or wide."

Viola thought back to the frightening, confusing few minutes that morning when gunfire had raged in the street. She couldn't remember seeing any of the towns-people falling to the bullets, but that didn't mean Chaco was telling the truth.

Maybe his men were just poor shots.

After a moment of silence, he went on, "If you need anything, tell me or Gabriel. We will see to it that you're treated decently, señorita. You must stay with us for now, but if you cooperate there is no need for you to suffer."

He left her and walked away. His back was stiff as he departed. She always seemed to offend him or embarrass him whenever he spoke to her.

Well, that was just too bad, she thought. She had been plenty embarrassed to spend half the day dressed only in a nightgown in the company of strange men.

Gabriel ambled over to her and sat down on another rock. He took a slender black cheroot from the pocket of his charro jacket and lit it with a lucifer he snapped to life with his thumbnail. When he had the cigar burning to his satisfaction, he took a deep draw on it and blew out the smoke. "You bother Chaco, little one."

"He bothers me," Viola snapped. "You all do."

Gabriel shook his head ponderously. "Now, that is where you are wrong. We could bother you. Many of us would like to *bother* you a great deal. But none would dare. Do you know why?"

"I'm sure you'll tell me," Viola said.

"I will. No one will molest you because Chaco passed among us and made sure everyone understood that he will kill any man who dares to lay a finger on you in an improper fashion."

Viola frowned. "He did that?"

Gabriel puffed on the cigar and then nodded. "He did."

"Why would he do that? Out of the goodness of his heart?"

"Exactly. You see"—Gabriel drew on the cheroot again—"our *amigo* Chaco used to be a priest before he decided he could serve *El Señor Dios* with a gun in his hand better than with a Bible."

"A priest? Really?"

"*Es verdad*," Gabriel said with a solemn nod. "Father Tomás. But when he put that aside he became Chaco again, as he had been since he and I were both *niños*. We grew up together, you see, in the same village. Different blood, but as close as *hermanos*. Brothers."

"How does a priest become an outlaw?" Viola asked with a frown.

A grin stretched across Gabriel's rugged face. "God works in mysterious ways His wonders to perform, eh? This is what the holy book says?"

"Don't tell me you used to be a priest, too?"

Gabriel took a last draw on the cheroot, dropped the butt, and ground it out with his boot heel. "Me, little one? No, I am an outlaw. I have always been an outlaw." He stood up. "You would do well to remember that."

It was unlikely she would forget.

Chapter 10

Slaughter's instincts warned him once again, and he had already started to throw himself aside as the gun blasted. The report was deafening and the shot was so close he felt the sting of burning grains of powder against his cheek as the slug whipped past his ear. It had missed him by an inch, no more.

He brought the Henry up, but before he could pull the trigger a rock rolled under the heel of his left boot and threw him off balance. The dark figure lunged at him and clubbed at his head with the gun that had almost put a hole in him.

Slaughter twisted aside so that the weapon didn't crush his skull, but the blow landed on his right shoulder with enough force to make his arm go numb. He fumbled with the rifle, but couldn't stop it from slipping out of his grip.

The attacker barreled into him. Slaughter went over backward. The light of the quarter moon was faint, but it was enough for him to spot the gun swinging toward him again. He pulled his head to the side just as the gun erupted for the second time. The bullet struck the ground next to his head and sprayed grit across his face. Some of the painfully stinging stuff went in his eyes, momentarily blinding him.

Slaughter struck out with his left fist, aiming the blow at the spot where he thought his assailant was. His instincts were right again. His knuckles hammered against the man's ear. Slaughter hit him again and heaved up from the ground. The weight of his attacker left him.

Unable to see or hear much, Slaughter rolled away. He thought he was headed in the direction of the streambed. That hunch proved correct as the ground suddenly dropped out from under him and he fell a few feet to land in the sandy bed.

He used his good arm to push himself up onto his knees and scrambled toward the bank. Although he wasn't as good a shot with his left hand as he was with his right, he reached across his body and drew the Colt. As he crouched next to the bank, he drew back the hammer.

Footsteps pounded toward him. A man shouted, "Sheriff! Sheriff Slaughter!"

It was Mose Tadrack. Confident it hadn't been Tadrack who attacked him, Slaughter called, "Mose, be careful! Find some cover! There's somebody else out here."

Feeling began to work its way back into Slaughter's

right arm and hand. He opened and closed his fingers to speed up the process. As soon as he felt like he could handle the gun again, he switched it to that hand.

As he stood up slowly, he swept the Colt from side to side. His keen eyes searched the shadows for any sign of movement. He didn't see anything. Either the attacker was hiding and waiting for another chance at him, or the man had fled once his attempt on Slaughter's life had failed and the rest of the group had been alerted.

More shouts came through the night as the other members of the posse approached to find out the meaning of the shots that had jolted them out of sleep. Luther Gentry called, "What in tarnation's goin' on out here?"

"Sound off," Slaughter ordered. "Who's out here?"

One by one the members of the posse called out until they were all accounted for. Slaughter figured the bushwhacker wouldn't make another try with all of them awake and on edge, so he climbed up out of the streambed.

"What happened?" Grover Harmon asked.

"Somebody snuck up behind me and tried to blow my head off," Slaughter replied. "When that didn't work he tried to bust my skull with his gun."

"Did he get away?" Pete Yardley asked.

Diego Herrara added, "Did you get a look at this *malo hombre*, señor?"

"Yeah, I reckon he got away," Slaughter said, "and no, I never got a good look at him. He was just a shape in the darkness. Fought pretty good for a few minutes before I got loose from him and he took off."

Gentry said, "You know what it sounds like to me? Those outlaws we're trailin' left a man behind to discourage us from comin' after 'em. He figured that if he killed you, Sheriff, there was a good chance the rest of us would turn around and light a shuck back to Tombstone."

"That's just what I was thinking, too," Slaughter agreed with a nod.

"Do you think he'll come back tonight?" Ross Murdock asked nervously.

Slaughter pondered that question for a moment, then said, "Now that he's lost the element of surprise, it's not likely. He'll probably try to catch up with the rest of the gang."

He looked around for his hat and rifle, found them, and went on. "You fellows go on back to your bedrolls and try to get some more sleep. I've got a hunch the excitement's over for tonight."

"You sure about that, Sheriff?" Harmon asked. "The rest of us could stay up, too, or at least somebody could take over what's left of your shift."

"I'm fine," Slaughter said somewhat testily. His right arm ached a little, but the feeling was back in it and he didn't have any trouble using it. "Who knows how long we'll be in the saddle tomorrow? Get your rest while you can."

Gentry nodded. "That makes sense, I reckon. Come on, boys."

Except for Mose Tadrack, the men returned to their bedrolls.

"Maybe we better stand guard together, Sheriff."

Slaughter reined in the urge to respond angrily. He was the sheriff, dadblast it, he thought, and here was a drunken swamper feeling sorry for him and acting like he shouldn't be alone.

"No, we'll each take one side of the camp, just like we were doing before," Slaughter said coolly. "I won't get taken by surprise again."

Tadrack shrugged. "Whatever you say, Sheriff." With his rifle under his arm he moved off to take up his previous position.

Slaughter stayed where he was. He abandoned his previous plan to scout around the camp. He didn't think another threat was going to come from the outside.

Despite what he'd said when Luther Gentry suggested one of the outlaws had lurked behind to ambush them, Slaughter had thought of another, more likely possibility as soon as things calmed down a mite.

With everyone supposedly asleep except him and Tadrack, one of the posse members could have crawled out of his blankets, catfooted after Slaughter, and bushwhacked him. During the commotion following the shots, the traitor could have hurried back and pretended to join the others as they came to see what had happened.

That theory made sense, but he had absolutely no proof of it. Still, he was going to keep a close eye on all of them from here on out. To his way of thinking, Jack Doyle was the most likely suspect. The gambler worked for Morris Upton, and Upton had a grudge against Slaughter. He could have told Doyle to volunteer for the posse and wait for an opportunity to dispose of the sheriff.

If Doyle was the would-be killer, he would make another attempt or do something else to slip up and reveal himself, and then Slaughter would have him.

Or maybe the bushwhacker really was one of the *bandidos* who had robbed the bank. Either way, the truth would come out eventually.

Until it did, Slaughter was going to proceed on the assumption that there might be a viper in their midst.

If there was, sooner or later he would stomp that snake.

The rest of the night passed quietly. Slaughter had all the men up while the sky was still gray with the approach of dawn. By the time it was light enough to see the trail they were following, they were in the saddle, ready to ride.

Jack Doyle wasn't acting suspicious, but that didn't mean anything, Slaughter decided. The man was a professional gambler. If Doyle was the bushwhacker, he had enough of a poker face not to give that away.

The mountains still looked tantalizingly close as the sun rose. They would reach the Mules today, Slaughter thought, and ought to make it all the way through them before nightfall.

The outlaws had probably camped somewhere up among the peaks. They would come down on the other side, hit the flats, and then it was only a few miles to the border. The feeling had grown stronger inside Slaughter that the posse wouldn't be able to catch up in time to keep the fugitives from crossing into Mexico.

He wasn't going to turn back, even if it meant giving up his job as sheriff. Viola was the most important thing in the world to him. He would stay on their trail all the way to hell and back if he had to, and he wouldn't stop until his wife was safe.

Mid-morning, Slaughter spotted a column of dust rising ahead of them and a good distance off to the east.

He wasn't the only one who saw it. Luther Gentry rode up alongside him. "Look over yonder, Sheriff."

"I see it."

"You reckon it's the bunch we're after?"

Slaughter's eyes narrowed in thought. "I don't hardly figure how it could be. That much dust has to come from a good-sized group of riders, all right, but they're coming toward us. Their course will cross ours if we keep going the way we are."

Gentry rubbed his angular jaw and frowned. "Yeah, you're right. But if they ain't them bank robbers, who in tarnation can they be?"

"One way to find out." Slaughter turned in the saddle. "Everybody make sure your guns are ready."

Then he heeled his horse into a faster pace and hurried ahead to intercept the strange riders.

Chapter 11

Viola didn't know if what Gabriel had told her about Chaco ordering the rest of the bank robbers to leave her alone was true or not, but no one came near her during the night other than the burly outlaw, who seemed to have been appointed her guardian and companion.

Gabriel brought her tortillas and jerky for her supper, and after not eating all day, even that meager fare was good. She ate hungrily and washed the food down with water from the spring-fed pool.

Then he brought blankets for her to make into a bedroll. When she stretched out, she thought it would be impossible for her to sleep under the circumstances, but exhaustion took over and a black tide of oblivion carried her away. She didn't wake until morning.

Her muscles were stiff when she got up, but they loosened when she stood up and stretched for a minute. As a girl helping her father and brothers drive cattle, she had spent many a night sleeping on the trail in a bedroll under the stars, so the sensation was nothing new to her.

As always, Gabriel was nearby.

"I need some privacy," she told him.

"Go behind those trees over there, but I'll be close enough to hear if you try anything."

Coolly, she said, "That's not really what I'd call privacy."

"It's the best you're going to get, *chiquita*," he said with a shrug.

Viola didn't think arguing would do her any good, so she went along with his suggestion and just tried to pretend that he wasn't there. When she came out from behind the trees she didn't look at him.

"Breakfast will be ready soon," he told her.

"And then what?"

"Then we keep going until we reach our destination."

"And where is that?"

Gabriel walked off as if he hadn't heard her, but she knew he had.

That brought a frown of consternation to Viola's face. She had assumed they were headed across the border into Mexico. But Gabriel had acted a bit odd when she'd questioned him, and she couldn't help but wonder what it meant.

Chaco came over to her. "Did you sleep well?"

"As well as can be expected . . . as a prisoner."

"I would prefer to think of you as a . . . guest."

"You can think of me however you like, Señor Romero, but it doesn't change the fact that I'm your captive."

"Perhaps not for much longer."

"It can't be soon enough to suit me."

Gabriel came up with her breakfast then—more tortillas, with some beans wrapped up in them—and Chaco moved off to supervise the men as they got ready to break camp.

"You should not hate Chaco," the big outlaw said as Viola ate. "He truly regrets having to put you through this."

"He didn't have to. He could have left me in Tombstone."

Gabriel's massive shoulders rose and fell. "It is true we did not plan to bring a hostage with us. But when Fate presented us with you, perhaps Chaco saw it as what *El Señor Dios* intended all along. *Quien sabe?* It would be good if Chaco had someone to make his life easier. He torments himself so."

Viola stared at him in disbelief for a moment before asking, "Are you really trying to play matchmaker between me and that . . . that outlaw?"

Gabriel grinned. "You are both young and easy to look at. You would have very beautiful babies."

"Oh. Oh!" Viola was so angry she could barely speak. She wanted to throw the tortilla in her hand in Gabriel's face. With an effort she controlled her emotions and said in chilly tones, "That will never happen."

Gabriel shrugged again. "It's something for you to think about, anyway, little one."

Viola wasn't going to think about it, not for one second. She was a married woman; she wasn't going to play up to another man, even if it might be to her benefit.

But if it slowed them down and gave John a better chance to catch up to them . . .

That thought came unbidden to her mind. She scolded herself for allowing it.

But when Chaco came over to her a short time later and asked if she was ready to go, she forced a faint smile onto her lips. "Could . . . could we wait just a little while longer? I'm still so tired from yesterday."

Chaco shook his head. "No. I'm sorry. You must mount up now."

Clearly his question had just been a formality. He didn't care if she was ready or not. They were going.

Viola turned her head and glared at Gabriel, who was already in the saddle. He shrugged and extended a hand to help her onto the horse.

So much for that big hairy Cupid's suggestion.

Chaco kept the group moving as quickly as possible through the mountains. They topped the pass at mid-morning, and from there Viola could see the slopes descending to the flats, which stretched for ten or fifteen miles to another range of mountains lower than the Mules. Those mountains, she knew, were across the border in Mexico.

Would John stop when he came to the border? Viola thought about her husband's personality and decided that was highly unlikely. As long as she was in danger, he would throw away his sheriff's badge if necessary and come after her. Even if it meant causing an international incident, he wouldn't stop until they were reunited.

That certainty made her feel warm inside because of the love she knew her husband had for her. At the same time, she didn't want him getting in trouble with the law.

Although it wouldn't be the first time, she reminded herself. More than once in his life, John Slaughter had been accused of being a rustler. She never questioned him too much about those incidents. On the frontier, the line between being an outlaw and being a law-abiding man was sometimes razor-thin and a matter of perception more than anything else.

From the top of the pass, Viola could also look back the way they had come. Chaco didn't slow down, so she had only a glimpse in that direction as Gabriel kept his horse moving, but she thought she saw dust hovering in the air.

That sight made her heart leap a little. It had to be a posse from Tombstone kicking up that dust, she thought. For the first time she had proof that someone was coming to rescue her.

But would they be in time?

The descent out of the mountains took until early afternoon. Once they reached the flats Chaco pushed the group even harder. He was anxious to reach the border, Viola thought. He probably believed that once he crossed that imaginary line, he would be safe.

That was because he didn't know Texas John Slaughter.

After a short time, something appeared on the horizon ahead of them. A few more minutes went by, and the dark blotch resolved itself into a cluster of buildings. There was a village there, Viola realized, one whose existence she hadn't been aware of.

With a frown, she turned to look at Gabriel. "Is that where we're going? To that village?"

"It's called La Reata," he said, which didn't really answer her question.

"It's still on the American side of the border, isn't it?"

"You'll see, little one."

She tried to control her impatience and annoyance with him. When she asked a question, she was used to getting an answer. She was, after all, the mistress of the great Slaughter Ranch and the wife of John Slaughter.

But these men didn't know that, and she didn't want them to. If Chaco knew who she really was, he might get the idea that he could hold her for ransom and raise money for his so-called revolution.

The village of La Reata had two streets, one running north and south and a smaller one running east and west. At the south end of the main street rose the bell tower of a small mission. It was the highest point for several miles around. The other buildings in the small settlement were all made of adobe, with either thatched or tile roofs. As the outlaws entered the village, Viola saw a stable, a blacksmith shop, a couple general stores, several cantinas, and the biggest building in town other than the church, a two-storied hotel with a covered gallery in front of it.

Chaco reined to a halt in front of one of the cantinas. The rest of the men followed suit.

Viola said to Gabriel, "Since you told me he used to be a priest, I thought he might go to the mission."

"Don't mention I told you that," the big outlaw said with a scowl. "Chaco might not like it. Anyway, none of the rest of us are priests, and we're thirsty. It's a hot day."

"Don't let me stop you from getting a drink." Viola smiled in mock sweetness. "I'll wait here and watch your horse."

"Haw! You'd like that, wouldn't you?"

Chaco swung down from the saddle. His booted feet had barely touched the ground when a woman appeared in the cantina's doorway and rushed out to put her arms around him and draw him into a hug.

She was beautiful, Viola thought, with a great mass of tightly curled black hair, flashing dark eyes, and a voluptuous body the lines of which were daringly revealed in the tight, low-cut dress she wore.

"Why would you try to interest me in Chaco when he already has a woman like that?" Viola asked Gabriel.

"Mercedes?" He laughed again. "Mercedes is his sister!"

"Really?" Now that Gabriel mentioned it, Viola could see a slight resemblance between Chaco and Mercedes, but they still seemed strikingly different.

"Just because a man is a priest doesn't mean his sister must be a nun. And believe me, Mercedes Romero is no nun!"

"I believe you," Viola said. No nun would ever be caught revealing as much cleavage as Mercedes was.

Gabriel dismounted and helped Viola down. The other men got off their horses, as well, and several of them headed into the cantina.

Chaco brought his sister over to Viola and Gabriel. In a formal voice he said, "Mercedes, this is Señorita Viola . . . I don't know your last name."

"Smith," Viola lied. That was the first name she thought of.

"Señorita Viola Smith," Chaco said. "You will look after her while we are here?"

"Of course," Mercedes said. "But I am surprised to see you with a woman, *mi hermano*."

Chaco gave a curt shake of his head. "It isn't like that. The señorita came with us from Tombstone."

"You *brought* me with you from Tombstone," Viola said. "You kidnapped me."

"Don't worry, Chaco," Mercedes told her brother. "I will see that this one is taken care of." She took Viola's arm and steered her toward the cantina entrance.

"*Gracias*," he said.

Into Viola's ear, still with a smile on her face, Mercedes said in a menacing whisper, "If you do anything to hurt my brother, *perra*, I will cut your heart out myself and feed it to the hogs!"

Chapter 12

Slaughter and his companions raised their own dust cloud as they crossed the flat, semiarid terrain, so whoever the other riders were, they had to be aware of the posse. The two columns gradually came closer to each other. Slaughter and his men drew even first, so at the sheriff's signal they reined in and turned their horses to wait.

After a few minutes, Slaughter spotted the guidon hanging limply from a staff in the hot air. The handful of blue-clad riders around it came on, and the lighter splotches of canvas-covered wagons hove into view behind them.

"It's the cavalry!" Pete Yardley exclaimed.

Slaughter had already come to that conclusion. He told the posse members, "Stay here," and heeled his horse into motion again. He rode forward to meet the patrol.

As he neared the cavalrymen, one of the riders spurred

ahead of the others and stopped when about ten feet separated him from Slaughter. The crossed-sabers insignia on the man's dark blue Stetson and the shoulder boards with their two pairs of double bars told Slaughter he was a captain in the United States cavalry.

Slaughter nodded. "Hello, Captain. I'm John Slaughter, Sheriff of Cochise County."

"Captain Brice Donelson, sir," the officer said with a polite nod. "You're almost out of your jurisdiction, aren't you?"

"No more so than you," Slaughter replied.

That brought a chuckle from Captain Donelson. "Yes, sir, we're both almost at the tail-end of our baili-wicks, aren't we?" He nodded toward the other men sitting on their horses in the distance behind Slaughter. "That looks like a posse to me. Are you out here chasing outlaws or renegade Apaches?"

"Outlaws. A bunch that robbed the bank in Tomb-stone yesterday morning."

Donelson took off his hat and mopped his forehead with one end of the dark blue bandanna he wore around his neck. He was around thirty, with dark, slightly wavy hair and a neatly trimmed mustache.

"I hadn't heard any rumors about bronco Apaches recently, so I figured it must be owlhoots. Sorry to hear about the bank." He waved the hat at the wagons behind him. "As you can see, my men and I are escorting a supply train from Fort Bowie to Fort Huachuca. If it weren't for that, I'd offer to give you a hand running those bank robbers to ground. They haven't crossed the border yet?"

"I don't know," Slaughter answered honestly. "They're somewhere ahead of us in the Mules, headed south."

Donelson made a face. "You've got your work cut out for you, then."

"It's worse than that. We're outnumbered by more than three to one."

"Well . . . far be it from me to tell you how to do your job, Sheriff, but if it was me I think I might turn around and head back to Tombstone. It's unlikely you're going to catch up to them in time anyway, and I'm not sure the bank's money is worth getting that many good men killed."

"I might consider it, if the blasted thieves hadn't also kidnapped my wife."

Donelson stiffened and sat straighter in the saddle. "What's that? Kidnapped your wife? My God! I'm sorry, Sheriff. They're holding her as a hostage?"

"I assume they are. All I know is that they carried her off when they made their getaway from Tombstone. So you can understand, Captain, why I'm not in a hurry to turn back."

"Yes, of course," Donelson said solemnly. He put his hat back on. "You have my sympathy, Sheriff. . . ."

As the officer hesitated, Slaughter considered what he ought to do next. In all his life, he had never been the sort of man who begged for help, even when he needed it. He hated the idea of doing it now.

On the other hand, Viola's safety was much more

important than his pride, and if he could persuade this cavalry captain to throw in with him, he could make a dash after the outlaws without having to wait for reinforcements from Tombstone to catch up.

Even if that happened, the odds of them catching up to the gang before the *bandidos* crossed the border into Mexico were slim. If Slaughter couldn't ask his posse men to invade another country, he certainly couldn't expect a U.S. cavalry patrol to do so. But with Viola's life possibly at stake, he had to do everything in his power to save her.

After a long moment of silence, Donelson said, "You know I'd like to help you, Sheriff, but it would mean going against my orders."

"I understand." Slaughter couldn't keep the bleak tone out of his voice.

Donelson looked like something had just occurred to him. "These bank robbers, did you get a good look at them?"

"Good enough. I killed one of them with a shotgun."

"Would you say that they were Americans?"

Slaughter leaned forward a little in the saddle. He thought he knew why Donelson had asked that question. "No, Captain, I would not. I believe they were Mexicans."

Strictly speaking, Slaughter knew that was an assumption on his part. There were plenty of *hombres* of Mexican descent north of the border, some who had been born and raised in the United States. Those vaqueros were just as American as he was.

From the way the gang had lit a shuck toward

Mexico, he had figured that was where they were from, and still believed that was the most likely possibility.

"An armed incursion onto American soil by foreign nationals isn't something to take lightly, Sheriff," Donelson said. "They could represent a threat to this supply train, and it's my duty to protect those wagons any way I see fit. It'll still take us several days to reach Fort Huachuca. I believe I can see my way clear to leaving a few of my men to guard the wagons while the rest of us accompany you after those invaders."

It wasn't like the Mexican army had crossed the border, but if Donelson wanted to rationalize his actions that way, Slaughter wasn't going to argue with him. The end result was that he now had an outside chance of rescuing Viola, and that was the only thing that mattered to him.

"Thank you, Captain," Slaughter said. "That would be a great help."

Donelson smiled tightly. "One thing, Sheriff. Under no circumstances will I lead my men across the border or venture into Mexico myself. I sympathize with your concern over your wife, but that's out of the question."

Slaughter nodded. "I understand. We'll catch up to them before they cross the border."

He added under his breath, "We have to . . ."

Captain Donelson had forty men in his patrol. He left fifteen of them with the supply train under the command of a grizzled sergeant and brought twenty-five of them with him as he joined Slaughter's posse. Combined with the men from Tombstone, that made the odds pretty close to even if they had to do battle with the outlaws.

The cavalry troopers had the look of seasoned fighters, and that made all the difference in the world. Slaughter felt better about their chances than he had since leaving Tombstone.

Luther Gentry rode alongside him as the group started into the mountains. "We was mighty lucky to run into these soldier boys, Sheriff."

Slaughter agreed. "Yes, we were. I hope that luck stays with us for a while."

If anything, Donelson pushed his men even harder than Slaughter did with the posse. They kept up the pace all day, stopping only occasionally to let the horses rest. When they reached the top of the pass, Slaughter called a halt, and he and Donelson used field glasses to search for any sign of the bandits ahead of them.

Slaughter's spirits sank a little when he didn't spot their quarry, but he refused to let himself lose hope or give up. Surrender just wasn't part of his personality.

"Are we going to push on?" Donelson asked quietly.

"Damned right we are."

By late afternoon, they had descended the southern slopes and reached the flats that led to the border. As they rode beside each other at the head of the combined posse and cavalry patrol, Donelson mused, "I wonder if there's any chance the men you're after stopped in La Reata."

Slaughter frowned. "You mean the little village that's up here a few more miles?"

"That's right. I went through there with a patrol a year or so ago. There's not much to it, but a gang of thirsty *bandidos* might want to stop there and cut the trail dust, maybe fool around with a few of the señoritas in the cantinas."

Slaughter hadn't thought about that. He had figured the outlaws would head straight for the border, but as he looked at the tracks they were following, he had to admit that the trail led toward La Reata.

He had tracked some rustlers there once and caught up to them in one of the cantinas. The three men had surrendered immediately when he confronted them, even though he'd been alone. Slaughter hadn't been a lawman for very long, but he'd already had a reputation. Lawbreakers who resisted arrest when he went after them seldom lived to stand trial.

Like Donelson, he remembered La Reata as being little more than a wide place in the trail, but it might be a good idea to check the village out. The border was close, and since they hadn't caught up to the bandits yet, Slaughter's last, best hope might be that they had stopped in La Reata.

"When we get close, I'll wait until dark and then take a few men to scout the place," he said. "If the bandits are there, I can send word back to you."

Donelson nodded. "That's a good idea. If they are there and have your wife with them, the last thing we want to do is spook them. That might set off a fight before we're ready."

"Yes, I'd like to get Viola out of there before any shooting starts if I can. Assuming she's there."

"Viola," Donelson mused. "A lovely name, Sheriff, if you don't mind me saying so." In a brisker tone, he went on, "If you can free your wife and signal me, I can lead the rest of the men into the village and hit the bandits hard."

"The harder the better." Slaughter's voice was like flint. "As long as I rescue Mrs. Slaughter and recover the bank's money, I don't care if I have any prisoners to take back to Tombstone."

Chapter 13

Chaco's men bellied up to the bar inside the cantina, led by Gabriel, who shouted for tequila. Several young, dusky-skinned women wearing low-cut blouses and long, colorful skirts circulated among them, laughing as the outlaws embraced them and swatted their rumps.

It was a raucous scene, but Viola wasn't particularly shocked. She had been raised around rough cowboys and knew their ways. These outlaws weren't much different.

Mercedes led her toward an arched doorway in the rear of the room. A beaded curtain hung over the opening. She pushed it aside and took Viola into a hallway with a door on each side. She inclined her head toward the door on the left. "My office." She opened the door on the right. "My bedroom. I thought you might like to wash off some of the trail dust."

After the way Mercedes had threatened her as they entered the cantina, Viola was a little surprised the woman was being nice to her. She wasn't going to turn down the chance to clean up, though.

For the back of a bordertown cantina, Mercedes' bedroom was well furnished with a thick woven rug on the floor, a four-poster bed, a dressing table with a chair and mirror, a wardrobe, a rocking chair, and colorful yellow and blue curtains over the single window. A gilt cross was mounted on one wall.

That was probably due to Chaco's influence, Viola thought, although it was possible Mercedes was religious, too. The fact that she ran a cantina and looked like a trollop might not be an accurate reflection of what was in her heart. Viola tried not to judge people, although sometimes it was difficult not to.

A basin of water and a cloth sat on the dressing table. Mercedes waved toward it. "Help yourself. There may be some clothes in the wardrobe that will fit you, too, if you'd prefer not to dress like a man."

"I'm fine with what I'm wearing." Viola realized that answer might have sounded curt, so she added, "Thank you for the offer, though."

Mercedes shrugged. "Suit yourself, Señorita Smith. If that's your real name."

Viola glanced sharply at her. "Why wouldn't it be? Don't you think I know my own name?"

"I'm just saying, a lot of people are called Smith who weren't born with the name. That's all."

Viola didn't press the issue. She went to the dressing table, took off her hat, and dipped the cloth into the basin. She wiped the wet cloth across her face and tried not to sigh at how good it felt to wash away the layer of dust that had settled on her skin.

"Come back out front when you're finished," Mercedes told her.

Viola eyed the window. "All right."

Mercedes laughed. "I know what you're thinking, señorita. But my brother isn't a fool. He has a man watching that window. If you climbed out, you wouldn't get ten feet before someone grabbed you."

"I'm not going to try to escape."

Mercedes made a scoffing sound, as if she found that hard to believe.

"Really, your brother and his men have treated me decently," Viola went on.

"Probably better than you had any right to expect. That is because Chaco is an honorable man. Someone had to be good"—Mercedes laughed—"and someone had to be the black sheep in the family, eh?" She went out and closed the door behind her.

Viola took advantage of the privacy to unbutton the shirt she wore and wash off more of the dust. By the time she was finished she felt considerably refreshed.

She still wasn't sure why the outlaws had stopped in La Reata instead of hurrying across the border where they would be safer. She could understand that Chaco might want to say hello to his sister, but from the way his men had acted, they were settling down to stay for a while.

Staying was just asking for the posse to catch up to

them. Clearly, they weren't afraid of John and the men he might bring with him from Tombstone.

When she had cleaned up as much as she could without a tub full of hot water—the thought of which was enough to make her groan—and had run her fingers through her hair to get as much of the dust out of it as she could, Viola went back out into the hallway. She carried the flat-crowned hat in her hand.

She paused in the corridor and darted a glance at the closed door to Mercedes' office. There might be a gun in there, she thought.

Unlikely, though, and the door was probably locked, to boot. Viola turned away from the office and pushed through the beaded curtain into the cantina's main room.

A number of Chaco's men were still at the bar. They tossed back shots of tequila almost as fast as the short, bald bartender could pour them. The fiery liquor didn't seem to affect them. To such men, tequila was probably like water.

Other members of the gang had taken bottles of tequila and whiskey and spread out to sit at tables with some of the serving girls. Laughter filled the room.

An old man with a drooping mustache sat on a stool in a corner and strummed the strings of a guitar. The music blended with the laughter to form a pleasing melody.

Gabriel and Mercedes sat at one of the tables. They didn't notice Viola at first, so she was able to see how Mercedes clasped Gabriel's big left paw with both of her hands. The smile on her face told how deep was the affection she felt for him.

Mercedes was in love with the big, ugly outlaw, Viola realized. Gabriel had said that he and Chaco were friends from childhood, so he had probably known Mercedes all her life. It was odd to see such a beautiful woman with a brute like Gabriel, but Viola knew better than to question the paths that a heart might take.

She had fallen in love with and married a man considerably older than herself, after all, and no couple had ever been happier than her and John.

The sausage-like fingers of Gabriel's right hand were wrapped around the neck of a tequila bottle. He lifted it to his mouth, took a long, gurgling swallow. When he lowered it, he saw Viola. "There you are, *chiquita*."

Viola frowned. He shouldn't refer to her with a term of endearment like that while Mercedes was right there doting on him. But that seemed to be Gabriel's way. He was big, crude, and unthinking . . . but not necessarily an evil man, as she was beginning to realize.

He thumped the tequila bottle on the table and pushed himself to his feet "Chaco wanted to see you. Come along." He bent over, planted a kiss on Mercedes' lips, and leered at her. "I will see you later, eh?"

"You know where to find me," she told him as she leaned back in her chair.

Gabriel took hold of Viola's arm and steered her toward the cantina's entrance.

She pulled away from him. "You don't have to

manhandle me, you know. I haven't tried to escape yet, have I?"

"And I wouldn't want you to start now," he said, but didn't take hold of her again. "Chaco would be very upset with me if I allowed you to refuse his, ah, hospitality."

"He can try to say that I'm his guest all he wants to, but it doesn't change the face that all of you kidnapped me."

Gabriel turned toward the mission at the end of the street. Viola walked alongside him. She knew that what Mercedes had told her earlier was true. If she tried to escape, she wouldn't get very far.

Besides, she was intrigued by what was going on in La Reata and wanted to find out the reason for it.

The doors of the mission were open. Before Viola and Gabriel reached the building, Chaco appeared in the doorway. His hat hung behind his head by its chin strap. He smiled at Viola as they came up to him. "Have you been treated well so far, señorita?"

"I suppose so." Viola didn't mention the threat Mercedes had made to cut out her heart and feed it to the hogs. The woman had been nice to her after that . . . although the menace had continued to lurk right under the surface.

Chaco leaned his head toward the mission. "Come inside."

She followed him while Gabriel stayed outside. The thick walls kept the heat out, making it cool inside.

The sanctuary was hushed and shadowy. The room was long and rather narrow, with tall windows on each side. Paintings and tapestries of religious scenes hung between some of the windows, while crucifixes decorated the walls in other places. Small statues of the Virgin Mary and other icons reposed in little nooks along the walls. The pews were arranged in two sections with an aisle between them leading to the altar at the front of the room. An elaborate candelabra hung from the high ceiling by a long rope.

"It's lovely," Viola murmured.

"La Reata is a small, poor village, but its people are very devout," Chaco said. "I always come here every time I visit Mercedes."

"Maybe you should live here and help her run the cantina, instead of risking your life as a revolutionary."

Chaco stared at her. "I could never do that. I could not abandon my countrymen in their time of need."

"Your countrymen are always in need," Viola said. "How many revolutions have there been? How many have been attempted that never even really began? If you and your men were to leave me and the loot from the raid here and scatter to the four winds for a while, the law would soon forget about you. It would be safe for you to return and make a life with your sister."

Chaco shook his head. "You don't understand. I swore a vow."

"You swore another vow and left it behind." The blunt words were out of Viola's mouth before she could stop them. She hadn't meant to betray Gabriel's confidence, but there it was.

Chaco was the one who had decided to leave the

priesthood. If he couldn't abide by that decision, he shouldn't have made it.

He looked sharply at her. "So Gabriel told you my secret, did he?"

"Don't be angry with him. He was just trying to convince me that you're really a good man."

"I could never be angry with Gabriel. Even though we do not share the same blood, we are *hermanos* and always will be." Chaco paused, then asked with a faint smile, "Was his effort successful?"

"At what? Making me believe that you're something more than a no-good, bank-robbing bandit?" Viola shook her head. "The jury is still out on that one." She strolled up the aisle between the benches. "How long are we going to be here?"

"Are you in a hurry to leave?"

"I just thought that you'd want to get across the border as quickly as you could. We're still in Arizona Territory."

Chaco laughed. "You are a very unusual hostage, Señorita Smith, urging your captors to carry you off into another country."

"I'm not urging anything of the sort. I'm just curious." Viola paused and turned to look at him. "Besides, you're an unusual kidnapper. I'm beginning to realize how unusual."

Chaco's eyes met and held her gaze for a long moment. Viola chided herself as she realized that he probably thought she was playing up to him. She hadn't intended to . . . but she couldn't fault him for feeling that way.

He looked away. "We will be here for a while. Tonight, maybe part of the day tomorrow. I cannot say for sure. And when we leave . . . you will stay here. I give you my word on that, señorita."

"You're not taking me across the border?"

"There will be no need."

Well, that was a relief, Viola thought.

She realized that the only reason the gang would stop for an uncertain amount of time was that they were waiting for someone and didn't know exactly when that person would arrive in La Reata. That meant there was more to this affair than a simple bank robbery. The potential existed for more trouble. A shiver of apprehension went down her spine.

She wished John would hurry up and get there. Even though she hadn't been mistreated so far, she was ready to go home.

Chapter 14

The lights of La Reata began to wink into view in the gathering dusk as Slaughter and Captain Donelson halted their party about a mile from the village.

"I'd better go ahead on foot from here." Slaughter leaned forward in the saddle to ease his muscles after two days of hard riding.

"How many men are you taking with you, Sheriff?" Donelson asked.

"Only a few. I'd go by myself and not risk anyone else's life, but I'll need someone with me to get word to you if I find Mrs. Slaughter."

Ross Murdock surprised Slaughter by saying, "Take me, Sheriff. I can do it."

Slaughter frowned. "I appreciate that, Murdock, but I was thinking about a more experienced man—"

"No offense, Sheriff," Gentry interrupted, "but you ain't got any more experienced men 'cept maybe me and Grover, and we're a mite too old to be dashin' around the prairie. Murdock there's got youth on his side, anyway."

Slaughter supposed the liveryman had a point. He wouldn't be counting on Murdock to do any fighting, only to carry a message to Donelson.

"All right, Murdock, if you want to risk it, you can come along. I can't guarantee your safety, though."

Murdock smiled. "There haven't been any guarantees since we left Tombstone, have there?"

The young bank teller had a point there.

Jack Doyle spoke up. "I can come with you, Sheriff. If there's trouble, I'm pretty good with a gun."

Slaughter remembered the attempt on his life the night before and his suspicion that Doyle might have been behind it. There was nothing to indicate that on Doyle's smoothly handsome face or in his bland voice, but Slaughter's suspicion remained.

"No, you stay here with the others, Doyle. How about you, Tadrack?"

The swamper's eyes widened. "Me? You want me to go?"

"You're pretty spry when you need to be, aren't you?" Slaughter asked.

"I suppose."

"Hold out your hand."

Tadrack did so, and Slaughter was pleased to see that it wasn't shaking as much as it had been the day before. He nodded. "You'll do."

"Take one of my men with you, too," Donelson suggested. "Corporal Winters has done a considerable amount of scouting for us. He can get around quietly. Can't you, Winters?"

"I reckon I can," one of the troopers drawled. The slow molasses of his voice indicated that he was from somewhere in the Deep South. He was too young to have been a Confederate soldier during the war, but Slaughter would have bet that his father was.

"All right. That makes four of us. That's enough."

"All right," Donelson agreed. "The rest of us will wait right here, Sheriff." He paused, then asked with a note of reluctance in his voice, "What are you going to do if you can't find your wife in the village?"

"It's only a couple miles to the border," Slaughter said grimly. "If Viola's not there, we'll camp here and I'll push on south in the morning." He looked around at the other men. "And I won't be asking anybody to go with me."

"I would if I could," Donelson said. "You know that." Slaughter nodded.

"Well, there's nothin' stoppin' the rest of us from goin' on." Luther Gentry gave the captain a belligerent stare. "Unless somebody takes it in his mind that he can't allow Americans to traipse across the border."

"I suppose according to regulations, I should put a stop to any sort of unauthorized incursion. But with Mrs. Slaughter—an American citizen, mind you—in possible danger, I think I can make an exception." Donelson looked at Slaughter. "If you run into trouble below the border, though, don't expect any help from the United States."

"I'm used to stomping my own snakes." Slaughter looked at the rest of the posse members. "How about the rest of you?"

Without any hesitation, Grover Harmon said, "We'll go wherever you lead us, Sheriff."

"You've been good for Tombstone, John," Pete Yardley said. "I don't plan on turning my back on you when you need me."

"That goes for me, too, señor," Diego Herrara added.

That left Chester Carlton and Joseph Cleaver. Slaughter could tell that the drummer and the bank teller were reluctant to promise they would accompany him into Mexico if he needed to pursue the outlaws across the border.

"It's all right," Slaughter told them. "I appreciate you coming this far with me."

"It's just that I have a wife and children who are depending on me," Carlton said. "I wanted to help out, and if those outlaws are in this La Reata place, I still will, Sheriff. But I don't think I should cross the border."

Cleaver pushed up the round-lensed spectacles he wore. "I sympathize, too, Sheriff, but I wouldn't even be here if Mr. Stockard hadn't told Ross and me we'd better volunteer to come along."

"We agreed we weren't going to say anything about that, Joe," Murdock said.

"Yeah, but I've reached the end of what I'm willing to do for Stockard. I'd like to take the bank's money back to Tombstone just as much as you would, but it's not worth getting in trouble with the government. Risking my neck is enough."

Slaughter said, "Nobody's going to hold that against you, Cleaver," although the way the other men glared at the young teller put the lie to that statement. "Stay here with Captain Donelson and the others, and if we need to cross the border in the morning, you and Carlton can head back to Tombstone. Actually, that might be a good thing. You'll probably run into Deputies Howell and Alvord along the way, and you can tell them where we've gone."

With that settled, Slaughter, Murdock, Tadrack, and Winters got ready for their foray into the village. Since stealth was vitally important, Slaughter thought it would be better if they didn't carry rifles. He borrowed a couple .45s and a .36 caliber Colt Navy from some of the other men for his three companions. They tucked the handguns in the waistbands of their trousers.

"Good luck, Sheriff. If I hear shooting, we'll come on in right away. Otherwise we'll wait to get word from you." Donelson shook Slaughter's hand.

"If we're not back by morning, you'll know something's gone wrong."

"In that case, La Reata will be getting a visit from the United States cavalry," Donelson replied with a grim smile.

Slaughter took the lead as the four men headed toward the village on foot. Like any good cattleman, he regarded any job that couldn't be done from horseback as a job not worth doing, but there were always exceptions to that rule. Slipping up on a bunch of dirty outlaws who had kidnapped his wife was one of them.

Still, his feet hurt before they had gone a quarter mile. The walk probably bothered Murdock and Tadrack less, since they were used to working on their feet.

There wasn't much cover to be found as they approached the settlement. A few mesquite trees and some even scrubbier bushes were about all that was any good. Slaughter used them and every shadow he could find to disguise their approach.

If the bank robbers were in La Reata, they probably had guards posted. But they might not, if they had stopped at the village for a debauch before crossing the border. Even if some of them were supposed to be standing watch, there was a chance the men would be sneaking drinks from bottles of tequila and would be less than fully alert.

Slaughter whispered orders to his men until they got within a hundred yards of the buildings on the village's outskirts. Then he used hand signals to indicate that they should proceed in a crouching run.

The closest building was an adobe barn. When the four men were in the deep shadows next to its rear wall, Slaughter felt a little better. Keeping his left hand on the wall and his right on the pearl-handled butt of his Colt, he moved to the corner and risked a look around it.

He could see a slice of La Reata's main street. Full night had fallen, and the town appeared to be sleepy and quiet. Faint strains of guitar music came from one of the cantinas.

Slaughter squinted his eyes. Where would the outlaws be holding Viola? They wouldn't want to let her out of their sight, so she would be wherever they were. One of the cantinas? A whorehouse? He hated to think about his wife being forced to endure captivity in such a place, but as long as she was alive and safe, that was all he really cared about.

If the outlaws were in La Reata, their horses had to be, too, he realized. Maybe in the very barn he was behind, especially if it was a livery stable.

"Come on," he whispered to the other three. As he drew his gun, he began to creep along the side of the barn toward the street.

When he reached the building's front corner, he paused again. He could look the entire length of the main street, all the way to the mission at the far end.

Lights burned in the sanctuary, but Slaughter paid little attention to them. If there was any place in La Reata he *wouldn't* find the men who had raided Tombstone, he thought, it was in a house of God.

He was more interested in the cantina located diagonally across the street. A number of horses were tied outside that building, enough to make Slaughter's heart slug a little faster in his chest. He supposed the animals could belong to vaqueros who worked on the ranches in the area, both above and below the border, but it seemed unlikely that many of them would be in town at the same time. La Reata was just a tiny village, not a town like Tombstone.

It made more sense to him that the horses belonged to the gang of outlaws, and as he was thinking that, a figure appeared in the doorway of the cantina and swaggered outside, a little unsteady on his feet. Light from inside spilled over him, and Slaughter stiffened as he recognized the burly outlaw who had galloped out of Tombstone with Viola perched in front of him.

It still didn't make sense to him why the outlaws stopped in La Reata when they could have been across the border in less than half an hour, but Slaughter accepted that good fortune. It was just a matter of finding Viola and figuring out a way to get her free.

He turned to his companions and was about to whisper the news to them when something hard pressed into his side. The words froze in his throat as he recognized the metal cylinder of a gun barrel.

"Sorry, Sheriff," Ross Murdock said. "This is as far as it goes."

Chapter 15

"Hey, what are you doing?" Mose Tadrack exclaimed.

"Shut up," Murdock snapped. "Tadrack, you and Winters throw your guns away, or I'll blow a hole through the sheriff."

Slaughter said, "You men stand your ground. Murdock is bluffing. If he fires, it'll bring the outlaws down on all of us."

"They're here?" Winters asked. "You're sure?"

"I'm certain," Slaughter said. "I just saw one of them come out of the cantina and recognized him from the raid yesterday morning. In fact, he's the one who carried off my wife."

"I'm mighty sorry about that, Sheriff," Murdock said, "but I can't let you interfere. Those men have to get away with the loot they took from the bank."

Murdock's double cross had Slaughter thrown for a loop, but that didn't stop his brain from working at a rapid clip. "You're the one who took that shot at me last night. I figured it was Doyle, but it was you, Murdock."

"I thought if you were dead, the others would turn back," Murdock said tensely.

"And that would work out well for you, because then no one would ever know that you've been embezzling from the bank." The theory had just clicked together in Slaughter's mind. "With the bank cleaned out, the loss would be blamed on the robbers."

"Hold on a minute," Winters said. "You mean the outlaws didn't get as much as they figured on?"

Slaughter didn't know why that would matter to the corporal. He ignored the question. "You'll wind up in a lot more trouble if you pull that trigger, Murdock. Put the gun down and we'll work this out."

"I-I can't." Murdock's voice shook from strain. "If Mr. Stockard ever finds out what I've done, he'll put me in prison. I-I know he will."

Keeping his voice calm and steady, Slaughter asked, "How much did you take, son?"

"Almost"—Murdock had to swallow before he could go on—"six hundred dollars."

Rage boiled up inside Slaughter. This boy had tried to kill him and now wanted to ruin his attempt to rescue Viola, all over *six hundred measly dollars*? That might seem like a fortune to Ross Murdock, but it wasn't the price of a man's life and a woman's safety.

"Listen to me, Murdock," Slaughter said as he controlled his anger with an effort. "Put the gun down and

I'll take care of this. Corporal Winters will be going with Captain Donelson and the rest of his patrol when this is over, and he won't have any reason to say anything about this to the law, will you, Winters?"

The trooper sounded amused as he drawled, "I reckon not, Sheriff."

"And Mose won't say anything," Slaughter went on.

"No, sir, I sure won't," Tadrack vowed.

"When we get back to Tombstone, I'll make up any discrepancy. Stockard doesn't have to know anything about it." Slaughter's voice hardened. "But you'll have to pay me back, and you'll have to give me your word that you'll never do anything so blasted stupid again!"

"I-I . . ." Murdock moaned, moving the gun away from Slaughter's side and pointing it at the ground. In a miserable voice, he said, "My God, Sheriff, I'm so sorry. I-I don't know what got into me. I never should have done it in the first place, and then it seemed like everything I tried to do to fix it just made it worse." The words babbled out of the young man's mouth. "If you'll do that for me, I swear I'll never, ever do anything like that again!"

Corporal Winters said, "No, you sure won't, you dumb idiot."

He brought up his borrowed .45, jammed the muzzle against the side of Ross Murdock's head, and pulled the trigger. The gun's boom was slightly muffled as the heavy slug shattered Murdock's skull, bored through his brain, and exploded out the other side. As Murdock dropped dead to the ground like a puppet with its strings cut, Winters took a fast step back and covered Slaughter and Tadrack with the revolver.

"Fella almost ruined everything," Winters said with a grin. "But I reckon it'll be all right now."

On the plains north of the village, gunfire erupted.

There was no law in La Reata, not even a local constable, and even if there had been, it seemed unlikely the outlaws would have worried about him. Judging by the way they swaggered around openly, they seemed to think that they owned the place.

Viola found out why that was during supper in the hotel dining room with Chaco, Mercedes, and Gabriel. Mercedes explained that in addition to trying to raise an army to throw off the yoke of the dictator Díaz, her brother had been helping her and the people of La Reata for several years.

"At one time, this was part of Mexico." Mercedes took a sip of wine from her glass. "To the people, it might as well still be. Treaties signed in Washington and Mexico City and borders shifting back and forth have no meaning to them."

"The Mission of San Lorenzo has been here for more than a hundred years," Gabriel added. "But it had fallen into disrepair until Chaco and I and the others helped restore it to what it once was. Chaco made sure a priest was sent here, as well."

Chaco looked more and more uncomfortable as his sister and his friend talked. "Good deeds are best done in the dark, so that no one knows about them."

"But people should know," Mercedes insisted. "The government calls you a bandit and sends the *rurales* to pursue you, but everything you do is for the good of the people."

Viola looked across the table at Chaco. "Can't you do good without breaking the law?"

"Honestly, these days in Mexico . . ." He shook his head. "No, señorita. I wish it were otherwise, but you cannot."

"I'm not sure I believe that."

"Believe it," Gabriel said. "If the *rurales* ever got their hands on us, they would have us up against a wall in front of a firing squad so quick—"

"That's enough," Mercedes interrupted. "I don't like talk such as that. Someday things will be different and good men won't have to worry about firing squads."

"I pray that you are right, *mi hermana*," Chaco said quietly.

Viola took a sip of her wine and thought about how bizarre the situation was. They were four people sitting around a table, having a conversation about politics, law, and good deeds, and it was easy to forget that less than forty-eight hours earlier she had been forcibly abducted by the two men who were now her dinner companions.

She knew she should hate them—and she was still angry with them for what they had done, no doubt about that—but she couldn't bring herself to feel about them as she had during those first few desperate hours of her captivity.

They were the only ones in the dining room. The hotel owner and his wife the cook had served them and then withdrew.

When the meal was finished, Gabriel grinned at Mercedes. "We go back to the cantina now, eh? You haven't danced for me in a long time, Mercedes."

She slapped his hand. "Stop that. There will be no dancing tonight. Señorita Smith will be coming back to the cantina with me."

"Actually," Viola said as she looked at Chaco, "I wouldn't mind taking a closer look at some of the paintings and tapestries in the mission. They seemed to be very beautiful."

He hesitated, then said, "I could show them to you. They are beautiful, and there is no more peaceful place that I know of."

"You won't let her get away, *amigo*?" Gabriel rumbled.

"I won't try to get away," Viola said.

Chaco looked surprised by that statement. "You give me your word on that, señorita?"

"I do. I think I've misjudged you, Señor Romero."

"I told you," Gabriel said with his leering grin.

Viola ignored the big outlaw and said to Chaco, "I'd like to hear more about your plans for helping your people."

He leaned forward and nodded. "I could tell you—"

"Be careful, Chaco." Mercedes looked narrow-eyed at Viola. "I think this one maybe should not be trusted."

"What am I going to do?" Viola demanded. "I'm unarmed, I have no horse, and Chaco's men are all over town. I'm not insane. He's promised me that when whatever brought him to La Reata is over and done with, I'll be free to go. I believe him."

"It's the truth," Chaco said. "Don't worry so, Mercedes. Señorita Smith will not cause any trouble."

Oddly enough, thought Viola, that was true. She was content to wait things out and see what happened.

Even more odd, she knew that big brute of a Gabriel wanted some time alone with Mercedes, and for some reason she wanted to help make that happen.

Matchmaking, it seemed, was contagious.

Mercedes still looked worried, but she didn't say anything else as Viola and Chaco left the hotel and walked toward the mission at the end of the street. He kept a small but circumspect distance between them as she put her hat on and tipped it jauntily to one side.

"I read a book a year or so ago about a man in England called Robin Hood. He was an outlaw, but he stole only from the rich and used the money to help the common people. Is that who you are, Señor Romero? The Robin Hood of Arizona Territory?"

"I only wish that were true," Chaco said. "Many of the people who had their money in the bank at Tombstone, they were not rich, I think. It is a bad thing we have done, even though we did it with good in mind. Good for my people, not yours." A slightly bitter tone came into his voice as he added, "You see, señorita, nothing in this world is completely pure, no matter how much we would like for it to be."

Not knowing what to say to that, Viola was silent as they walked the rest of the way to the mission.

Once they were inside, she actually enjoyed looking at the paintings, the tapestries, the icons, and the relics with which the mission was furnished. While she was looking around, a brown-robed priest came out of a room in the back and spoke briefly to Chaco.

When the priest was gone, Chaco went over to Viola. "Father Fernando was telling me how the work is going around here."

"The work of the Church?" Viola asked. "Or the work of your revolution?"

"God does not want the people ruled by a dictator—"

Chaco stopped short as somewhere in the village a gun suddenly boomed. Viola stiffened as the crackle of gunfire in the distance followed that single shot.

"What—" she exclaimed.

A look of genuine surprise passed over Chaco's face as he reached out and took hold of her arm. "Stay here," he urged. "There was not supposed to be any violence." He let go of her and started for the doors.

"Chaco, wait!"

He paused and looked back at her. "Stay here, I beg

of you, señorita. It may not be safe on the streets of La Reata tonight."

Viola stood in the aisle tensely as he rushed out of the mission. Chaco might be surprised and puzzled by the shots, but to her they had only one possible meaning.

John Slaughter had arrived.

Chapter 16

Luther Gentry and Grover Harmon hunkered on their heels and smoked quirlies as they waited for Sheriff Slaughter to return to the posse and cavalry patrol. They traded whoppers as they puffed on the cigarettes. It helped pass the time.

Gentry said, "I once saw a fella bucked so high off a bronc he was tryin' to break that the hoss had time to swap ends before he came back down. When he landed he was bass-ackwards in the saddle."

"That ain't nothin," Harmon replied. "I knowed a bronc peeler who got throwed so high the other hands was able to lasso that buckin' devil and lead him away and put another un in his place before the varmint lit in the saddle again."

"Well, this fella I knew got so tangled up once with a hoss that he wound up wearin' the saddle and the hoss had the *hombre*'s hat on his head by the time it was all over!"

The two old-timers continued swapping lies. Pete Yardley drifted over to join them, followed by Diego Herrara and Chester Carlton. The bank teller and the gambler still stood apart, waiting near their horses.

Captain Donelson, followed by half a dozen of the troopers under his command, approached the group of posse members. Gentry and Harmon stood up and nodded to the officer.

"Something we can do for you, Cap'n?" Harmon asked.

"Sheriff Slaughter's been gone for a while. I thought we would have gotten word from him by now, or he'd be back to report that the outlaws aren't in La Reata after all."

"We got to be patient," Gentry said. "You got to take it slow and careful-like when you're skulkin' around. The sheriff's a good man. He knows what to do."

"I've heard of him. He already has a reputation as an excellent lawman."

Harmon snorted. "I reckon he's done more to clean up things around Tombstone than anybody else ever has. Folks always talk about the Earps, but shoot, they stirred up as much trouble as they ever put a stop to. Maybe more. Odds are Tombstone would've been a more peaceful place if Virgil and Wyatt and them other boys hadn't ever rode in."

Gentry added, "Some say they was no better than outlaws their own selves. Nobody can claim that about Texas John Slaughter, though. Man's straight as a die."

"Although I do recollect hearin' that when he was younger he got accused a time or two of runnin' a few cattle with iffy brands," Harmon put in. "Don't know if there's anything to those stories, though."

"An honest lawman," Donelson mused. "That must be a good thing for a community to have."

"It sure makes a difference." Gentry's eyes narrowed slightly as he looked toward the horses. Several more troopers had drifted up behind Doyle and Cleaver.

There was nothing unusual about that, Gentry supposed, but he thought that it looked for all the world like those soldier boys were sneaking up on the gambler and the bank teller.

That had just occurred to him when the flat sound of a shot came from somewhere in La Reata. Several of the men jerked their heads in that direction, and Pete Yardley exclaimed, "Blast it! The sheriff might be in trouble. We'd better—"

Donelson slid his revolver smoothly from leather and the troopers with him raised their rifles and pointed them at the men from Tombstone. It happened so quickly that Gentry and the other posse members hardly knew what was going on.

"That's not exactly the signal I told Winters to give us," Donelson said, "but I don't think we can afford to ignore it. You gentlemen stand where you are and don't try to use your guns!"

"What the devil—" Harmon began.

"Look out! The gambler—" one of the troopers cried.

The soldiers who had moved up behind Doyle and Cleaver had thrown down on them when Donelson pulled out his gun. Jack Doyle didn't cooperate, though. He suddenly darted between two of the horses so that the animals shielded him from the troopers' rifles.

As he grabbed a horse's reins, Doyle stuck a foot in the stirrup and took hold of the saddle horn with his left hand. His right flashed to his pistol. Orange flame spouted from the muzzle as he fired at the cavalrymen and scattered them.

"Stop him!" Donelson bellowed as the spooked horse burst into a gallop with Doyle desperately clinging to him. "Don't let him get away!"

In the dark, if only a couple men had opened fire on Doyle he might have had a chance. But fully a dozen of the soldiers triggered rounds from their Springfields at the gambler. The bullets tore through his body, making him lose his grip on the saddle horn.

A couple slugs creased the horse's rump. In pain, the animal lunged ahead faster in a panic-stricken dash. With his foot still stuck in the stirrup, Doyle's corpse bounced crazily as the horse dragged it across the plains.

With that commotion going on, Gentry tried to lift his rifle, but Donelson sprang forward and swung the revolver in his fist. The barrel crashed into the side of the liveryman's head and drove him off his feet. Blood welled from the cut the gun sight opened up and flowed down Gentry's leathery cheek.

"Dang it!" Harmon yelled angrily as he dropped to

one knee beside his fallen friend. "Did you have to do that?"

"I could have just killed him and been done with it," Donelson said in cool, menacing tones. "I might still do that if you fools don't cooperate."

"You fellas ain't real soldiers, are you?" Yardley sounded stunned by the sudden turn of events.

That question brought a chuckle from Donelson. "As a matter of fact, we are. Or rather, we were, if you want to be precise about it."

"Deserters!" Harmon spat. He lifted Gentry's bleeding head and cradled it on his leg. "Bunch o' no-good deserters!"

"Your insults don't mean anything to me, old man," Donelson said with a smug smile. "All of you put your guns down and step away from them."

Gentry groaned. He had dropped his rifle already, and so had Harmon. Yardley, Herrara, Carlton, and Cleaver followed Donelson's orders. Even in the faint light from the moon and stars, it was obvious that the drummer and the bank teller were terrified. Yardley just looked mad, and Herrara's squarish face was impassive and hard to read.

"What are you varmints gonna do with us?" Harmon demanded. "Murder us like you did Doyle?"

"The fool would still be alive if he hadn't tried to escape. We're here to get rich, not to kill people. We'll just take you into La Reata with us while we conduct our business. Once we're gone, you'll be free to go, too."

"Business," Harmon repeated. "What in blazes are you talkin' about?"

"We're going to meet those outlaws you've been chasing all the way from Tombstone. They're our . . . partners, I suppose you'd say." Donelson jerked his gun in a curt gesture. "Enough talk. Get Gentry on his feet. They're waiting for us in town."

Fury welled up inside Slaughter as he looked from Murdock's body to the gun in Corporal Winters' hand. The urge to try a shot at Winters was almost impossible to overcome.

What made him rein in that impulse was the knowledge that Viola was somewhere in La Reata and still needed his help. He couldn't risk his life just yet.

"Wha . . . what's going on here?" Tadrack said.

"Put your gun on the ground, mister," Winters ordered without answering the swamper's question. "Slaughter, you drop that fancy gun, too."

"Tell me, Corporal," Slaughter said coolly as he followed Winters' order and put his Colt on the ground, "are you an actual cavalry trooper? Or just another outlaw?"

"I was a trooper until a few days ago," Winters drawled. "Reckon now the army figures I'm a deserter. But I'm gonna be a rich deserter pretty soon."

Again, the wheels of Slaughter's brain revolved rapidly, as they had when he'd figured out that Ross Murdock must have embezzled money from the bank, but he couldn't come up with an answer. Whatever Winters was up to was a mystery to him.

Judging by the flurry of shots that had sounded in the distance, the rest of the cavalry patrol was in on it, too.

He never should have trusted Captain Brice Donelson, Slaughter realized.

It was too late for thoughts like that. He shoved them aside, deciding to find out as much as he could and wait for the right moment to make his move.

Mose Tadrack still held the borrowed revolver. Winters snapped, "I won't tell you again to put that gun down, Tadrack."

"Sheriff?"

"Do what he says, Mose," Slaughter said quietly. "We can't do anybody any good by getting ourselves killed."

"That's sure enough true," Winters said.

Tadrack had laid the weapon at his feet and stepped back away from it.

"All right, we'll just wait right here for the others to show up," Winters told them.

"Did you have to kill Murdock?" Slaughter asked. "You could have gotten the drop on him, too."

"He was already on edge and primed to shoot somebody. I don't like to take chances. Besides, what do you care, Sheriff? Hell, he admitted that he was a thief and tried to bushwhack you last night."

"He was foolish, but he didn't deserve to die over six hundred dollars."

"Well, it's too late to worry about that now, ain't it?"

Slaughter's eyes narrowed. He didn't feel a great deal

of sympathy for Murdock, but he vowed that he would see justice done for the young man's murder, anyway.

First, there was the little matter of surviving whatever plans Winters and his treacherous fellow cavalrymen had made for their rendezvous in La Reata.

Chapter 17

Despite what Chaco had told her, Viola followed him to the door of the sanctuary and watched as he strode into the street. Gabriel hurried up to join him. The big outlaw's burly figure was impossible to mistake. More members of the gang emerged from other buildings along the street and gathered with Chaco and Gabriel.

A soft step behind her made Viola gasp and turn around. She relaxed slightly when she saw the sad-faced priest standing there in his brown robe and sandals.

"You should come away from the door, my child," he said in softly accented English. "I do not think there will be trouble, but one never knows."

Father Fernando, that was what Chaco had called him, Viola recalled. "Father, do you know what's going on here? What was that shooting about?"

The padre shook his head. "Chaco's plan for tonight was a peaceful one. But sometimes circumstances force plans to change."

"So you *do* know what he's doing."

"Bringing justice to a country in desperate need of it. That is his intention, at least."

Viola looked out in the street again. What appeared to be the entire gang had congregated in front of the hotel. They stood tensely, some with rifles in their hands, others holding pistols. They were ready for a fight, if one developed.

Fear for her husband's safety filled Viola. When she had heard the single shot, then the flurry of gunfire, she had been sure the reports heralded John's arrival. She'd expected him to come barreling into La Reata at the head of a posse, with guns blazing.

That hadn't happened, and from Chaco's reaction and the way his men had flocked to him, something else was going on. Her thoughts were confused as she tried to figure it out.

Father Fernando's hand plucked at her sleeve. "Please, come away—"

More movement from up the street caught Viola's eye. Several men moved out into the open from the shadows next to a building. As they walked toward Chaco, Gabriel, and the rest of the gang, Viola realized that two men were being prodded along at gunpoint by a third man.

And one of those men under the gun was—

"John!" she cried as she burst out of the mission and broke into a run up the street.

Slaughter's breath caught in his throat when he heard his wife's voice. He saw her emerge from the mission at the end of the street and start toward them. Involuntarily, he took a quick step forward to meet her.

"Hold it, Sheriff!" Winters barked. "I'll put a bullet in you if you try to run."

A shiver went through Slaughter. Part of it was anger, but most of the reaction was the need to grab Viola and draw her into his arms. He controlled it with an effort. It wouldn't help anything if he got gunned down.

Gabriel stepped forward and caught Viola as she ran by him. She struggled and pounded her fists against his barrel chest, but she had no chance of breaking out of his grip.

Slaughter recognized him as the big man he'd identified a few minutes earlier.

"Go ahead," Winters ordered, "but take it easy, Sheriff. Don't get carried away and do something foolish."

With his jaw tight from strain, Slaughter started walking forward slowly again.

"That's Miz Slaughter," Tadrack said beside him. "Thank God it looks like she's all right, Sheriff."

"Yes," Slaughter said. "For now."

It was true. Judging by the way Viola had run down the street, she seemed to be uninjured. She was dressed much differently from when she had been kidnapped from Tombstone. Denim trousers, a faded shirt, moccasins, and a flat-crowned hat had replaced the long white nightgown. As she struggled with the big outlaw, the hat had been knocked back so that it hung by its chin strap, and her dark hair was loose around her shoulders.

It may been relief at seeing she was alive, but Slaughter didn't think she had ever looked more beautiful.

Winters herded him and Tadrack up to the gang of outlaws in the street and raised his voice to ask, "Which one of you *hombres* is Chaco Romero?"

The lean, darkly handsome man stepped forward. His hand rested on the butt of the gun at his hip. "I'm Romero," he said curtly. "Who are you?"

"Ex-Corporal Lonnie Winters at your service, señor," the deserter said in a dryly amused tone. "Cap'n Donelson sends his respects. He'll be along directly, I expect."

"With the rifles? I did not expect you until tomorrow."

"Well, the cap'n don't have the rifles with him right now, but they'll be here, don't you worry about that."

Slaughter had been busy searching his wife's face, making sure she was all right, but he heard enough of the conversation that things began to make sense to him again. He looked back over his shoulder at Winters. "Those so-called supply wagons are full of stolen rifles, aren't they?"

"You're a little late figurin' that out, Sheriff," Winters drawled mockingly, "but like they say, better late than never, eh?"

The man called Romero seemed a little less tense, although he didn't take his hand off his gun. He nodded to the big outlaw who had hold of Viola. "I think you can let go of Señorita Smith now, Gabriel. I believe she wants to see her . . . old family friend."

Gabriel chuckled and turned Viola loose. She crossed the intervening ground in a flash and came into Slaughter's arms. He folded her tightly in an embrace as she buried her face against his shoulder. He brought a hand up and tenderly stroked her midnight-dark hair.

"Somehow I don't think he's just an old friend, eh, Chaco?" Gabriel said. "The señorita, she has been lying to us. If she *is* a señorita."

As soon as Romero had referred to Viola as Señorita Smith, Slaughter had known what was going on. She had hidden the fact that she was a sheriff's wife. He wasn't sure what her motivation for that deception had been, but he trusted her instincts. He knew how keenly intelligent she was.

However, her reaction on seeing him had rendered her pose as "Señorita Smith" moot. Anybody who had eyes could see that the two of them loved each other.

Indeed, Romero said, "The sheriff here is your husband, isn't he, Viola?"

It made Slaughter bristle to hear this outlaw refer to her in such a familiar manner. Of course, she had been their prisoner for two days and a night, so much worse things could have happened than for him to call her by her given name. Slaughter had sworn to himself that it would not change what was between them . . . but the reminder was unwelcome anyway.

As if she were reading his mind, Viola ignored Romero's question, lifted her head, and looked into Slaughter's eyes "Nothing happened, John. I swear it."

"Of course, my dear." His voice was a little stiff, and he knew it was because he wasn't a hundred percent certain that she wasn't trying to spare his feelings. "It need not be spoken of again. Ever."

"No, John." A new intensity was in her tone. "*Nothing happened.* I'll explain it later, but it's the truth."

Slaughter smiled. He didn't have to bend much to brush his lips across hers. "I believe you," he whispered. Then he circled an arm around her shoulders and leveled his cold gaze at Romero. "This is my wife, sir, and when you speak to her, I'll thank you to do it in a respectful tone."

Romero smiled. "Of course, Sheriff Slaughter."

"Well, this is a mighty touchin' reunion," Winters said, "but I could've told you these two was married, Romero. Me and the cap'n and the rest of the boys ran into a posse from Tombstone this mornin'. Cap'n Donelson agreed to join forces with Slaughter to help him chase down the no-good bandits who robbed the bank in Tombstone and carried off his wife."

That seemed to strike the ex-corporal as hilarious. His voice trailed off into laughter.

The sound of hoofbeats drifted down the main street of La Reata. Everyone turned to look as a large group of riders appeared at the northern end of the street and proceeded slowly along it.

Slaughter's heart sank slightly as he saw the remnants of his posse riding in front of Donelson and the other deserters. Luther Gentry's leathery old face was smeared with blood, but he seemed to be the only one who was hurt.

Slaughter counted quickly and realized that the posse

was one member short, not counting the murdered Ross Murdock. It took him only a second to figure out that the missing man was the gambler, Jack Doyle.

Had Doyle gotten away somehow? If he had, he might be able to find Stonewall and Burt and the rest of the reinforcements that Slaughter hoped fervently were on their way south from Tombstone.

But even if those men showed up, would there be enough of them to do any good? It didn't seem likely. The *bandidos* and the group of deserters together added up to approximately sixty men . . . and that wasn't counting the troopers Donelson had left with the supply train.

Donelson moved ahead of the prisoners and urged his horse to a faster pace. He drew up in front of the group waiting in the middle of the street, eyed Viola appreciatively for a second, and then said, "I'm looking for Chaco Romero."

"I'm Romero."

Donelson touched the brim of his hat in a casual sketch of a salute. "We haven't met, but I'm Captain Brice Donelson. Former captain, I should say, although I'm still in command of this patrol. It's a pleasure to make your acquaintance, Señor Romero. I believe we have some business to conduct."

Romero nodded. "Of course. As soon as we deal with these prisoners."

But Chaco didn't look all that pleased about it, Slaughter thought.

Donelson grinned at Slaughter. "Hello again, Sheriff. I suppose this lovely lady is your wife?"

"I don't have anything to say to a traitor like you, Donelson," Slaughter snapped.

"I don't see any need to be unpleasant, but have it your own way." Donelson glanced at Winters. "Where's the other one, Corporal?"

"I had to shoot him," Winters replied. "There's a good story goes with that, Cap'n. I'll tell you all about it later."

Donelson grunted. Clearly, the news that Winters had killed Ross Murdock meant less than nothing to him. He turned back to Romero. "What did you have in mind to do with them?"

"My men can hold them in the church," Chaco said. "You and I will go in my sister's cantina and discuss our arrangement."

"Cantina, eh?" A broad grin stretched across Donelson's face. "Best idea I've heard all day!"

Chapter 18

The other members of the posse had dismounted, and they trudged along dispiritedly with their heads down. The big outlaw called Gabriel, along with several more of Chaco's band and some of Donelson's troopers, herded the prisoners down the street toward the mission.

Slaughter kept an arm around Viola. He was anxious to have a chance to talk with her in private, but he didn't know when or if they would get that opportunity. He wanted to know everything she could tell him about the bandits. He hadn't given up on the idea of turning the tables on their captors and needed as much information as he could gather.

A balding, brown-robed priest stood in the mission's open double doorway with a worried frown on his somber face. "Gabriel, I don't like to see so many guns in the Lord's house. It's disrespectful."

"I'm sorry, Father. We have to guard these prisoners to make sure they don't do anything to ruin Chaco's plans."

"All right," the priest said reluctantly. "But please, there can't be any violence in here."

Gabriel nodded. "I know Chaco agrees with you about that, Father." He motioned with the revolver in his hand. "All right, move on in there, *hombres* . . . and Señora Slaughter."

"I didn't intentionally lie to you at first, Gabriel," Viola said. "I just let you and Chaco assume that I wasn't married."

"We should have known." Gabriel smiled and sighed. "All the beautiful ones are taken. My Mercedes, she is married to that cantina of hers, I think!"

The prisoners sat down on the pews, all on one side of the aisle so the guards would be able to keep an eye on them more easily. A gilt carving of Christ on the cross was mounted on the wall practically right above their heads.

Slaughter and Viola sat down next to Gentry, who had Grover Harmon on his other side. Slaughter leaned over. "What happened to you, Luther?"

"That damn Donelson—" Gentry stopped short, then muttered, "Shouldn't ought to cuss inside a church, I reckon. What I meant to say was, that no-good polecat who called hisself a cap'n pistol-whipped me when I tried to get my gun on him."

Harmon put in, "Luther bled like a stuck pig, too. I started to worry it was all gonna leak out."

"I'm fine," Gentry insisted. "Better than Jack Doyle, that's for sure."

"I noticed he wasn't with you," Slaughter said grimly. "What happened to him?"

"He tried to get away," Harmon said. "Made it onto a hoss, but then the varmints shot him to pieces. If that wasn't bad enough, when he fell off, his foot hung up in the stirrup, so his horse dragged him off across the plains when the nag bolted."

"So there's no chance he survived."

Harmon shook his head. "It'd be a pure-dee miracle." He looked around and sighed. "Despite our surroundin's, I got a hunch those are in mighty short supply tonight!"

The cavalry troopers and the *bandidos* went into the cantina and bellied up to the bar. The sounds of raucous laughter and loud talk filled the room, punctuated by the squeals of the serving girls as they were slapped on the rump or pulled onto the laps of lecherous men.

It was an odd thing, Chaco thought as he looked around the room. Under different circumstances, these two groups of men would be trying to kill each other. Greed on one side and practicality on the other had made them allies.

He called his sister over. "The captain and I would like to use your office, Mercedes."

"Of course." She eyed the cavalry officer, who returned the look with a frankly appraising stare that seemed to find much to approve of.

With some reluctance, Chaco introduced the two of them. "Mercedes, this is Captain Brice Donelson. Captain, my sister, Señorita Mercedes Romero."

"The pleasure is all mine, señorita." Donelson took Mercedes' right hand in both of his and held it a little longer than Chaco thought was necessary.

"Send Gabriel to the office when he gets back from the mission," he told Mercedes.

"All right." She took that as an excuse to extricate her hand skillfully from the captain's.

"This way, Captain." Chaco gestured toward the beaded doorway leading to the cantina's back rooms.

Donelson wasn't ready to give up. "I'm sure I'll be seeing you again while we're here, Señorita Romero."

"If *El Señor Dios* wills it," Mercedes murmured.

Chaco steered Donelson into the rear hallway and then into the office, which was rather sparsely furnished with a desk and a couple chairs. The only decoration on the wall was a small painting of the Madonna and child, but a vase with several red and yellow wildflowers added a spot of color to the room.

Chaco went behind the desk and waved Donelson into the chair in front of it. He took off his hat and dropped it on the desk next to the vase. Tired of small talk, he began the discussion. "Your corporal tells me that you don't have the rifles with you, Captain."

"You know, you don't have to address me by my rank. I suppose when you get right down to it I'm not a captain anymore since I've, ah, left the army."

"But it simplifies matters, does it not?"

"Well, that's true." Obviously at ease, Donelson cocked his right ankle on his left knee and leaned back slightly in the chair. "You know, a drink might be nice. I've found that business discussions often go better when a man's throat is properly lubricated."

"But our arrangement is already settled. The price for the guns was agreed to by our intermediaries."

"Yes, of course."

"It would be unwise to try to change the details of the agreement now," Chaco said softly.

He saw a flash of steely anger in Donelson's eyes, but the man's faintly arrogant smile never wavered. "That's not my intention, *amigo*. I'm just trying to keep things on a friendly basis here."

"Of course." Chaco resisted the impulse to tell Donelson that they weren't friends and never would be. He didn't like the fact that Donelson's men had killed two members of Sheriff John Slaughter's posse.

Unfortunately, true change usually could not be brought about without bloodshed. The dictator Díaz would not relinquish his power willingly. The people would have to take it from him, and that meant more men would die. Women and children, too, more than likely. Chaco knew he would carry that stain on his soul for the rest of his life.

That was the price he must pay for doing what had to be done.

Donelson went on. "I hope you're not worried because I got here ahead of the guns. My plan was for all of us to stay together while we brought the wagons here, but then we ran into Slaughter and his pitiful excuse for a posse. I decided it might be better to split my force and come with him, just to make sure he didn't cause any trouble with our deal. The wagons—and the rifles— ought to be here sometime tomorrow."

"That's good to hear." The mention of Sheriff Slaughter made Chaco's thoughts stray to Viola. He had sensed all along that she might not be telling him the truth about who she was, but never would he have dreamed that she was married to a man so many years older than her.

Although to be fair, from what he had seen of John Slaughter, the man possessed a vitality that made him seem younger than he really was and larger than his compact stature. His courage and determination were easy to see. Chaco would have been pleased to have such a man as his ally in his quest to bring freedom and justice to Mexico.

That was almost certainly never to be. Even though Viola's capture had been a fluke of circumstances, Slaughter wouldn't forgive what had happened to his wife. Chaco hoped she would be able to reassure her husband that she had not been mistreated during her time with the revolutionaries.

The noise from the cantina swelled up as the door opened and Gabriel came into the office.

"The prisoners are secure in the mission?" Chaco asked his old friend.

Gabriel nodded. He had his left hand wrapped around the neck of a tequila bottle. "I left several of our best men guarding them. I think we have nothing to fear from them, Chaco."

"Good. If they'll just be reasonable, they can leave here safely once our business is concluded and we're gone." Chaco looked at Donelson again. "I hope you will be able to keep your men under control while we're waiting for the rifles to get here, Captain."

"Well, you have to remember they're not duty-bound to follow my orders anymore," Donelson replied. "They'll want to blow off some steam. After all, they risked their lives stealing those guns and they've made themselves fugitives. They'll never be able to go back to their families and their old lives."

"And they are being well paid for that sacrifice," Chaco snapped. "My men have sacrificed much as well and will risk even more in the future, simply because they want to do the right thing."

"It's their country," Donelson pointed out. "Not mine or my men's."

Chaco shrugged.

"If they want to get drunk or bed some whores, I'm not going to stop them," the captain went on.

"Tell them to leave the respectable citizens of La Reata alone," Chaco said tensely.

"You can't expect them to tell one pretty señorita from another." Donelson looked up at Gabriel, who lounged with his back against the wall next to the desk. "How about sharing that bottle, *amigo*?"

Gabriel glanced at Chaco, who gave him a curt nod. He handed the bottle to Donelson. The officer tilted it to his mouth and took a healthy swallow. He licked his lips and said, "Ah," as he gave it back.

Chaco wished he didn't have to deal with a man such as this in order to get what he needed. But once the rifles arrived in La Reata, they could make the exchange, and he would never have to have anything to do with Brice Donelson again.

That time could not come soon enough to suit Chaco.

Chapter 19

Father Fernando asked the guards if he could bring wine and food for the prisoners, and when they agreed he retreated into the rear of the mission and came back with cups, a jug of wine, and a platter full of tortillas.

"It is simple fare, my friends, but all I can offer you," the priest told them.

"We appreciate it, Father," Slaughter said.

"I had supper earlier," Viola added, "but I'd love a cup of wine."

As they sat and sipped their drinks, Slaughter stretched his legs out in front of him and crossed them at the ankles. "I can't tell you how relieved I was to see you, my dear. I say, Viola, I've spent the past two days more worried than I've ever been in my life. You're sure you weren't harmed?"

"Positive. The only thing that might have hurt me was riding for such a long time, and you know that being in the saddle doesn't bother me, John."

"You've always been an excellent rider, ever since I've known you," Slaughter admitted. "But I find it hard to believe that such rough men didn't . . . well . . ."

"I told you, you can put your mind at ease on that score." She laughed softly. "I wouldn't go so far as to say that Gabriel was a perfect gentleman, but if he was a bit forward at times, I think it was inadvertent. Most of it, anyway. As for Chaco—"

"Yes, what about Chaco?" Slaughter asked crisply. "The two of you seem to be on excellent terms."

That brought another laugh from Viola. "Why, John, if I didn't know better, I'd say that you're jealous."

"Nonsense. I don't believe for one second that you'd throw me over for some *bandido*."

"Of course I wouldn't. Chaco Romero isn't some run-of-the-mill bandit, though. He used to be a priest, and he's still very devoted to good works. He gave his men firm orders that I was not to be harmed or molested in any way."

"And they went along with those orders?"

"That's how much they respect him."

"He's still a bank robber," Slaughter said.

"Yes, and I don't condone that. He's going to use the money to buy guns for the revolutionary army he's trying to raise."

Slaughter nodded. "I figured that out. I'm not going to admire him because he's a rebel, though. He's funding his revolution with the money of honest, hardworking American citizens. No matter how you look at it, that's outright thievery, and Romero has to answer for it."

"That's going to be difficult, as outnumbered as you are," Viola pointed out quietly.

Slaughter frowned. He knew what she said was true, but he hadn't given up on the idea of turning this debacle around somehow.

He looked around at the men from his posse. Luther Gentry still appeared pretty shaky after being pistol-whipped, but he would come around. The old liveryman was tough as whang leather. So was his friend Grover Harmon. Slaughter knew he could count on them, and he figured that Pete Yardley probably wouldn't let him down, either. Pete had been in Arizona Territory for a long time, and it bred toughness in a man.

The same held true for Diego Herrara. Slaughter couldn't be absolutely sure the cook would back any play he made, but he suspected Herrara would.

That left Joseph Cleaver and Chester Carlton, both of whom looked scared enough to piss in their boots, and Mose Tadrack, who was still an unknown quantity. Tadrack didn't exactly seem scared, but he was pale and drawn and kept licking his lips. The strain of being a prisoner might be making his thirst worse.

Gabriel had left five men from Romero's group to stand guard over the prisoners. Two were at the double doors, one was posted at the door leading into the rear of the mission, and the other two lounged on benches across the aisle from where the prisoners were gathered. All of them seemed reasonably alert, but as the night wore on and they grew more tired, it might be easier to take them by surprise.

The problem was that it was a long way from the mission to the livery stable. Even if the prisoners could manage to escape from the building where they were being held, it might be very difficult to reach some horses and get away from the village.

As always, Viola seemed to know what he was thinking. She said quietly, "Chaco promised to let us go once his business was done and he and his men headed for the border. I know you want to stop him and recover that money, John, but it might cost all of us our lives."

Slaughter frowned. "Are you saying we shouldn't fight?"

"I'm saying you should consider everything before you make a move."

"I always do."

"And if it does come down to a fight . . . make sure you've got a gun for me, too."

Now *that* was the Viola he knew.

Donelson left Romero and the big brute called Gabriel in the office and went back into the cantina to look for Mercedes. He spotted her behind the bar and started in that direction, but Lonnie Winters intercepted him along the way.

"Get everything settled with those greasers, Cap'n?" the former corporal asked with his usual cocky grin.

"I think so." Something occurred to Donelson and he suggested, "Let's sit down and have a drink."

"Now that's somethin' I never say no to."

As they took chairs at one of the empty tables, Donelson told Winters the same thing he had told Romero. "You don't have to call me captain anymore, you know."

"I suppose I could call you boss, since we're pretty much outlaws now and you're still ramroddin' the bunch, but you know, *cap'n* just sounds better to me for some reason. I guess it's what I'm used to. Of course, if you don't like it—"

Donelson waved that idea away. "No, it doesn't bother me. What bothers me are these two-bit revolutionaries we're dealing with."

"I was never partial to bean-eaters, myself." Winters looked around speculatively. "I got to say, though, some of these curvy little brown-skinned gals look good enough to eat."

Donelson grunted and lifted a hand to signal to one of the young women Winters referred to. As she came over to the table, he had to agree that she was rather delectable. Her skin was a little darker than honey, her hair was a tumbled mass of raven curls, and her eyes were the warmest, deepest brown Donelson had ever seen. She was several years short of twenty, he judged, but a full-grown woman nonetheless, as demonstrated by the tantalizing half-moons of her upper breasts revealed by the low neck of her white blouse.

"*Cerveza, por favor*," Donelson ordered and gestured to indicate that the girl should bring beers to them.

"Most of the other fellas are drinkin' tequila," Winters pointed out as the girl went to fetch the drinks.

"Yes, but I can't have you falling into a drunken stupor, Sergeant."

Winters frowned slightly. "I was a corporal."

"Well, now you're a sergeant." Donelson laughed. "Hell, I think I'll make myself a colonel."

"Why not a general?"

"I don't want to get ahead of myself. In time, Sergeant, in time."

Winters leaned back in his chair. "You sounded like you've got a job for me, Cap'n . . . I mean Colonel."

Donelson grew more solemn. "I was talking to Romero just now. He indicated that he plans to leave those prisoners in the mission when he and his men ride out tomorrow. That troubles me, Sergeant. Sheriff Slaughter and his men know who we are."

"Well, I reckon that by now the army has a pretty good idea we've done deserted and made off with all them rifles," Winters pointed out. "They're gonna be lookin' for us, anyway."

"I know, but the idea of leaving witnesses behind still rubs me the wrong way. Quite possibly it wouldn't make any difference . . . but why take unnecessary chances? Besides"—Donelson paused for a second—"did you get a good look at Mrs. Slaughter?"

Winters grinned again. "She's a mighty pretty woman,

all right, Colonel. Were you thinkin' you might take her along with us as a bonus?"

"The idea crossed my mind," Donelson admitted. His voice hardened slightly as he added, "But I'd be taking her along with *me*."

Winters held up both hands, palms out, and shook his head. "That's fine with me. I can appreciate the lady's good looks without wantin' to be saddled with her. I don't reckon she'd cooperate too much if you took her away from her husband."

"I can teach her to cooperate," Donelson said, his voice flinty, "if she knows what's good for her."

The serving girl brought mugs of beer to the table and set them down in front of the two men. Winters reached up, slid an arm around her waist, and tugged her onto his lap. She laughed as he nuzzled his face into the soft valley between her breasts, then she gracefully slipped out of his grasp. Clearly it wasn't the first time she had dealt with such advances.

"You an' me, we're gonna get together later, señorita," Winters called after her as she danced away from the table.

Donelson picked up his mug and downed some of the warm beer. It wasn't very good, but it eased the dryness in his throat.

Winters took a drink, too. "Why are you tellin' me this about the prisoners?"

"I was impressed by the way you handled things when you came into town with Slaughter and those other two,

Winters. You saw a situation that needed to be dealt with, and you took care of it quickly and efficiently."

"You mean when I blowed that stupid varmint's brains out."

"Exactly. Do you think you could find, oh, half a dozen men among the troop who can be counted on to do what needs to be done?"

"I reckon I probably could. What's the job you've got in mind?"

"I think you know," Donelson said. "Once we have the money, take the detail you put together and go to the mission. Take charge of Mrs. Slaughter and bring her to me . . . but not until you've killed the rest of the prisoners."

Chapter 20

At Donelson's suggestion, Winters began circulating through the cantina to sound out some of the other men and see if they would be up to taking on the bloody task the captain had laid out. Although the troopers were all deserters and had been willing to go along with Donelson's plans in return for a share of the money from the sale of the rifles, some of them might balk at the prospect of mass murder.

Not all of them, though. Donelson shared Winters' conviction that they could find enough men to take care of what needed to be done.

Since he was alone at the table, Donelson caught the eye of the girl who had brought them the beer earlier and crooked a finger at her. She looked a little tentative. He supposed that was because he wasn't quite as young and handsome as Winters.

But he would soon be a rich man. Richer than any of

his men even suspected, if everything went according to plan.

He wasn't interested in her, though, no matter what she might think. His taste ran to more mature females.

"You wish something, señor?" the girl asked as she came up to the table. "More beer? Tequila? Mescal?"

"Actually, I want you to deliver a message to your employer for me," Donelson said.

"My employer?"

"Señorita Romero."

"Ah," the girl said, brightening. "Señorita Mercedes."

"That's right. Tell her I'd like to speak with her. Ask her if she would be so kind as to join me."

The girl looked doubtful and shook her head. "The señorita, she does not often drink with the customers—"

"Just tell her, *por favor*." Donelson's voice hardened slightly as he spoke.

"Of course, señor. Is there anything else?"

"Not right now." Donelson took a coin from his pocket and laid it on the table in front of the girl. "But later . . . you make my young friend happy, understand?"

The coin disappeared, swept deftly off the table so that it vanished into a hidden pocket in the voluminous skirt. "I understand, señor. *Gracias*." The girl turned and walked away.

Donelson sipped his beer and thought about Viola Slaughter and Mercedes Romero. They were both very beautiful women, but Viola was more the sort he would want to take away from here and keep with him for a while. Mercedes would be good for passing the time while he was in La Reata waiting to be a rich man. He would enjoy her company very much, he thought.

After a few minutes, Mercedes appeared. She came up to the table and regarded Donelson coolly. "Estellita said you wished to see me, Captain."

"That's right." Donelson gestured at the empty chair Winters had occupied earlier. "Please, have a seat and join me."

Mercedes shook her head. "I don't really do that, señor."

"You won't have a drink with a good customer?"

"I only met you tonight, Captain," she reminded him. "And from what I've heard, you plan to leave tomorrow. You probably won't be visiting my cantina again."

"All the more reason to make this visit memorable. I was thinking that perhaps you could show me your living quarters. . . ."

Mercedes leaned toward him slightly. While her dress wasn't as low-cut as the peasant blouses her serving girls wore, its neckline dipped enough to give him an enticing glimpse of the smooth brown valley between her breasts.

She said softly, "Captain Donelson, while my brother may be doing business with you, I am not . . . except for selling drinks to your men. I have no interest in spending the night with you, and I will tell you what I would tell any man making unwelcome advances toward me— leave me alone or I will slice off your *cojones* and throw them to the hogs for a treat. A tiny treat. *Comprende?*"

She smiled, so that no one looking on would guess

what she was saying. But as she spoke, rage welled up inside Donelson. He stiffened and started to stand up.

"Keep your seat." Mercedes moved a hand slightly, and light from the candelabras that hung from the ceiling flashed on the blade of the dagger she held.

Donelson began, "I ought to—"

"You ought to forget this happened, Captain. You and my brother need each other. Don't let the weakness of the flesh interfere with your arrangement."

"What if I told him you threatened me?"

"Then I would tell him what you just suggested, and he would kill you. That would ruin everything, would it not?"

"You didn't have to act so insulted," Donelson said sullenly.

"If you want a girl, there are others to choose from."

"I don't want a girl. I want a woman."

Mercedes smiled again. "That is almost flattering. Almost. *Buenas noches*, Captain Donelson." She slipped the dagger back wherever it had come from, turned, and walked away from the table.

With an effort that tightened his jaw and made a shiver go through him, Donelson controlled his anger. Before this was over, Mercedes Romero would regret speaking to him that way, he vowed. He would see to it that she was sorry.

It was almost dawn when Gabriel Hernandez slipped out through the cantina's rear door. He stretched and yawned. A pleasant lassitude gripped him. The night he had just spent with Mercedes had been very enjoyable, as usual. She had seemed a bit distracted by something at first, he thought, but then his kisses had warmed her as they always did. Nay, they had enflamed her!

A huge grin stretched across his ugly face at the memory.

He knew he was ugly, and it was a miracle from *El Señor Dios* that Mercedes did not consider him so. She loved him and he loved her, and once Chaco's revolution was over and done with and the dictator Díaz had been unseated, Gabriel planned to come back to La Reata. Father Fernando at the mission would join him and his beautiful Mercedes in marriage, and he would live out the rest of his life happily running the cantina with her. It was a consummation devoutly to be wished.

But there was still a revolution to begin and a war to be waged, and that began with an army, and an army began with men and guns. Chaco had the men, and as soon as those army wagons arrived, he would have the guns.

Gabriel strolled toward the mission. He wanted to check on the prisoners and their guards, and then maybe he would go up to the livery stable, crawl in a pile of hay, and sleep until the wagons rolled into the village. It was an appealing prospect.

Although the eastern sky held a faint rose tinge heralding the approach of the sun, shadows were still thick around the buildings in the village. When he heard voices up ahead, Gabriel stopped and stood unseen in the gloom next to a closed mercantile. Some instinct warned him.

A moment later, a whiff of tobacco smoke drifted to him. That didn't have to mean anything other than the fact that someone was up early, but Gabriel had learned to trust his gut. He stayed close to the wall and moved forward with a degree of stealth uncommon in such a big man.

The words he heard were in English, and one of the voices was familiar—the cavalry captain called Donelson.

"—got everything lined up?"

"I surely do, Cap'n."

Gabriel knew that soft drawl, too, he realized. It belonged to Corporal Winters, the trooper who had killed one of Sheriff Slaughter's posse men and then taken Slaughter and Tadrack prisoner.

"I'm glad to hear it, Sergeant," Donelson said. "Remember, no harm is to come to Mrs. Slaughter. You make sure of that."

"I understand," Winters said. "Me and the other fellas will make sure the sheriff and the rest of 'em are dead."

Gabriel stiffened in surprise and anger. The two cavalrymen were talking about murdering the prisoners. Chaco had forbidden it. He had promised Señora Slaughter—Gabriel had to remind himself not to think of her as Señorita Smith or Viola anymore— that they would be left behind safely in La Reata when the revolutionaries headed back across the border. Chaco had made that clear to the captain as well.

It was clear that Donelson planned a double cross. He was going to wipe out the other prisoners and take Señora Slaughter with him.

Gabriel could not allow that.

He wanted to confront the two plotters then and there, but he forced himself to wait and listen to see if they said anything else. It would be better to tell Chaco about this startling discovery. He would know what to do.

Winters went on. "You want us to wait until we've done the deal for the rifles, right?"

"That's right," Donelson told him. "But as soon as we have the money, take your detail to the mission and carry out your orders."

"What if them greasers try to stop us?"

"What do you think?" Donelson snapped. "Kill them, too."

Caramba! Gabriel thought. The man really was evil. Donelson's treachery was liable to cause a great deal of trouble, but one way or another, Chaco had to have those guns. The revolution couldn't begin without them.

Gabriel drew back deeper into the little niche where the store's entrance was located as he spied movement in the shadows ahead of him.

Donelson stepped out of the shadows. He was taller and bulkier than Winters, and Gabriel recognized him. With a cigar clenched between his teeth, Donelson looked back. "You've done good work, Winters. I won't forget this."

He strode across the street without a glance toward the doorway where Gabriel stood. The big man waited until he disappeared into the hotel before moving from the shadows.

He had to get to the mission and warn Chaco. That meant going past the alley where Donelson and Winters had had their rendezvous. Gabriel let a few more minutes go by, then slid along the wall of the building and risked a look around the corner into the alley.

In the faint gray light, he saw it was empty. Winters had left in the other direction.

Gabriel took a step toward the mission, then stopped as pain bit deep into his back.

Even as big as he was, the sudden agony might have knocked him to his knees if an arm hadn't clamped around his neck from behind like a bar of iron. He felt the blade's cold fire as someone shoved it even deeper into his body.

"I thought I smelled you, greaser," a voice whispered in his ear. "Spyin' on me and the cap'n, were you? I reckon you heard more than you need to know, but that's all right. I got a hunch all you dirty bean-eaters are gonna wind up dead 'fore this is over. I'm just gettin' a head start with you!"

Gabriel tried to struggle. He willed his muscles to move, but they refused. It outraged him that a scrawny gringo like Winters could defeat him, but never before had he known such pain. It froze the blood in his veins, stiffened his body, and sent waves of darkness rolling through his brain.

"Mer . . . cedes . . ." Gabriel whispered.

Then he knew nothing more.

Chapter 21

Leaning against the back of the bench, Slaughter woke with his arm around Viola and her head pillowed on his shoulder. His arm had gone to sleep, but under the circumstances the numbness was more than welcome since it was due to the warm presence of his wife.

Light had started to filter into the sanctuary through the stained glass in the tall, narrow windows. The sun was up. Sometime today the supply wagons full of stolen army rifles would arrive, he thought. The wagons had had to take the longer way around the Mule Mountains.

Without turning his head, Slaughter looked around. He seemed to be the only one of the prisoners awake. The others were stretched out on the benches, using blankets that Father Fernando had provided.

It wasn't surprising that Slaughter was awake first. He usually rose before everyone else, although the hour was later than normal.

A different set of guards stood watch over the

mission. Chaco Romero was talking quietly to the ones by the double doors.

Slaughter frowned as he pondered the situation. He didn't want Romero and the other would-be revolutionaries getting away into Mexico with a load of rifles stolen from the U.S. Army. On the other hand, political shenanigans south of the border weren't really any of his business except as they affected law and order in Cochise County. He had wanted to recover the money stolen from Tombstone, but now that he'd been reunited with Viola, it was really the only reason he was there.

He was more outraged by what Donelson and the rest of the deserters had done. They were responsible for the deaths of two of Tombstone's citizens, and they were traitors to the oath they had sworn.

Not only that, but if the deal for the rifles was completed as planned, Donelson and his men would have the money. When Slaughter weighed everything, he knew that if it came down to a decision, he would allow Romero and the rest of the bandits to escape if it meant bringing Donelson's bunch to justice and recovering the loot.

Of course, most people would think he was insane for even considering these things, he mused, since he was unarmed, vastly outnumbered, and a prisoner. But a man had to be prepared for fate to turn everything upside down. Otherwise, he wouldn't be ready when the unexpected happened.

Viola stirred in his embrace. She murmured sleepily, "John?"

"I'm right here, my dear." Slaughter pressed his lips to her head and tightened his arm around her shoulders.

"I was dreaming that we were back in our own bed on the ranch. But we're not, are we?"

"I'm afraid not. But we're together and we're all right. That's all that matters right now."

She sat up a little straighter, turned her head, and kissed him. Then she slipped out of his embrace and sat beside him on the bench. He moved his arm around to get some of the feeling back into it.

Chaco noticed that they were awake and went over to them with a solemn look on his face. "I know better than to ask you if you slept well, my friends. My apologies for the accommodations. The church was meant for worship, not to serve as a hotel. But it was the best place to keep you all together."

"And the easiest place to keep us under guard," Slaughter said. "I probably would have done the same thing if the circumstances were reversed."

Chaco smiled faintly. "I'm glad you understand, Sheriff."

"I didn't say I approved," Slaughter responded dryly. "Do you intend to feed us this morning?"

"Of course. I've already arranged for breakfast and coffee to be brought to you from the café."

Viola asked bluntly, "When will the rifles be here?"

"Captain Donelson assures me the wagons will arrive

by midday. Shortly after that, all of you will be free to return to your homes."

"If you expect us to thank you for that, you'll have a long wait," Slaughter said.

Chaco shook his head. "I expect no thanks for trying to do what is right, Sheriff. When my people are free, that will be reward enough." He left the mission as the other prisoners were waking up.

True to Romero's promise, several women arrived carrying platters of scrambled eggs, peppers, sausage, and tortillas, as well as mugs of coffee. The breakfast was passed around to the prisoners while the guards stood nearby with their rifles ready to make sure no one tried anything.

"How are you feeling this morning, Luther?" Slaughter asked Gentry.

The liveryman slurped coffee from the mug in his hand. "Better, Sheriff. Had a headache when I woke up, but I think it's goin' away."

Grover Harmon asked, "Are those varmints still sayin' they're gonna turn us loose today?"

"As soon as they've gotten their rifles and hightailed it across the border," Slaughter replied. "I suspect that Romero plans to leave a few men guarding us until the others have time to get away. Then they'll light a shuck as well."

"What about those bluecoats?" Pete Yardley asked.

"I figure they'll take off for the tall and uncut, too."

Despite what he told Yardley, Slaughter was uneasy

about the renegade cavalrymen. He knew that Donelson couldn't be trusted, and the deaths of Jack Doyle and Ross Murdock proved that the troopers didn't draw the line at murder.

He looked around at his fellow prisoners and hoped they didn't all wind up in front of a firing squad. He wouldn't put that past Donelson at all.

The morning dragged by. Slaughter was used to staying busy, and the forced inactivity gnawed at his nerves and his gut. He kept watching for a chance to get his hands on a gun and maybe turn the tables on their guards, but Romero's men knew what they were doing. They remained alert, and they never came close enough for any of the prisoners to jump them.

Slaughter's frustration grew.

Romero looked just as upset, when he came into the mission late in the morning and asked the guards, "Has Gabriel been here?"

The men responded that they hadn't seen the big *bandido* all day. Viola heard that exchange and looked interested. She stood up, and Slaughter came to his feet beside her, causing a couple guards to turn toward them and lift their rifles.

Romero motioned for them to take it easy. "What is it, Señora Slaughter?"

"Is Gabriel missing?" Viola asked.

"No one has seen him today. He left my sister's cantina early this morning, before dawn, and seems to have disappeared after that."

"Maybe he rode out for some reason," Slaughter suggested.

"Gabriel would never do that without telling me. He had no reason to leave." Clearly worried, Romero left the mission.

Slaughter and Viola sat down again, and he asked her, "What's bothering you about that big galoot being gone?"

"Chaco and Gabriel have been friends since they were little boys," Viola said quietly. "And Gabriel is in love with Chaco's sister. Chaco's right. If Gabriel is missing, it must be because something happened to him."

"I know what you said about Romero's sister, but maybe Gabriel's just holed up somewhere with one of the, ah . . ."

"Whores?" Viola laughed humorlessly. "You should know by now, John, that you can say words like that without shocking me. And I don't believe it. He could have treated me much more disrespectfully than he did. He's devoted to Chaco, and I think he's equally devoted to Mercedes."

"Maybe he ran afoul of one of those deserters. I don't trust Donelson and his men."

"We're in complete agreement about that," Viola said with a firm nod. "I have a bad feeling about the way this is shaping up, John."

Slaughter looked at her, then glanced at the other prisoners. "If there's trouble, you stay close to me, you hear?"

"Just try getting me away from you."

A short time later, another of Romero's men appeared at the door and spoke to the guards. Slaughter couldn't hear the words they exchanged, but the guards looked more tense and excited. Something was going on, and he had a pretty good idea what it was.

Viola sensed it as well, and so did the other prisoners. They all got to their feet.

Mose Tadrack said, "Something's happenin', Sheriff."

Slaughter nodded. "You're right, Mose. Unless I miss my guess, those wagons full of rifles just rolled into La Reata."

Chapter 22

Gabriel woke up expecting to feel the searing heat of hellfire and hear the cackling laughter of *El Diablo*'s imps. Given the life he had led despite his best intentions, he considered it his inescapable fate to have his immortal soul consigned to the deepest pits of Hades.

To his complete surprise, he discovered that instead of brimstone, Hell smelled like a hog wallow. And Satan's imps . . . well, they grunted like hogs.

Was it possible, he began to wonder, that he was not dead after all?

Memories began to seep back into his brain. The first was pain. Horrible, breathtaking pain, so bad that for several moments it created a high wall so impenetrable that he could recall nothing before it.

He had been stabbed in the back. On several occasions in the past, Gabriel had felt the bite of a blade during a fight, so he knew what it was like. None of those times had been as bad as what he had experienced just before he passed out, but the sensation was unmistakable.

Winters. The deserter was the one who had driven the knife into his body. Once that realization came clear in Gabriel's brain, the rest of it rushed back to him—the two renegade cavalrymen talking, the plot to murder all the prisoners except Señora Slaughter, the threat to Chaco and his men if they interfered.

Gabriel had been on his way to the mission to warn Chaco when he was attacked from behind. The urge to alert his old friend to the danger was still there, uppermost in his mind.

He was lying on hard ground with something rough against his face. He tried to heave himself to his feet and discovered that he couldn't move. Something weighed him down. Normally, his strength was such that he could practically move a mountain. At the moment. he was weak as a newborn kitten.

Gabriel lay there panting from the futile effort he had made to get up. He forced his eyes open to look around.

At first, he couldn't see anything. Then glimmers of light began to appear here and there, but still not enough to show him his surroundings. Finally, he realized that he was covered up with something. The rough texture against his cheek where his head was turned to the side suggested that it was burlap.

Somebody had piled sacks of feed on him. That was the only explanation that made sense. Winters had believed he was dead from that stab wound in the back, and he had hidden the body by dragging it into a barn and covering it with heavy sacks of feed.

That explained the smell, too. There was a hog pen close by.

A groan welled up Gabriel's throat, but he tightened his jaw and clamped his mouth shut so it couldn't escape. Chances were, Winters was long gone and none of Donelson's other men were around close enough to hear him, but he didn't want to take that chance. Winters believed he was dead, and Gabriel wanted to use that mistake to his advantage.

The pain in his back was intense, but the fact that he was still alive told him the deserter's knife hadn't hit anything vital, nor inflicted enough damage to make him bleed to death. He really wasn't hurt that bad, he told himself.

As long as he believed it, he could keep going.

Calling on the strength in his massive body, he moved his hands underneath him and tried again to heave himself up. He thought the weight on him shifted slightly. He heaved again.

The terrible burden moved. Gabriel twisted his right shoulder a little and slid that hand into a tiny gap between the burlap sacks filled with grain. He got hold of one of the sacks and tugged on it, trying to lessen the weight on him.

The effort seemed to take forever, but finally the sack moved. Not much, but enough to make it easier for Gabriel to breathe. He lifted his shoulder, made more room that way, and got hold of another sack. He grunted and pulled and thought he sounded like one of those hogs rooting around in the mud somewhere nearby.

The second sack shifted. He was making progress, Gabriel told himself. He got both hands under him again and tried once more to push himself upright.

His body lifted off the ground, and he heard rasping movement as more of the weight fell to the side. He had shifted the balance of the sacks piled on top of him, and they were sliding off each other. He couldn't hold back a bellow as his muscles bunched and he surged upward to his feet.

The light coming through the open side of the shed blinded him. He lifted a shaky arm to block some of it from his eyes. Judging from the brightness of the glare, the hour was midday or close to it.

As Gabriel's eyes began to adjust, he shambled forward. He had to find Chaco. There was no time to waste.

Despite the worry Chaco felt over Gabriel's disappearance, he turned his attention to the arrival of the guns that were so vital to his plans. One of the guards he had posted around the outskirts of the village had spotted the wagons approaching and had hurried to bring the news to him.

Chaco walked toward the northern end of the street to meet the wagons. Donelson had come out of the hotel and was headed in that direction, too. All over La Reata, members of Chaco's band as well as troopers from

Donelson's renegade patrol emerged from buildings and began to gather in the street.

Mercedes hurried out from the cantina to intercept him. His sister had a shawl wrapped around her shoulders and wore a worried look on her face. "Chaco, have you had any word from Gabriel?"

"I haven't found him," he replied with a shake of his head.

"Something has happened to him, I know it has. He knew how important this is to you, to all of us. He would be here if he could."

Chaco nodded grimly. "I know."

His suspicions were directed toward the deserters. As soon as he had met Donelson, every instinct in his body told him not to trust the man. Nothing had happened in the time since then to change that opinion.

He put a hand on Mercedes' shoulder and squeezed for a second to reassure her. Then he strode on to meet the wagons.

Donelson grinned at him. "I told you they'd be here, Señor Romero. As you can see, my word is good."

A dozen wagons made up the supply train. Each wagon carried four crates, with twenty rifles in each crate. Nearly a thousand rifles in all, Chaco thought. Many more would be needed before the revolution was over, but it was a start, he told himself. A good start.

The wagons also contained boxes of ammunition. It pained Chaco to think that those bullets would wind up in the bodies of his countrymen, but Díaz's soldiers had made the decision to throw their support behind the dictator. Like everyone else, they would have to bear the consequences of their actions.

As the wagons rolled to a stop, Donelson said, "I believe we can conclude our deal now. Here are the guns. You have our money—"

"Not yet," Chaco snapped. His instinctive distrust of Donelson, along with Gabriel's mysterious disappearance, made him more wary. "I'm not a fool, Captain. I must see what I am buying."

A brief look of annoyance passed over Donelson's face, but he didn't hesitate. "Of course. I'd be glad to have my men open a few of the crates and show you—"

"Not a few of the crates. All of them." Chaco lifted his left arm and leveled it as he pointed to the far end of the street. "Have your men take the wagons down there and unload the crates. Take them into the mission."

Frowning, Donelson didn't try to hide his reaction. "What? That's insane, Romero! Why unload all the crates when you'll just have to load them up again to take them across the border?"

Normally, Chaco would have thought that Donelson was right. But he had given in to the impulse and was going to stand by the decision. Besides, the delay would give him more time to search for Gabriel.

He wasn't going to leave La Reata without his old friend, or at least without having found out what had happened to him.

The two leaders traded cold stares as Chaco said, "I will need to inspect all the rifles before I turn the money over to you, Captain. If the guns are as you say they are, it will be a minor delay and nothing more, eh?"

"I'm not sure how minor. It'll take quite a while to unload all those crates and open them."

Chaco shrugged. "I don't have anywhere else I have to be right now. Do you?"

"I might," Donelson snapped. "The army's going to be looking for us pretty soon."

"You'll be gone by nightfall with your money."

The tension between the two men seemed to communicate itself to their followers. Chaco's men began to draw away from the deserters. Rifle barrels swung more toward the troopers, and a few hands rested on pistol butts.

Donelson's men reacted the same way. Their stance made it obvious they were getting ready to fight if they needed to.

"All right, fine," Donelson said loudly. He waved the wagons forward. "Take them down to the church and unload the rifles like Señor Romero wanted."

"*Gracias*," Chaco said.

Quietly, Donelson said, "This had better not be some sort of trick, Romero. Neither of us will be pleased with the outcome if it is."

"If you've been dealing in good faith with us, Captain, you have nothing to worry about." Chaco paused. "By the way, have you seen my friend Gabriel Hernandez?"

Chaco thought he saw a flicker of something in Donelson's eyes—guilt? worry?

"You mean that big fella who looks like somebody hit him a few times in the face with a board?" He shook his head. "I haven't seen him since we were all in the cantina last night."

Chaco thought the man was lying. He was glad he had given in to the whim of demanding to inspect all the rifles before handing over the money. Before they left La Reata, he would get to the bottom of Gabriel's disappearance.

"You know, I'm starting to think you don't trust me." Donelson's tone was pleasant, but his eyes were full of hatred.

"There is a time and place for trust," Chaco said. "This is not it."

With the teamsters shouting and lashing at their mules, the wagons lurched into motion again.

Chapter 23

Slaughter wanted to know what was going on. He told Viola, "Stay here with the others," and took a step toward the mission doorway.

She stopped him with a hand on his arm. "I'm coming with you, John."

Slaughter shook his head. "Not this time. I need you to stay out of the line of fire."

"And where in this village is that?" she responded. "It seems to me that trouble could break out anywhere."

He couldn't argue that point. With a curt nod, he said, "All right, come along."

The other prisoners waited where they were while Slaughter and Viola approached the guards at the double doors. One of the men noticed them coming and turned to face them with his rifle held slanted across his chest, which was crisscrossed by bandoliers of ammunition.

"Halt, Sheriff," the man ordered. "You and your señora should go back with the rest of the gringos."

Diego Herrara called from the middle of the sanctuary, "I am no gringo, *cabrón*." He looked around at the others. "But these men are my *amigos*, I am proud to say."

Slaughter told the guard, "I just want to know what's going on out there. We have a stake in this, too, you know. Your leader has promised that we'll go free after your business here is done."

The guard thought about it. He looked over at the other sentry, who shrugged as if to say that the decision wasn't up to him. Then the first guard said sullenly, "All right, you can come up here where you can see. But don't try anything funny." He paused, then added, "Maybe you can figure out what this is about, Sheriff, because I have no idea."

Slaughter took Viola's hand and held it as they stepped into the doorway with the guards. He frowned in surprise as he saw the line of canvas-covered wagons rolling slowly along La Reata's main street toward the mission.

"It looks like they're coming here." Viola sounded surprised, too.

"So it does," Slaughter agreed.

Romero and Donelson walked beside the lead wagon's team of mules. Both men appeared to be angry. Slaughter wondered if their deal had developed some kinks in it.

If that was true, he might be able to turn the potential rift to their advantage. . . .

The first wagon pulled up in front of the mission doors. Romero said, "Sheriff, señora, please go back with the others and stay out of the way." To the guards he added, "Watch them closely, all of them."

Slaughter and Viola retreated and joined the other prisoners, but not before Slaughter saw some of Donelson's troopers reach into the back of the wagon and pull out one of the crates. A moment later, the blue-clad men carried the crate through the open doors into the mission.

"Stack them up there, in front of the altar," Romero ordered.

The deserters hesitated and looked at Donelson, who jerked his head in an angry nod to indicate they should obey Chaco's command.

Whatever was going on, Donelson evidently didn't like it but didn't have any choice except to go along with it.

Father Fernando bustled out of the rear of the mission as the troopers set the crate on the hardwood floor in front of the altar. He hurried along the aisle to Romero and asked agitatedly, "Chaco, what is this? You know I support your cause, but you cannot bring these . . . these instruments of violence into a house of God!"

"We won't be leaving them here, Father," Romero assured him. "As soon as I've checked them all and settled a few other details, we'll put them back on the wagons and depart from La Reata."

"What other details?" Donelson snapped. "The price was settled a long time ago. You're not going to weasel out of it now, Romero."

"I'm not trying to weasel out of anything, as you put it."

They might be doing business together, thought Slaughter, but these two definitely didn't like each other anymore, if they ever had.

Romero's voice was cold and hard as he addressed Donelson. "One of my men is missing, as you might recall."

"I don't know anything about that, and it's none of my affair, anyway."

Slaughter suddenly got the impression that Donelson was lying. He couldn't say why he felt that way, but it was a definite hunch. Judging by the suspicion in Romero's eyes, the bandit leader felt the same way.

Donelson went on. "If you're bound and determined to inspect all those rifles, why don't you get started? You don't have to wait until they've all been brought in."

"*Es verdad,*" Romero said.

As Donelson's troopers brought in the other crates from the wagon, the bandit leader went to the first one, drew the heavy-bladed bowie knife from the sheath at his waist, and used it to pry loose the top. He let it slide to the side.

From where Slaughter stood, he couldn't see into the crate. He watched, as Romero moved packing material aside and withdrew a long, oilcloth-wrapped object. He unwrapped it and used some of the packing to wipe away grease. Then he held up what Slaughter recognized as a Springfield army rifle.

"Brand-new Model 84s with the Buffington rear

sight," Donelson said. "With it you can draw a bead on an enemy up to 1,400 yards away. You won't find a better weapon for ambushes. Fires a .45-70 round, and you're getting plenty of them, too. Arm your men with these, and in six months you'll be running Mexico, Romero."

"You underestimate *El Presidente* Díaz," Romero said as he ran a hand over the rifle's smooth wooden breech and stock. "But with these we will have a chance . . ."

The Springfield was a breech-loading single-shot weapon. Romero worked the action to see how smoothly it operated and raised the rear sight as well. Finally he nodded in satisfaction, obviously impressed by the rifle.

"You're not going to inspect each one that closely, are you?" Donelson asked. "If you do, we're going to be here until next week!"

"No, I just want to make sure the rifles are what you say they are."

"Some men would be insulted by a comment like that." Donelson slid a cigar from his pocket and clamped his teeth on the cylinder of tobacco. Around it he added, "Don't try my patience, Romero, any more than you already have."

"Just have your men continue to bring in the crates," Romero said.

He gave the other rifles in the first crate a much more cursory examination, just enough to make sure they were the same model as the one he had looked at closely.

As the deserters continued to carry in the crates,

Slaughter wondered how Donelson had managed to put his hands on so many rifles. When the posse first ran into the supply train, Donelson had claimed they were on their way from Fort Bowie to Fort Huachuca. There might have been some truth to that, Slaughter mused. It was possible the guns had been intended for the troops at Huachuca. The more Slaughter thought about it, the more likely the explanation seemed. In that case, it might be several days before the army realized that Donelson had diverted them elsewhere.

The prisoners couldn't expect any help unless Stonewall, Burt, and more men from Tombstone showed up. Burt was an excellent tracker and would follow the trail to La Reata, but Slaughter had no way of knowing if a second posse had even started out.

He had to assume that whatever would be done, he and his companions would have to do it themselves.

Slaughter's eyes narrowed slightly as he looked at those crates being lined up in front of the altar. If they could get their hands on some of those rifles and a few boxes of ammunition . . .

"John," Viola said, "I don't like the look on your face. It looks to me like you're a little too eager for trouble."

"Just thinking, my dear. Just thinking."

Mercedes was furious with her brother. She knew that concluding the deal for the rifles was important to

Chaco and didn't blame him for that, but she was more worried about Gabriel's disappearance.

Mercedes wasn't particularly vain, but she was practical enough to know that she was a beautiful woman. Beautiful enough to have any man she wanted, even without the added attraction of owning a cantina.

But despite that, she had chosen to give her heart to a big, ugly outlaw. She had loved Gabriel Hernandez since she was ten years old, and that would never change.

She stood in front of the cantina and looked down the street toward the mission. All the crates had been unloaded and carried into the church. Chaco's men and Donelson's troopers stood around outside, gathered on opposite sides of the street. Tension still hung in the air. Mercedes supposed that Chaco and Donelson were still inside putting the final touches on their deal.

Only a few of the locals were in the cantina, drinking desultorily in the middle of the day. Mercedes heard a sudden commotion from them, and her bartender called urgently, "Señorita!"

She turned quickly and stepped through the entrance. As usual when coming from midday sunlight into the shadowy coolness of the thick-walled cantina, her eyes had to adjust and for a few seconds she couldn't see very much.

Then she spotted the massive form lurching through the beaded curtain leading to the rear hallway, and she cried out, "Gabriel!"

With her heart hammering in her bosom, Mercedes rushed across the room toward her lover. The bartender got there first and grabbed Gabriel's arm to steady him as he swayed drunkenly.

Mercedes knew that Gabriel wasn't drunk. She had seen him swig down a seemingly endless amount of tequila and show no effect from it. Something else was wrong with him.

Very wrong.

The bartender wasn't strong enough to keep Gabriel on his feet, but he was able to keep the big outlaw from crashing to the floor. Both of them went down in what seemed like slow motion. As Mercedes dropped to her knees beside them, she saw the large, dark bloodstain on the back of Gabriel's shirt. He was badly hurt, just as she had suspected the moment she saw him.

She tugged his head and shoulders into her lap and bent over to rain kisses down on his rugged features. His eyes were closed.

"Gabriel!" she said, fearful that he was dead. "Gabriel!"

His eyes fluttered open. He stared around blindly, uncomprehendingly for several seconds before he was able to focus on her. Then a grin broke out on his face and he whispered, "*Mercedes, mi amor.*"

"Gabriel, what happened? Who did this to you?"

He didn't answer her questions. "Chaco . . . I have to find Chaco . . . Donelson . . . double-cross . . . going to kill . . ."

He sighed and his eyelids slid closed again. Once more Mercedes felt fear's cold touch stab through her.

But when she rested her hand on his chest, she felt his great, valiant heart still beating. She looked over at the bartender and ordered, "Find my brother and bring him here! Now!"

Chapter 24

Romero was still checking the rifles in each crate and was about halfway through the job when one of his men ran into the church, went directly to him, and said something so quietly that only Romero could hear.

Slaughter was watching. He knew from the way Romero's head jerked slightly at the words that the news was unexpected and unwelcome. Romero turned away from the crates and followed his man out of the mission. He was almost running by the time he reached the doors.

Viola saw the same thing and murmured, "John, something's wrong."

"I know," Slaughter said quietly.

Romero had left the lids off the crates as he opened them with his knife. Slaughter assumed they would be hammered on again later, when the bandits were ready to load them back into the wagons. The first rifle Romero had examined, the one he had cleaned off with the packing material, lay diagonally across a corner of that open crate. A box of ammunition was right beside it.

Slaughter wanted that rifle loaded and in his hands. He wanted it very badly. Every instinct in his body told him that all hell was about to break loose.

Donelson frowned as Romero rushed out. Whatever the other bandit had reported, it had upset Romero. That didn't bode well. Donelson rolled the unlit cigar to the other side of his mouth, took it out, and sidled closer to Winters. A handful of troopers had lingered inside the church after unloading the crates, and Donelson knew they were the men Winters had selected to wipe out the prisoners . . . with the very important exception of Viola Slaughter.

"Get ready for that special detail of yours, Sergeant," Donelson said from the corner of his mouth. "I think I may be calling upon you to carry out those orders very soon now."

"I got the same hunch, Colonel," Winters drawled.

"You're sure you killed that bandit who was spying on us early this morning?"

"Mighty sure. Stuck my knife right in his heart, I did. Then I dragged him into a shed and covered him up with sacks full of grain. He was such a big galoot it wasn't easy, either. Nobody's gonna find him until he starts to stinkin', and we oughta be long gone from this greaser hellhole by then."

Donelson gave a minuscule nod. "I just wanted to

be sure no one could tip off Romero to what we have planned."

"Must be somethin' else that got him all hot an' bothered, Colonel."

"All right. Be ready for trouble anyway, beause one way or another it's coming."

Winters stroked his fingertips along the breech of the rifle he held, which was a Springfield like the ones in the crates. "Me and the boys are ready. Whenever you give the word, Colonel, that's when the killin' will start."

Chaco's heart plummeted when he ran into the cantina and his sister looked up at him with tears running down her face. She sat on the floor with her colorful skirt spread around her and Gabriel's head pillowed in her lap. His face was pale and washed out under his permanent tan.

"Is he—" Chaco was unable to go on.

"He's alive," Mercedes said, "but I don't know for how long. He's badly hurt, Chaco. I think someone stabbed him in the back."

Chaco went down on one knee beside them. "Whoever did this, I'll find him and kill him."

His first thought was that Gabriel might have gotten into an argument with one of the other men. No one in the group would fight him head-on. None of them was that foolish. But someone nursing a grudge might lie in wait and drive a knife into his back.

The likelihood of that was small, Chaco realized. He

hadn't heard of any trouble among them. Gabriel got along well with all the other men. If the clash was bad enough to prompt an attempted murder, surely he would have heard rumblings about it among the men.

That left the residents of La Reata—again a very unlikely possibility in Chaco's estimation—or the soldiers as suspects in the attack on his old friend.

The troopers, Chaco thought as his jaw tightened. He could easily imagine one of Donelson's men doing this.

"Where did you find him?" he asked Mercedes.

She shook her head. "I didn't find him. He came here. He stumbled in from the back and collapsed."

"Did he tell you anything before he passed out? Did he say who did this to him?"

"All he said"—Mercedes stopped and took a breath before she could go on—"was that Donelson was going to double-cross you and kill someone. Probably you, Chaco. He probably plans to kill you and your men, take the money, and keep the rifles. He can sell them again!"

That theory made sense. It would explain Donelson's shifty behavior and the instinctive distrust he felt for the man.

He put a hand on the shoulder of the senseless Gabriel and squeezed, even though he knew his friend probably couldn't feel it. "Can you take care of him?" he asked Mercedes.

"Of course," she answered without hesitation. "I'll have some of the men put him in my bed. Then I can see how badly he's hurt."

Chaco nodded. He had faith in his sister. La Reata

had no doctor, not even a *curandero*, but in the past Mercedes had patched up enough bullet and knife wounds to become fairly proficient at it. If anyone could save Gabriel, she was the one to do it.

And no doctor would ever fight harder for a patient than she would for her big, ugly brute of a lover.

"I need to get back down to the mission and find out what Donelson's plan is," Chaco said as he got to his feet. "Stay here and take care of Gabriel. No matter what you hear outside, Mercedes, stay in the cantina until you're sure all the trouble is over. These walls are thick enough to stop anything smaller than a cannonball."

She reached up and clutched at his sleeve. "Be careful, Chaco," she urged. "That gringo Donelson is a bad man."

"I know, but I'm afraid the time for being careful may be over."

Slaughter continued to edge closer to the crate with the rifle lying across it. While he wasn't nearly as familiar with the Springfield as he was with his favorite Henry or his shotgun, he had fired one before and knew how to load and operate the weapon. He figured he could snatch up the rifle, use the butt to smash the top of the ammunition box, grab a handful of cartridges, load the Springfield, and have it ready to fire in a matter of ten seconds or so.

Under normal circumstances, facing an armed enemy meant he would be dead two or three times over—at least—by the time he had the Springfield ready for action.

He was counting on some sort of distraction to give him a chance to arm himself. If trouble erupted between Romero and Donelson, all eyes in the church would be on them for a moment. If gunplay broke out, the bandits would side with Romero and the troopers would join in on Donelson's side.

Slaughter wanted to be ready to protect himself, Viola, and his posse no matter which of the two groups won the fight.

One by one, he caught the eye of each member of his posse. With each man, he nodded slightly toward the open crates of rifles until he thought they got his drift. He couldn't be sure how they would react when the time came, but at least maybe they had some idea what he had in mind.

Chaco Romero appeared in the doorway.

From the look of grim anger on his face as he strode into the church, Slaughter knew things were about to break loose.

"Donelson!" Romero cried.

"What the hell is it now?" Donelson snapped back at him, openly displaying his own anger and impatience. "You've stalled on giving us our money long enough. I'm starting to think you're trying to double-cross us." The last sentence came out in a snarl as the two men faced each other in the aisle between the benches.

A few yards away, Slaughter did a quick head count and saw that Donelson had six men, in addition to himself, while only three of Romero's men were on hand. Given the history of how Romero's men had treated Viola while she was their captive, Slaughter would have preferred that those numbers were reversed. He had no sympathy for the bandits, but he trusted them slightly more.

A cold, humorless laugh came from Romero. "Double cross! You are the one trying to pull the double cross, Donelson. You tried to kill my friend Gabriel!"

That brought a gasp from Viola.

"That's a damned lie," Donelson rasped. "I never touched the man."

"Then you ordered one of your lackeys to do it. He condemned you with his own lips."

Donelson's eyes flicked toward one of his men.

Slaughter saw the reaction and recognized the man as Corporal Winters, the trooper who had murdered Ross Murdock in cold blood. Winters was capable of trying to kill Gabriel Hernandez, Slaughter had no doubt about that.

"I don't know what you're talking about," Donelson insisted stubbornly, "but you're not going to weasel out of our deal. You've got your rifles"—he waved a hand at the crates—"now hand over our money . . . *now!*"

Romero stepped back with his hand poised over the butt of his revolver, ready to hook and draw.

Winters exclaimed, "Watch it, Colonel, that greaser's goin' for his gun!"

The rifle in Winters' hands flashed toward Romero

and spouted flame as Romero's gun flickered from its holster and roared in return.

Slaughter shoved Viola to the floor between two of the benches and made a dive for the rifle on the open crate as more gunshots echoed from the adobe walls and stained-glass windows behind him.

Chapter 25

The other prisoners were right behind him, as Slaughter snatched up the Springfield and brought its butt down hard on the top of the ammunition box. The wooden top splintered under the blow. Cartridges scattered from the impact, spinning, bouncing, and rolling across the hardwood floor.

Slaughter bent and scooped up a handful of cartridges and shoved them all in his pocket except one. He fumbled a little as he opened the rifle's breech, simply because of his unfamiliarity with it. But the mechanism came open, and he slid the cartridge into the firing chamber, and snapped it closed.

He felt as much as heard a bullet burn past his ear. When he glanced up he saw a cavalrymen drawing a bead on him. Slaughter let his instinct guide his aim and got his shot off first.

The .45-70 round bored into the man's chest, driving

him backward as he squeezed the trigger. The bullet went harmlessly into the ceiling as he fell.

Father Fernando rushed into the sanctuary and shouted in Spanish. Slaughter barely heard him over the gun thunder, but he understood enough to know that the padre was pleading with them to stop shooting, to cease spilling blood in the house of the Lord.

It was a shame, Slaughter thought, but that wasn't going to happen.

Diego Herrara had started to go after one of the rifles like the other posse men, but as Father Fernando started down the aisle, waving his arms frantically, Herrara tackled him. As they fell to the floor, several bullets screamed through the air where the priest had been an instant earlier and smashed into the altar.

Since the crates had been placed in front of the altar, the benches provided a little cover for the posse men as they armed themselves. The shots that came their way were from a couple of Donelson's men. The other troopers were busy trading slugs with Romero's men.

Slaughter knelt beside one of the benches as he reloaded. About halfway down the aisle, Chaco Romero crouched and fired his revolver at Donelson as the renegade officer retreated toward the doors. Slaughter saw a bright crimson stain on Romero's left side. The bandit leader wasn't giving up the fight, despite being injured.

Slaughter fired again and saw a trooper's arm jerk as the bullet drilled it. The wounded man stumbled through the open doors and disappeared.

Blood flew from Romero's right thigh as he was hit again. His leg collapsed underneath him and sent him spilling into the aisle. The impact as he hit the floor knocked the gun out of his hand.

Viola appeared, darting out from between the benches and scooping up Romero's gun. She fired it one-handed at the deserters while she used her other hand to catch hold of Romero's shirt and drag him behind a bench. Slaughter knew he couldn't reach them to help, so he reloaded as fast as he could to give them some covering fire.

More shots began to bark and crack from the front of the sanctuary. Slaughter glanced over his shoulder as he reloaded and saw that Gentry and Harmon, his most experienced men, had gotten rifles from the crates, cleaned them off enough to use them, and loaded the weapons.

To his surprise, Tadrack was already in the fight, as well. A moment later, Yardley joined in. Carlton and Cleaver were trying, but neither man was familiar with firearms and didn't really have any idea what he was doing.

As Slaughter brought the loaded rifle to his shoulder, he saw that Viola and Romero had reached the relative safety of the narrow space between two benches. The sheriff looked around quickly. Donelson was gone and two of his men were down. He counted heads as he watched a trooper duck through the opening. Two others had obviously reached the doors and fled, leaving only

Winters. Slaughter took a quick aim and fired at the killer, just as Winters squeezed off another shot, too.

Both bullets missed. Slaughter saw splinters fly from the doorjamb as his slug chewed into it. At the same time, the bullet from Winters' rifle whipped past Slaughter's head. He heard a man grunt in pain and knew that while Winters had missed him, the deserter had scored a hit after all.

Winters ducked through the doorway and was gone.

First things first. Slaughter reloaded. He gathered up several of the cartridges that he had knocked out of the box when he busted it open and slipped them into his pocket. It never hurt to have extra ammunition.

As the guns fell silent and that quiet echoed eerily, he called urgently, "Viola! I say, Viola! Are you all right?"

"I'm not hurt, John," she replied, "but Chaco was hit a couple times and he's bleeding a lot."

"Do what you can for him, but keep your head down," Slaughter told her. Without taking his eye off the open doors, in case Donelson's men attacked again, he went on. "Luther, Grover, what's the situation back there?"

"That drummer fella's got a bullet hole in him," Harmon reported, "but it don't look fatal to me. Couple creases here and there amongst the rest of us, but nothin' serious."

That was a relief. The actual battle had lasted only a couple minutes, although it had seemed longer, but enough lead had been flying around to kill them all. Clearly, luck had been with them, Slaughter thought, although they were a long way from being out of trouble. As far as he could tell, Donelson had lost only one man in the exchange. The captain and the rest of the deserters were still out there. So were the rest of Romero's men.

Instead of the battle royal between the two groups Slaughter might have expected, an ominous silence reigned. Any hopes Slaughter might have had of both bunches wiping each other out were dashed.

He didn't know what was going on, but the quiet gave him a strong hunch that it couldn't be anything good.

Donelson's brain worked furiously as he stumbled out of the church and veered to one side so that he would be out of the line of fire from any bullets flying through the open doorway.

There had to be a way to fix it. The rifles were inside the mission with his enemies, and he had no idea where the money was. He and his men could mount up and gallop away from La Reata, but they would do so empty-handed.

That was unacceptable. Donelson was damned if he was going to leave with nothing.

He wanted it all.

Including Viola Slaughter.

"Hold your fire!" he called to the men he had left outside. "Hold your fire and take cover! Get behind those wagons!"

The outburst of gunfire from inside the church had escalated the tension in the street tenfold. The troopers on one side and Romero's men on the other had their guns pointed at each other, and all it would have taken was a small spark to set off an all-out war between them.

Donelson knew he had to prevent that. An idea was already taking shape in his cunning mind.

Winters was the last man out of the church. Donelson waved for him to follow and started across the street in a crouching run toward Romero's men. Winters looked shocked, but after a second followed his commander.

Donelson was uncomfortably aware that almost three dozen Mexican bandits had him in their gun sights as he approached. He was no coward, though. He holstered his gun and held out his hands in front of him to show the *bandidos* that he wasn't attacking them. They had taken cover at the corners of buildings and behind water troughs and rain barrels. Donelson didn't know who any of them were, but he headed toward the largest group he could see.

"Hold your fire, *amigos*!" he called, hoping that at least some of them spoke English. "We're on the same side, remember?"

As long as Romero and the other three bandits were still inside the church, the men had no way of knowing that Donelson wasn't telling the truth. They hadn't seen what happened in the sanctuary.

One of the men leveled a revolver at Donelson and snapped in heavily accented English, "Talk fast, gringo. What's going on here?"

"Sheriff Slaughter and the other prisoners got loose. They got their hands on some of those rifles and killed

Romero and your other men in there, as well as one of my men. The rest of us barely got out alive."

A torrent of rapid Spanish exploded from the man. Most of it was probably cursing, Donelson thought. But as far as he could tell, the bandit had swallowed the lie completely.

"We're going to have to work together to get those rifles for you and avenge your compadres," Donelson went on. "What do you say, *amigo*?"

"I hate to spill blood in the house of *El Señor Dios*, but none of those gringo dogs will get out of there alive!" the bandit said as his mouth twisted in a snarl of hate.

That was exactly what Donelson wanted to hear. "Pass the word to your men. Let them know what's going on. I'll talk to my men, and we'll figure out our plan of attack. For now, throw some lead through those doors so I can get back across the street without one of those prisoners picking me off."

The outlaw nodded in agreement and started issuing orders in Spanish. A moment later, guns began to hammer again as the Mexicans fired at the mission.

Donelson and Winters sprinted back across the street to rejoin the other deserters.

As Donelson reached the cover of a supply wagon, he dropped to one knee to catch his breath. Winters hunkered beside him and grinned. "That was some mighty fast thinkin', Colonel. If them pepper-bellies knew the truth, they'd want to kill us mighty slow and painful-like, but you got the stupid bastards on our side!"

"We're still going to win, Winters. But there's one wild card that could still ruin everything for us—Hernandez."

A grim look came over Winters' face as he said, "Listen, Colonel, I'm sorry. I thought sure that varmint was dead—"

"He may be by now," Donelson cut into the apology. Winters' previous failure didn't matter at the moment. "But we have to be certain he can't tell anyone else the truth. Find him and make sure he's dead. If he's not, kill him . . . and anyone else he may have talked to."

Winters nodded. "I understand. I'll take care of it. Good and proper this time."

"See that you do."

As Winters scurried off on the deadly assignment he'd been given, Donelson looked again toward the mission. The guns were in there, and somewhere in the squalid little village was a small fortune in stolen loot. When he rode away from La Reata, he intended to have it all with him, including the beautiful Viola Slaughter.

But if he had to give something up . . . well, soon he was going to be a very rich man who could have any woman he set his sights on.

"It would be a great shame, Mrs. Slaughter," he murmured. "But if you have to die, then so be it."

Chapter 26

In a crouching run, Slaughter was on his way to check on Viola and Romero when shots exploded again outside. Bullets traveling at different angles screamed through the open doorway like a cloud of angry lead hornets. Slaughter flung himself to the floor as the barrage threw splinters from the alter into the air, smashed statues, and thudded into the benches.

"Everybody stay down!" Slaughter bellowed.

The way those shots were coming from both sides of the street confirmed something he had worried about. Donelson must have lied about what happened inside the church and blamed everything on the prisoners. He had fooled Romero's men into helping him attack the place. The *bandidos* knew nothing about Donelson's planned double cross.

But Gabriel Hernandez knew the truth, Slaughter thought as he kept his head down and the shooting continued. Gabriel was out there somewhere, if he was still alive, and could ruin all of Donelson's schemes.

Donelson was smart enough to know that, too. There was a good chance he would send someone to find Gabriel. The cold-blooded killer Winters, more than likely.

Slaughter hoped Hernandez would be all right, but there was nothing he could do to help the big outlaw.

What he had to do was get those doors closed. As long as they were standing wide open, it gave the men outside a perfect target to shoot at. They could keep the air inside the church full of flying lead.

Warning bells went off in Slaughter's brain as the gun thunder abruptly stopped. The most logical thing to follow such an intense barrage was a rush. He came up on one knee and called, "Get ready for an attack! Don't everybody fire at once!"

That was the problem with single-shot rifles. A concentrated volley would empty their weapons and they would all have to reload at the same time. If they had been armed with repeaters it would have been a different story. He wished he'd had the chance to explain some tactics to his companions.

At least some of the men had experience fighting Apaches, so it wasn't their first battle. Slaughter knew he'd have to hope for the best.

Some of the bandits hit the doorway then, yelling and shooting as they tried to force their way into the church.

Coolly, Slaughter drilled the first man through the head. His falling body blocked the others for a second, and that gave the posse time to fire a ragged burst of shots that ripped through several more of Romero's men. That blunted the attack and forced the others to fall back. The charge was over almost as soon as it began.

As soon as the doorway was clear, pistols and rifles began to roar again outside.

Bullets whined and sizzled through the air not far over Slaughter's head as he crawled toward the doors. He paused and looked to the side as he passed the place where Viola and Romero lay between benches. Romero was either unconscious or dead. Viola's face was pale and drawn, but she meet Slaughter's gaze without fear and even summoned up a faint smile of encouragement. He nodded to her and kept crawling.

Each had said plenty during that brief moment their eyes met, even though they hadn't uttered a word.

When Slaughter was close enough, he used the Springfield to extend his reach and stretched his arm out to hook the nearest door with the tip of the rifle barrel.

Outside, Donelson shouted, "Don't let them close those doors!" as the door began to swing shut.

As soon as the door had moved enough to give him a little protection, Slaughter sprang to his feet and put his shoulder against it. He shoved the heavy wooden panel until it slammed closed. He felt the vibration as it shivered under the impact of dozens of bullets. The wood was too thick for the slugs to penetrate.

From the corner of his eye he saw Joseph Cleaver dash along the aisle and grab the other door. The bank teller was slender, and he moved fast enough that he didn't present a good target for the gunmen outside. He swung the other door closed with a crash.

Slaughter threw the heavy iron bolts attached to the doors. Brackets were on either side of the doors so a bar could be placed in them to make the entrance more secure. The old missions had been built so they could be defended against Indian attacks. Slaughter didn't know where the bar was, but Father Fernando probably did.

Outside, the guns fell silent again. Donelson would need a battering ram or possibly even a cannon to breach the doors.

Slaughter had barely turned away from them, however, when the stained glass in several of the windows shattered and exploded inward. With one avenue of attack closed off to them, the attackers had switched their approach.

Each side wall of the sanctuary had four of the tall, narrow windows. Slaughter called to his men, "Spread out, one man to each window! Take several rifles with you and load all of them before you start shooting. That way you can keep up a steadier fire!"

He had seven men, so with himself as the eighth, they could cover all the windows. He didn't know how much help he could count on from Chester Carlton, but if the man could load a rifle, point it in the right general direction, and squeeze the trigger, at least he would keep some of the attackers occupied.

Cleaver had demonstrated some unexpected courage dashing down the aisle to close the other door with bullets flying all around him. He was inexperienced, but he might make a fighter yet.

As the other men scattered to the windows, Slaughter ran to Father Fernando's side. The priest knelt in front of the altar, praying fervently.

"Father, is the rear door securely barred?" Slaughter didn't like to interrupt a prayer, but he needed to know the situation.

Pale and haggard, Father Fernando looked up at him and nodded. "Yes, Sheriff Slaughter, it is. Is there any way we can put an end to this violence?"

"Not just yet, I'm sorry to say. What about the bar for the front doors?"

"In the storage room," the padre said. "The Indians have been peaceful since I've been here. We haven't needed it."

"We do now," Slaughter said grimly.

"I'll get it."

"Keep your head down whenever you're moving around," Slaughter warned him.

"The Lord will protect me, my son."

"I don't doubt it, Padre, but give Him a hand and keep your head down, anyway."

The defenders began to fire from the windows. The shots cracked on a fairly steady basis.

Slaughter hurried over to Viola and Romero. Viola was sitting up and had tugged Chaco's head and shoulders into her lap. He stirred and opened his eyes as Slaughter knelt beside them.

"My men!" Romero exclaimed as he tried to sit up.

"I must—" He fell back into Viola's lap as his strength deserted him.

"Take it easy, Romero," Slaughter said as he rested a hand on the man's shoulder. The bandit leader had lost a lot of blood from the wounds in his left side and right thigh, but if he could regain consciousness long enough to call out to his men and tell them to attack Donelson and the other deserters instead of the mission, the fight would change in a hurry.

That hope was dashed as Viola said, "He's passed out again, John. But I think the bleeding has stopped."

"Do what you can for him," Slaughter said. "Try to bring him around again. If he can put a stop to his men attacking us and turn them against Donelson, we might actually have a chance here."

"I'll do my best," she said with a nod.

Slaughter took half a dozen rifles and a box of ammunition to the lone unattended window. Shards of stained glass crunched under his boots. He loaded all six rifles. With as many Springfields as they had inside the church, if he'd had a dozen loaders he and his men could have kept up a steady fire on the attackers for a long time. As it was, they could still put up a good fight.

The mission was the southernmost building in La Reata. As Slaughter looked out the window he saw that the attackers had drawn a couple supply wagons even with the church and were using the heavy vehicles for cover. The mule teams had been unhitched and led away. He felt sure they had done the same thing on the other side of the mission.

Bullets still flew through the broken windows, but the barrage was no longer constant. The return fire from Slaughter's men made the killers duck. If the mission had been a few miles farther south, it would have been a true Mexican standoff, Slaughter thought with a grim smile as he brought one of the Springfields to his shoulder and sent a .45-70 round tearing through the canvas cover on one of the wagons.

The question had become whether he and his companions could hold off their enemies until something happened to change the stalemate.

Chapter 27

It had taken four men to pick up Gabriel and carry him to Mercedes' bed. Once there, they had placed him on his stomach so that she could get to the wound in his back. She cut away the heavily bloodstained shirt to expose the injury.

Her initial guess appeared to be right. He didn't have a bullet hole in his back. The narrow wound had been made by a large knife. She was a little surprised that the weapon hadn't pierced his heart and killed him instantly. The angle of the thrust must have been wrong and caused the knife to barely miss that vital organ.

El Señor Dios had been watching over Gabriel and protecting him, Mercedes thought, and for that she sent a heartfelt prayer of thanks heavenward as she sat on the bed beside the big outlaw.

"Bring me a bottle of whiskey and a clean rag," she told her bartender, who had helped carry Gabriel to the bed.

Since the wound had stopped bleeding, she couldn't do much for him except clean it and keep him comfortable. He would have to rely on his own fierce determination and iron constitution to see him through.

The bartender returned with the whiskey and the rag. Mercedes soaked the piece of cloth and swabbed away the dried blood around the injury. Then she carefully parted the edges of the wound and dribbled the fiery liquor into it. Even though Gabriel was unconscious, he groaned as he felt the whiskey bite into his raw flesh.

Tenderness filled Mercedes as she looked down at him. Gabriel and her brother were the only ones who could still provoke that feeling in her. For a woman to be successful running a bordertown cantina, she had to harden her heart. She couldn't allow herself to be ruled by her emotions.

But with Gabriel it had always been different, ever since they were children. Mercedes accepted this. And of course she loved her brother, as well. Their parents were long since dead, so Chaco and Gabriel were the only people she had left to care about.

She worried about Chaco. As soon as she laid eyes on Donelson, she knew the gringo cavalryman was not to be trusted. She understood that Chaco had to do business with him in order to get the rifles he needed for the revolution, but she wouldn't feel good about things until the deal was done and the captain was gone from La Reata.

The attack on Gabriel made things worse. Mercedes felt sure one of Donelson's men was responsible.

A sudden burst of gunshots from down the street in the direction of the old mission made her leap to her feet. "Chaco!" she exclaimed.

She hated to leave Gabriel's side, but he was unconscious and she had done what she could for him. She rushed out of the bedroom and into the main room of the cantina. It was empty except for the heavyset bartender. Mercedes figured her customers had scurried for home as soon as the shooting had started.

"My rifle!" she snapped at the bartender.

He reached under the bar, picked up the repeater, and tossed it to her. Mercedes caught it. Most women wouldn't have been able to handle a heavy weapon like the Winchester with such ease, but as she liked to point out to Gabriel, she was not most women.

A pang went through her. She couldn't stand it if Gabriel died.

She forced that worry out of her mind and hurried to the entrance. As she looked out carefully, in case any bullets were flying in her direction, she saw the tense confrontation of Chaco's men on one side of the street and Donelson's on the other.

Donelson and some troopers rushed out of the church, firing through the open doors behind them as they fled. They hunted cover, but Donelson stumbled to the side. He waved to another of the deserters and surprised her by running across the street to join some of Chaco's men.

For a second, the urge to lift the rifle to her shoulder

and put a bullet in the captain gripped Mercedes, but she checked it because she didn't know what was going on. She was sure that Chaco had been headed to the mission to confront Donelson when he left the cantina, and the fact that he didn't emerge from the church made fear for him stab through her.

Donelson was talking to Chaco's men, and there seemed to be a truce forming between them, which was puzzling. It might be better to wait, she decided reluctantly, until she had a better idea of what the situation really was.

Over her shoulder, she told the bartender, "Go keep an eye on Gabriel. Let me know if there's any change in his condition."

"*Sí, señorita.*"

She stayed where she was by the door, watching warily. Donelson and the trooper with him—the one called Winters, Mercedes thought it was—ran back across the street to join the other cavalrymen. A few minutes later, riflemen from both groups opened fire on the mission.

Mercedes' hands tightened on the Winchester. Chaco was still in there. She was sure of that. Donelson was trying to kill her brother, just as he or one of his men had tried to kill Gabriel.

As the battle raged, she snugged the rifle's butt into her shoulder and rested its barrel against the doorjamb.

Just let that gringo dog Donelson show his face

again, she thought, and she would put a bullet through his head.

Lonnie Winters cursed bitterly as he looked in the shed where he had hidden Gabriel's body and saw the stack of grain sacks shoved aside. He didn't understand why the big bastard wasn't dead. Winters had killed men before by stabbing them in the back like that, more than once, in fact.

Somehow, Hernandez had lived. In order for Winters to redeem himself in Donelson's eyes, he had to remedy that.

The injured man had dragged his feet as he left the shed, so his trail wasn't difficult to follow. The marks were obvious on the dusty ground. After following them for a while behind the buildings, Winters realized that Hernandez had been heading for the cantina.

That didn't come as any surprise. Winters figured if he had been hurt, he might have tried to reach the cantina run by that lushly beautiful señorita. She looked like she could nurse a man back to health, sure enough. Just being around a gal like that was enough to boost any man's vitals.

In addition to the marks left by the bandit's dragging feet, drops of dark brown blood were visible here and there. Winters came to a place where the dust was more disturbed and a larger patch of blood appeared to have soaked into the ground. Hernandez must have collapsed and passed out again before regaining consciousness once more and struggling onward.

Why hadn't he just gone ahead and died, Winters asked himself? That would've simplified matters, and Romero never would have known what the colonel really had in mind.

Winters wasn't completely sure he knew all of the colonel's plans himself. Donelson played his cards pretty close to the vest. But Winters was confident that in the end he would make them all rich men. It was all Winters cared about.

Well, that and warm brown señoritas and the chance to kill a man every now and then.

The trail resumed, confirming his hunch about Hernandez passing out for a while. As Winters suspected, it led to the rear door of the cantina. He put his right hand on the knife sheathed at his waist as he used his left to try the latch.

No one had thought to bar the door. It swung open easily to his touch. He tensed and drew the knife.

He looked down a short hallway with a beaded curtain at the far end and an open doorway on each side. It was empty. Winters slipped inside.

He glanced through the doorway to his right. It led into what appeared to be an office that was empty at the moment.

The doorway on the left opened into a bedroom. As Winters turned in that direction, a short, fat, bald man unexpectedly appeared. His eyes opened wide in shock, and he opened his mouth to yell a warning.

Winters struck like a rattlesnake, plunging the knife into the man's belly and ripping upward. The man sagged forward. His mouth worked, but he was unable to make a sound as a crimson stain spread rapidly on the grimy apron he wore. Winters took him for the cantina's bartender.

He pulled the knife out of the man's body and stepped back. The bartender fell to his knees and then pitched forward on his face. Blood spread in a pool underneath him.

Winters looked into the room and saw Gabriel Hernandez sprawled facedown on a bed. The big outlaw was starting to stir. He moved one arm and moaned.

This time he wasn't going to make any mistakes, Winters thought as he stepped into the room. He was going to put his left hand under Hernandez's chin, yank his head back, and cut his throat from ear to ear.

"Let's see you live through this," he whispered viciously as he stepped toward the bed.

Chapter 28

Mercedes was still waiting to get a clear shot at Donelson when she heard beads rattle behind her. Thinking that Gabriel had regained consciousness and the bartender was coming to tell her, she looked over her shoulder toward the arched doorway on the other side of the room.

She saw the bartender, all right, but the front of his apron was soaked with blood and in a vain attempt to keep himself from falling he made a grab at the beads as he stumbled through them. The cords on which the beads were strung snapped under the man's weight and he sprawled on the floor.

Even so, he had succeeded in alerting Mercedes that something was wrong. She sprang away from the entrance, dashed across the room, and hurdled over the unfortunate bartender's recumbent form. Her sandal-clad feet slid a little on the floor as she reached the door of her bedroom.

Instantly, her eyes took in the scene—the blue-uniformed trooper looming over the bed as he reached for Gabriel, the knife in his other hand poised to strike, the faint movements Gabriel made as he came to, evidently unaware of the deadly threat hovering over him . . .

"Gringo!" Mercedes cried as the rifle in her hands came up.

The man whirled toward her as she fired. In that same split second, his arm flashed forward, his reactions lightning fast.

Mercedes felt the impact as the knife struck her, but no pain at first. She saw blood leap from the side of the trooper's head.

Then agony exploded through her, radiating out from the spot where the blade was buried in her left shoulder. She staggered, and the Winchester started to slip from her hands. With no warning, it had grown too heavy for her to hold up.

A second later the trooper crashed into her and drove her over backward. Her head hit the floor with enough force to stun her and render her powerless for the moment.

Frenzied curses spewed from his mouth as he locked his hands around her throat and began to squeeze. The terrible pressure made Mercedes' eyes bulge out. The whole world was blurred and spun crazily around her. A tiny voice screamed in the back of her brain, warning her that she was only moments away from death.

Her vision cleared and her eyes locked on the face of

the man whose weight pinned her to the floor as he strangled her. Blood dripped from the right side of his head and splattered on her face. She saw that the bullet from her rifle had torn away a good-sized chunk of his ear.

Mercedes couldn't move her left arm. The pain from the wound rendered it helpless.

But she snaked her right hand through the narrow gap between their bodies and closed her fingers around the knife's bone handle. She began working it free, doing more damage as the razor-sharp edge sliced her flesh. She would have screamed from the pain if she could have, but the death grip he had on her throat prevented any sound from escaping.

Finally the knife came free. She fumbled slightly as she tried to turn it, evidently warning Winters what she was trying to do. The trooper started to pull back.

With every ounce of strength she had left, Mercedes rammed the knife upward. The point pierced the soft hollow of his throat under his chin, went through his tongue and the roof of his mouth, and on into his brain. Blood filled his mouth and spilled out like a fountain, showering her in gore. His fingers lost their strength and slipped off her throat. She saw his eyes widen with the realization that he was dead.

Then life was gone and he toppled to the side as she heaved up against him. His body hit the floor with a dull thud.

Mercedes lay there with her back arched for a few seconds as she drew great gasping breaths of air back into her lungs. Weakness made her collapse. She couldn't get up, couldn't do anything except listen to her heartbeat hammer loudly inside her head.

She heard Gabriel groan. Summoning strength from somewhere, she rolled onto her right side and got that hand underneath her. With a great effort she pushed herself to her knees and started to crawl toward the bed.

When she was close enough she lunged forward, reached out, and grasped the sheet so she wouldn't fall. She pulled herself closer. Her throat hurt where Winters' brutal grip had bruised it, but she was able to rasp, "Gabriel . . ."

"*Chiquita* . . ." His hand groped for hers, grasped it.

Mercedes laughed softly. Both of them were in bad shape, maybe dying, but they were alive and together and Winters was dead. She turned her head enough to see the trooper lying there, his sightless eyes staring at nothing, the lake of blood slowly spreading around his head.

She squeezed Gabriel's hand and whispered, "Rest, *mi amòr*, rest. . . ."

If you had to be trapped in a siege, Slaughter thought wryly, there were worse places to be than inside a church with thick adobe walls, plenty of rifles, and thousands of rounds of ammunition. Several times during the afternoon, the deserters and Romero's men had charged the mission, but withering fire from the defenders had forced them to retreat on each occasion.

Slaughter had passed the word to the others to try not to kill the would-be revolutionaries from south of the border. He was convinced that Donelson had duped them somehow in order to get them to join forces with him and his men. Although Slaughter hadn't forgotten how they had raided his town, robbed the bank, and shot up the place, he also knew that they hadn't killed anyone in Tombstone and hadn't mistreated Viola while she was their prisoner. He didn't think they deserved to die just because they wanted to throw off the oppressive yoke of the dictator who ruled Mexico.

It was impossible to guarantee anyone's safety with so many bullets flying around, of course, but the deserters and the bandits tended to attack separately so the defenders inside the church could aim high or low and try to drive Romero's men back without fatally injuring any of them. Slaughter hoped it would end without too many casualties among them.

Another advantage to being inside the mission's thick walls was that it was cooler. As the afternoon dragged past, the temperature outside climbed higher and higher. The men using the wagons for cover didn't have much protection from the blazing rays of the sun.

During a lull in the fighting, Slaughter went over to Viola. She still sat beside Romero, who was stretched out on the floor between benches with his head pillowed on a folded blanket that Father Fernando had brought from his living quarters in the rear of the church.

Viola had half a dozen loaded Springfields close at hand. If Donelson's men got into the church, she would be ready to fight. Slaughter had no doubt that her aim would be cool and steady.

"Romero hasn't come around yet?" he asked as he knelt beside her.

Viola shook her head. "He's stirred a few times and muttered a little, but he hasn't been coherent. If he could just talk to his men . . ."

Slaughter nodded. "That would make a difference, all right. If Romero's men turned on Donelson, the odds would be on our side for a change."

Viola had a basin of water and a rag, also provided by Father Fernando. She wiped Romero's face with the cool, damp cloth. "I'll keep him comfortable. That's about all I can do right now."

Slaughter nodded again. Viola had bound up Romero's wounds earlier. The bleeding had stopped, but not before he lost enough blood to weaken him severely. More than once, Slaughter had seen men die from that.

"If he wakes up and you think he's strong enough for us to get him to a window, let me know. We'll have to hold them off until then."

"Or until Stonewall and Burt get here."

Slaughter had told her about his hope that a second posse from Tombstone would arrive. Quietly he said, "We can't count on that. For the time being, we're alone in this."

"Not completely alone. We have the men you brought with you."

Slaughter looked around the sanctuary. What she said was true. The posse men's faces were grimed with powder smoke. Most of them had cuts from flying glass or bullet burns where a slug had come close enough for them to feel its fiery kiss.

But they were all grimly determined. Scared, sure, but a man who didn't feel fear wasn't brave, he was an idiot. Courage was doing what had to be done no matter how scared you were.

The old Mission San Lorenzo was full of courage on that day.

Slaughter patted Viola's shoulder. He would have liked to kiss her, but it wasn't the time or place.

Besides, that was when Luther Gentry called out, "Looks like they're gettin' ready for another charge, Sheriff."

"Keep your head down," Slaughter told Viola for what seemed like the hundredth time. He went back to his position in a crouching run.

Something was up, all right, he saw as he risked a look at the wagons on his side of the church. It was the side where Donelson's renegades had congregated. Some of them were moving around behind the wagons. Slaughter got ready to open fire if they rushed the mission.

He was taken by surprise as Donelson called out to him.

"Slaughter! Slaughter, do you hear me in there?"

He hadn't expected Donelson to try to negotiate. Everyone inside the church knew that Donelson didn't intend to leave any of them alive, with the possible exception of Viola. What he might have in mind for her would be even worse.

Besides, the mission's defenders had the best bargaining chips—the crates full of rifles. Donelson didn't have much to offer.

Slaughter supposed it wouldn't do any harm to find out what Donelson wanted. He wasn't going to trust anything the renegade captain had to say, though.

"I hear you, Donelson!" Slaughter shouted through the window. "If you've got something to say, spit it out!"

"Oh, I've got something to say, all right," Donelson replied. "I want all of you to march out of there right now with your hands empty and over your head!"

"Why in blazes would we do that?"

"Because if you don't, my men are going to start shooting villagers. Surrender, or by nightfall La Reata will be a ghost town!"

Chapter 29

Father Fernando heard Donelson's ultimatum and rushed to the window where Slaughter crouched with one of the Springfields ready in his hands.

"*Dios mio,* this cannot be!" the priest exclaimed. "Not even a man such as Capitan Donelson would do such a horrible thing!"

"I wouldn't bet on that, Padre," Slaughter said grimly. "I think Donelson would do just about anything to get what he wants."

Judging by the angry shouts he heard outside, Donelson might have overplayed his hand. Some of Chaco's men might well have relatives in La Reata. Even the ones who didn't would be sympathetic to the villagers and unwilling to stand by while they were murdered in cold blood.

The fact that Donelson would make such a threat showed how desperate he was getting. Slaughter knew that if he and his companions could hold out a while longer, the pendulum might begin to swing back toward them.

Slaughter gave that pendulum a little push by shouting, "You're insane, Donelson! You know you tried to double-cross Romero and his men! You can't fool them anymore!"

"That's a damned lie!" Donelson called from behind the wagons. "You murdered Chaco Romero!"

From behind Slaughter, Viola said urgently, "John!"

Slaughter looked over his shoulder and was surprised to see Viola standing there with her arm around Romero's waist, helping to support the wounded revolutionary. Diego Herrara was on Romero's other side, also holding him up. Romero was pale and hollow-eyed, but he was conscious and seemed to know what was going on.

"How can I . . . help . . . Sheriff Slaughter?" he gasped.

It was what Slaughter had been waiting for. With excitement coursing through his veins, he stepped forward to take Viola's place at Romero's side. "Come on. Let's get you to the door so all your men can hear you."

"John, be careful with him," Viola urged as Slaughter and Herrara turned Romero toward the entrance. "He just regained consciousness and he's very weak."

"I know, but he's the only one who can put a stop to this."

As they half-dragged, half-carried Romero toward the double doors, Slaughter told Yardley and Harmon to take down the bar. Mose Tadrack unfastened the latches and gripped the handle on one of the doors.

"Just say the word, Sheriff, and I'll open it."

"Now, Mose," Slaughter said. "But not too wide. We don't want a bunch of bullets flying through there."

Tadrack heaved on the thick door. It moved back slowly, scraping a little on the floor.

Donelson's claim that Slaughter had murdered Chaco Romero was the last thing that had been said. That accusation hung tensely in the air.

Slaughter looked over at Romero. "Are you up to this?"

Romero drew in a deep breath and nodded. Slaughter and Herrara helped him closer to the door. He called out, "*Amigos! Amigos,* listen to me!"

Hearing Romero's voice when they had all thought he was dead prompted startled shouts from the bandits. Romero leaned closer to the open door. "Donelson is the traitor! He plans to murder us all and steal back the guns! You must stop him!"

With that, Romero's eyes rolled up in their sockets and he passed out, sagging in the grip of Slaughter and Herrara.

But the deed was done. When shots began to roar again outside, the bullets fired by the would-be revolutionaries were directed at Donelson and the rest of the deserters, who fought back desperately.

War had truly come to La Reata.

Donelson cursed bitterly. All his plans had fallen apart. Winters had allowed that brute Hernandez to live, and Romero had put on the finishing touches. Donelson would have sworn that Romero was dead. Just how many times did a man have to be shot before he died?

"Fall back!" Donelson roared to his men as he fired his revolver and saw one of the Mexicans fall as the slug blew away a good-sized chunk of his head. "Get to the horses!"

Retreat was the only option left to them. His forces were pretty evenly matched with those of Romero, but the survivors of the posse who were holed up in the church had to be taken into account. They had opened fire on the deserters again, which meant that Donelson and his men were under attack from two directions.

They had to get out of La Reata. They would be lucky to do it with their hides intact.

Donelson still had one thing working in his favor. His men might be deserters, greedy bastards who had gone back on their oath for the promise of a big payoff, but they were still well-trained cavalrymen. Most of them had been in fights with the Apaches in the past, so they were cool under fire and obeyed orders well. The retreat toward the stable was an orderly one, not a rout, and the men continued to fight as they pulled back.

Their horses were in the big corral next to the livery stable. Donelson crouched behind a water barrel, drilled another charging bandit with a round from his Colt, and called out to several of his men to get the horses saddled. The others would hold off the Mexicans.

The old man who owned the stable rushed out of the barn as several of the troopers charged up to the building. He shouted at them in Spanish, yelling too fast for Donelson to make out what he was saying over the roaring guns.

But it didn't really matter because one of the troopers raised his rifle and shot the old man in the chest. The stableman clapped his hands to the blood-spouting wound, staggered back a couple steps, and collapsed in the dust.

The deserters bounded past the dead man as they hurried into the barn to grab some saddles.

The fight was a fierce one. Donelson saw several of his men fall and knew that his force was being whittled down. He knew it was callous, but he didn't really care as long as he made it out alive.

He had to live in order to put the rest of his scheme into motion. His plan had always had another part to it, right from the start, although he hadn't let any of his men in on it. They didn't have to know until the right time came. This debacle at La Reata had just sped things up, that was all, he told himself.

As he reloaded his revolver and looked around the street, he realized that he hadn't seen Winters since he'd sent the former corporal to find Gabriel Hernandez and make sure the big outlaw was actually dead. That no longer mattered—Hernandez couldn't ruin things that were already ruined—but Donelson would have liked to have Winters by his side. The Southerner was like a vicious dog—handy to have around when you needed to turn him loose on somebody and command him to kill.

But if Winters got left behind when the rest of them pulled out, or if he had fouled up and gotten himself killed somehow, that was just too bad. Donelson was looking out for his own hide first.

"Horses are saddled, Cap'n!" one of the men shouted to him.

A bullet burned past Donelson's ear as he made a run for the stable. Another man swung the gate open enough for the troopers to pour into the corral and grab the horses' reins. All the shooting had spooked the animals, so they were dancing around making it difficult to mount up.

Several horses stampeded for the partially open gate. One of the deserters screamed as he was knocked down. Steel-shod hooves slashed and pounded at him. The scream was cut off abruptly as the horses trampled the fallen man to death. They hit the gate, knocked it the rest of the way open, and bolted out of the corral.

Only about half of the men had managed to mount before the stampede, but Donelson was one of them. He leaned forward over his horse's neck to make himself a smaller target and twisted to fire his revolver back at Romero's men.

A cloud of dust boiled up from the horses' hooves and helped shield the escaping deserters from view. Donelson guided his mount expertly and worked his way to the front of the group. He hauled hard on the reins and sent his horse lunging into the village's lone cross street. As soon as they had flashed past the few buildings, Donelson turned south toward the border.

Nothing lay north for him except a military prison and quite possibly a firing squad.

But south . . . ah, south lay another opportunity for riches, and almost as important, for revenge.

Romero and Slaughter believed that he was beaten, he thought with a savage grin as he galloped toward the border.

They would soon learn that Brice Donelson was just getting started!

Chapter 30

The shots began to die away after the deserters fled from La Reata on horseback. Slaughter opened the doors of the church wider and looked out at the scene of battle. Bodies littered the street. Some were Romero's men, but most belonged to deserters who had been killed in the fighting.

The sporadic reports of gunfire told Slaughter that the bandits were finishing off Donelson's men who had been left behind. It was a brutal business, but after everything that had happened, as well as the possibility of the atrocities that Donelson had threatened to carry out, Slaughter couldn't blame them too much.

Viola came up beside him. "We took Chaco back to Father Fernando's quarters and put him to bed. He came to again for a minute and said that he wanted to see his men."

"They're still a little busy at the moment," Slaughter said with a grim smile, "but when they've finished with

Donelson's men, I'm sure some of them will come to see how he's doing."

With things evidently under control for the moment, Slaughter turned away from the doors to check on the members of his posse. He found Grover Harmon tying a rag around Joseph Cleaver's upper left arm to serve as a bandage.

"Bullet knocked a hunk o' meat outta the kid's arm," Harmon explained as he tightened the makeshift bandage.

"But I'll be all right." Cleaver was pale and haggard like the others, but seemed to be steady on his feet.

Chester Carlton also sported a new bloodstained bandage. It was tied around his head. "I got creased again, Sheriff." His voice held a note of pride. "This was the most exciting thing I've ever done. I can't wait to tell my wife I was injured in a gun battle!"

Slaughter grinned and clapped a hand on the drummer's shoulder. "She may not think that you coming that close to getting killed is as exciting as you do," he warned Carlton.

With a rueful smile, Carlton said, "Well, it's not anything I'd want to go through again. It was also the most frightening thing I've ever done!"

All the injuries were minor, which was a relief to Slaughter. The men had known when they left Tombstone that they might be in danger before it was all over, but he'd wanted to keep the casualties to a minimum. He had lost Jack Doyle and Ross Murdock. That was enough, and he was going to mourn them.

Well, maybe not Murdock quite so much, since the young man had tried to kill him, but Slaughter still wished that Winters hadn't gunned him down in cold blood. With Slaughter's help, Murdock might have been able to put right what he had done.

Viola had gone into the rear of the mission to check on Romero again. When she came back, she told Slaughter, "Chaco wants his sister brought here, John. Do you think you could go find Mercedes?"

Slaughter hadn't heard any shots from outside for several minutes. He nodded. "I'll take a couple men with me. She's bound to be at that cantina of hers."

He told Yardley and Tadrack to bring rifles and come with him. Even though it was hot outside, after being cooped up in the church all day, it felt good to step out into the late afternoon sunlight.

The three of them had gone only a few yards before several of Romero's men rushed up and leveled Winchesters at them.

Slaughter muttered, "Stay calm," to his companions, then stepped out in front to meet the bandits. "Chaco Romero is inside the church," he told them in fluent Spanish. "He's wounded, but I think he's going to be all right. You can go see him if you think I'm not telling the truth. You heard him with your own ears when he said that Donelson was the one who shot him."

The tension in the air eased slightly. The men lowered their rifles, but didn't point them at the ground just yet.

"You pursue us all the way from Tombstone," one of

the men said, "and now you want us to believe that you are our friend?"

"I never said we were friends," Slaughter replied bluntly. "You robbed the bank in my town. But circumstances have made us allies. Donelson and his men are our true enemies."

"The man Donelson is gone, along with those of his dogs who still live." The spokesman's rifle barrel tilted up again slightly. "And now we must deal with you."

Slaughter grimaced in disgust. "You can do it after we've taken Romero's sister to him."

He stepped around the bandits and motioned for Tadrack and Yardley to follow him.

The two men looked a little nervous about that—and who could blame them, Slaughter thought, with hard-eyed bandits staring at them over the barrels of repeaters?—but they fell in step behind him as he headed for the cantina.

After a moment, Romero's men lowered their weapons and followed.

Slaughter was a little surprised that Mercedes hadn't already emerged from the cantina and come looking for her brother, now that the shooting was over. Maybe she was just being cautious . . . although caution didn't strike him as being that big a part of her makeup.

As he stepped into the building his eyes had to adjust from the bright sunlight outside, as usual, so for a moment he couldn't see much. About all he could make out was that there were no customers.

Then he spotted the bloody, huddled shape lying on

the floor just inside the arched door to the rear hallway. Beads from the damaged curtain were scattered on the floor around the body.

"Good Lord!" Slaughter exclaimed, hurrying across the room.

Tadrack, Yardley, and the three bandits were close on his heels.

Slaughter bent over the fallen man and recognized him as the bartender. His pale, waxy face and sightlessly staring eyes, along with the large pool of blood underneath him, were mute testimony to the fact that he was dead.

"Señorita Romero!" Slaughter called as he straightened. "Mercedes!"

No answer came from the back rooms. A couple swift steps along the corridor brought him even with the open doorways. Instantly, he saw Mercedes lying on the floor next to the bed in the room to his right. The massive form of Gabriel Hernandez lay on the bed. He was facedown, like Mercedes.

A few feet away, Winters' corpse was sprawled on its side. A knife had been driven into the former corporal's throat all the way up to the hilt.

Slaughter ran into the room and dropped to one knee beside Mercedes. He placed the rifle on the floor, then took hold of her shoulders and carefully rolled her onto her back. Blood covered the area around her left shoulder. He could tell that it came from a knife wound high on that side of her chest.

When Slaughter looked closely, he could see her

breasts rise and fall as she breathed. She was alive. Her wound had added to the rivers of blood spilled that day, but she might be all right with some prompt medical attention.

Gabriel was alive, too. Slaughter heard the big man's breath rasping in his throat.

He turned his head and told Tadrack, "Run back to the mission and fetch Mrs. Slaughter and Father Fernando." Slaughter looked at Romero's men and added in Spanish, "One of you go with him so the rest of your men won't think they need to shoot him."

Tadrack nodded and left the room, followed by one of the bandits.

Blood was still seeping from the wound in Mercedes' shoulder. Slaughter tore a piece off the sheet, folded it, and pressed it to the injury. She moaned a little as he put pressure on it. Her eyelids fluttered, then opened.

"I'm sorry it hurts," Slaughter told her. "Looks like you've already lost enough blood for one day."

He didn't know if she understood what he said or even heard him. Her eyes rolled around wildly and had trouble focusing. Her breasts heaved harder. He figured she was in quite a bit of pain.

Finally her gaze seemed to locate him. She whispered, "S-Señor . . . Slaughter?"

"That's right, señorita. I've sent for my wife and Father Fernando—"

"The priest! I . . . I must . . . make my confession. I have been . . . an evil woman . . ."

"I don't know you that well, señorita, but somehow

I doubt that. I didn't send for the priest so he could administer last rites. He'll just help Señora Slaughter patch you up. You're going to be fine."

She lifted her right hand enough to clutch at his sleeve. "Gabriel . . . ?"

"He's alive." Slaughter added honestly. "I don't know how bad he's hurt, but he's definitely alive."

"He will be . . . all right. He is strong . . . like an ox." Her thoughts seemed to be more in order. "If you are here . . . the fight must be over. Where is . . . my brother?"

"Down at the mission. He was wounded, too. Shot a couple times. My wife has been taking care of him."

"What happened to . . . that gringo captain?" Several curses followed her question about Donelson.

When she paused in her tirade, Slaughter said, "I hate to admit it, but Donelson got away. He galloped out of here with about a dozen of his men. I didn't see which way they went, but my guess would be south."

"Over the border."

Slaughter nodded. "Exactly. The army will be looking for him and the others on this side of the border. They'll be better off getting into Mexico."

"Did he get . . . the money?"

"Not a bit of it. He left here empty-handed, without the money or the rifles. He saved his own hide, but that's all."

"Someone will . . . catch up to him. Justice . . . will be done."

Slaughter hoped that was true.

"It was Donelson's rabid dog . . ." Mercedes motioned with her good hand toward Winters. ". . . who tried to kill my poor Gabriel. Then he . . . came back and . . . killed my bartender . . . stuck his knife in me . . . but I paid him back . . . gave him a taste of . . . his own steel . . ."

Slaughter glanced at the way Mercedes had driven the knife up through Winters' mouth into his brain. "I'd say you certainly did. Winters won't ever murder anyone again."

Before either of them could say anything else, Viola and Father Fernando hurried into the room, followed by Tadrack and the *bandido*.

"Dear Lord!" Viola exclaimed when she saw the blood on Mercedes' dress and bare shoulder. "Is she alive?"

"She is," Slaughter said solemnly. He lifted the cloth he had pressed to the wound. "Looks like the bleeding has just about stopped. But she's going to need some cleaning up."

"That wound will need some stitches, too." Viola looked at the priest. "Can you find me needle and thread, Padre?"

"Of course," Father Fernando said. "I believe you'll need to do some sewing on poor Gabriel, as well."

"I'll leave them in your capable hands, my dear." Slaughter picked up the Springfield he had set aside earlier, got to his feet, and motioned with a jerk of his head for Tadrack and Yardley to follow him as he left the room.

Romero's men came with them. Slaughter took note of that and reminded himself that not all of the problems had been settled.

There was still the question of what to do about all the loot that had been stolen from Tombstone.

Not to mention an entire load of contraband army rifles.

Chapter 31

Donelson didn't slow his horse until he had covered several miles. That ought to be far enough to be sure he had crossed the border into Mexico, he thought as he slowed the exhausted animal to a walk.

The men who'd fled out of La Reata with him followed his example. In their desperate flight, they had almost ridden their mounts into the ground. Much farther at that pace and the horses would have started collapsing and dying.

Unlike Texas, where the Rio Grande formed a distinct boundary between the United States and Mexico, in Arizona Territory the only line was an imaginary one.

You couldn't look around and tell from the terrain that you were in Mexico. The landscape looked the same as it did north of the border—flat and semiarid, brown and sere, with occasional clumps of sparse grass, sage, and scrub brush, and lots of hot, dusty sand.

Unappealing country to be sure, Donelson thought.

But he was glad to be there. For the moment, he was safe from the reach of the United States Army.

Some of his men didn't seem so glad. Several of them crowded their horses up alongside his. One of them demanded angrily, "What the hell are we gonna do now, Donelson? Half the boys are dead, and you never did get our money from those greasers!"

"That's Captain Donelson," he said coldly, thinking it might not be wise to mention the promotion in rank he had given himself while talking to Winters. "We may not be in the army anymore, but we all agreed that I was still in command."

"That was before everything went to hell." The speaker was a squat, balding trooper named Armstrong.

The first man who had spoken had enlisted under the name Jones, but that could have been an alias. Both were privates, and both had been in trouble in the past and spent time in the stockade.

Armstrong waved a beefy arm. "We don't even have most of our gear. All we've got are the damned army shirts on our backs!"

"Settle down," Donelson said sharply. He had to maintain discipline if he was going to have any chance of salvaging the situation.

And it could still be salvaged, he reminded himself. He hadn't played all his cards yet. One still remained up his sleeve that he hoped would turn out to be an ace.

Jones said, "If you want to keep givin' the orders, *Captain*, you'd better tell us what you plan on doin' about this mess. As far as I can see, we're worse off now than when we were actually in the army. We're stuck in Mexico with no money and damned little ammunition."

"Enough to find a bank somewhere and rob it, maybe," Armstrong said.

Donelson didn't care at all for the sarcastic tone of Jones's voice when the trooper had addressed him by his rank, and he ignored Armstrong's ridiculous suggestion except to say, "We're not going to rob a bank. We're going to keep riding until we reach those hills ahead of us."

The heights he mentioned were several miles away. They were primarily brown and tan and gray, indicating that they were barren of vegetation for the most part, but there were splotches of green that looked welcoming.

"What's in those hills?" Jones demanded with a scowl.

"Our salvation," Donelson replied softly. He wouldn't say anything else, and after a few minutes the other men stopped pressing him about it. They muttered and grumbled, but they kept riding with him.

They stopped and rested the horses only once on their way to the hills.

It was late afternoon before the deserters reached the slopes. Donelson led them into a narrow pass between two humpbacked hills. He had been given directions in a letter, and he thought it was the right route.

"What in blazes are you doin', Cap'n?" Armstrong asked, sounding slightly less rebellious. "Are we gonna camp in here?"

"More than likely," Donelson replied, "but that's not

the only reason we're here." He supposed he might as well go ahead and tell the men the rest of the plan that had brought them to Mexico. "You see, we were coming here all along, even if things had gone exactly as planned in La Reata. This is where we were going to deliver those guns."

"But we delivered them to those Mex rebels in that village," Armstrong said with a confused frown.

"We just didn't get paid for 'em," Jones added acidly with a disgusted look on his face, as if he had just bitten into something rotten.

Donelson shook his head. "No, this was their actual destination all along. You see, Chaco Romero isn't the only one I've been doing business with. I had another . . . arrangement. If everything had gone as planned, we would have turned those rifles over to Romero and his men and gotten our money for them . . . and then we would have killed those fools and taken the rifles back."

"A double cross!" Armstrong said. He slapped his thigh. "I like that way of thinkin', Cap'n."

"I thought you and the other men might," Donelson said smugly. "Once we had recovered the rifles, we would have brought them down here and delivered them to my other business partner—"

"And double-crossed him, too!" Armstrong enthused.

"Well, no. I think that would have been unwise. We would have honored the agreement I made with him."

"Who's this so-called business partner of yours?" Jones wanted to know. He still sounded skeptical.

Before Donelson could answer, a strident yell sounded in the canyon. "*Alto!*"

The command to halt was repeated, or maybe it just sounded like that because of the way it echoed. Donelson hauled back on the reins and brought his mount to a stop. So did the others.

As they did, uniformed figures appeared above them on the rocky slopes of both sides of the canyon. Rifles were cocked and leveled. Curses and exclamations of surprise came from the deserters as they realized they were under the guns of approximately fifty men.

A man wearing a uniform resplendent in the late afternoon sunlight even under the dusty conditions stepped out from behind a boulder. He clasped his hands together behind his back and called down, "Capitan Donelson?"

"Gentlemen, meet my real partner," Donelson drawled to his men. "General Alphonso Montoya."

General Montoya and his men led Donelson and his band to their camp higher in the hills. It was in a little grassy bowl next to a spring that was probably the nicest spot within a hundred miles. Cottonwood trees around the spring had provided shade for his men and horses while they'd waited for Donelson's arrival. Montoya hadn't known exactly when Donelson was going to get there with the guns, so he'd been prepared to wait for several days.

Donelson looked around. He suspected that Montoya

cared more about the shade protecting his horses than he did about the comfort of the men. The general could always get more men.

Montoya stopped in front of the tent he had brought with him—his headquarters—although his men had to make do with bedrolls. In the comfortable spot, it didn't really matter. He pointed out the area Donelson and his men should make their camp, and they moved off in that direction.

Night had fallen by the time Montoya sent for Donelson and had him brought to the tent.

Donelson's nerves were taut as he stepped into the tent. He had looked into the background of the man he was doing business with, of course, and discovered that the general had a reputation for ruthlessness, even brutality.

Donelson didn't mind that. He was ruthless himself, and he could be brutal when he needed to.

A small table was set up in the middle of the tent. Montoya's bunk was at the rear. Food waited on the table, a platter of tortillas and bowls of stew. Montoya was pouring tequila from a bottle into cups.

The general turned and held out one of the cups to Donelson.

"*Gracias.*" The captain nodded his head.

Montoya waved Donelson into one of the empty chairs at the table. "I apologize for the simple fare, Captain. Traveling in this godforsaken wilderness is not easy. Providing any sort of reasonable amenities is even more difficult."

"I assure you, General, this looks very good to me," Donelson said as Montoya sat down across from him. "Especially considering the way things could have turned out."

"Yes," Montoya said. "I want to hear all about that while we dine. I could not help but notice when you rode into the hills that you did not bring the rifles as we agreed. What happened, Captain?" The general's voice hardened. "Bear in mind that my men still have plenty of weapons for a firing squad, if not for a revolution."

Even though Donelson recognized the clearly implied threat, he couldn't help but think in a moment of grim humor that everyone in Mexico must be born wanting to overthrow the government. That had been the overriding goal in Chaco Romero's life, and General Montoya—an officer in *El Presidente* Díaz's own army—felt the same way.

The weapons carried by Montoya's men were old and sometimes unreliable. His uprising would stand a much better chance of succeeding if his forces were armed with new, modern Springfields.

In the end, of course, Díaz would probably crush Montoya's would-be revolution anyway, but Donelson didn't care one whit about that.

He admired Montoya at least a little, however. Romero had prattled on about overthrowing Díaz for the good of the people. Montoya just wanted more power. Donelson could understand and sympathize with that.

He took a sip of the tequila. "It's true the guns aren't here, General, but I know where they are."

Montoya's eyes narrowed in the lamplight. "Please tell me you would not be foolish enough to try to change the terms of our agreement at this late date, Captain Donelson."

"Of course not. We just ran into some difficulties on our way to fulfill our end of the bargain."

For the next few minutes, Donelson explained what had happened in La Reata.

Montoya grimaced in disgust when Donelson mentioned Chaco Romero. "Peasants," he spat when Donelson concluded. "They are like *la cucaracha*, the cockroach. Do you know why I say that, Captain?"

"Um . . . not exactly sir."

Montoya tossed back the rest of the tequila in his cup. "It's not so much what they carry off as what they fall into and ruin." He set the empty cup on the table. "So, these peasants have my guns, do they?"

"I'm afraid so."

"Then in the morning we will go to La Reata, all of us . . . and we will crush ourselves some cockroaches."

Chapter 32

By nightfall, Chaco Romero had been taken to the hotel on a makeshift stretcher and carefully placed on the bed in one of the rooms. Mercedes was carried over there as well, although she objected strenuously to being separated from Gabriel, who was left behind in her bed in the cantina.

Viola and Father Fernando had tended to them, cleaning and stitching up the wounds and making them as comfortable as possible.

While that was going on, Slaughter took de facto command of the forces in the village. The bodies of Romero's men who'd been slain in the fighting were taken to the mission. They would be laid to rest in a respectable fashion first thing the next morning. Slaughter regretted that he and his men were responsible for some of those deaths, but circumstances had dictated their actions.

Besides, Brice Donelson's treachery was truly responsible for what had happened in La Reata.

The deserters who had been killed would be buried properly, too, although a part of Slaughter wanted to find a gully, toss the corpses into it, and leave them for the scavengers. That would be a barbaric thing to do, however, and he wasn't going to give in to the impulse.

The men digging the graves were going to be mighty busy, come morning.

With that taken care of, Slaughter posted guards on all four sides of the little settlement. The way Donelson and his men had been routed, there was a good chance the deserters would cross the border and just keep going, but as long as there was a possibility they might double back, caution was advisable.

The sentries were a mix of the men from his posse and members of Romero's group. Some of the bandits were reluctant to take Slaughter's orders, but they knew his wife was caring for Romero, Mercedes, and Gabriel, so they were willing to cooperate . . . for now.

Satisfied that he had done all he could for the time being, Slaughter went to the hotel and climbed the stairs to the upper floor.

Romero was sitting up in a bed with pillows propped behind him. The would-be leader of the revolution was pale and drawn, but seemed to be alert. He nodded to Slaughter and smiled faintly. "I hear that I have you and your lovely wife to thank for saving my life, Sheriff."

"Viola's the one who kept you from bleeding to death. After that, you saved your own life by calling off your men. They're the ones who ran off Donelson before he could finish the job of murdering you."

"He got away, then?"

Slaughter nodded. "Unfortunately, he did. I was pretty sure I saw him ride out of town. Since things have settled down, we've searched the entire village and the area around it, just to make sure he wasn't hiding out somewhere. I'm afraid he's lit a shuck."

"Which way did he go?"

"The trail he and the other survivors from his bunch left leads south toward the border."

Romero nodded solemnly. "It makes sense that he would flee the United States. He is a deserter from the army, after all." Romero's face hardened. "When I have recovered, I will see to it that he is hunted down and dealt with as justice demands. His man Winters tried to murder my sister and my friend."

"Winters came pretty close to succeeding, too, but Viola tells me she thinks they'll be all right. They just need time to rest and recuperate, like you."

"How many of my men were killed? Do you know?"

"Seven dead," Slaughter replied. "Another dozen or so wounded, some of them pretty badly, but it looks like they'll all pull through."

"That is more for Donelson to answer for."

"He's responsible for the deaths of two of my men. I'd like to see him hang for that. I'm practical enough to re-alize that's pretty unlikely, though. He'll probably never set foot in this country again."

"Sooner or later, justice will find him no matter where he goes. I believe this."

Slaughter wished he shared Romero's certainty, but he had seen evil men escape their just deserts too often in the past and he was sure he would again. Some said that final justice would be dealt out in the next life, but that was too far beyond the pale for him to consider. He was a supremely practical man and dealt in the here and now.

Slaughter picked up the single ladder-backed chair in the room, turned it around, and straddled it. As he rested his arms on the chair back, he said, "There's something else we need to talk about, Romero."

"The money?" Romero guessed shrewdly. "The rifles?"

"Both, actually. I know where the rifles are."

Romero chuckled. "The money is hidden. Donelson never would have found it until I was ready to turn it over to him—which I would have done, had he not betrayed his true nature by trying to double-cross us."

"I figured as much. You want to tell me where it is?"

Romero's eyes narrowed. "Why would I do that?"

"That money belongs to the people of Tombstone. And you don't need it anymore. You already have the rifles you were going to buy with it."

"Bought with the blood of my men, instead."

"Blood is the currency of revolutions," Slaughter said. "If you don't know that, you might want to reconsider trying to overthrow Díaz."

"I know full well the price that must be paid," Romero

snapped. "But I also know that money could still do the revolution much good in other ways, now that we no longer need it to purchase the rifles."

"If you want any sympathy for your cause on this side of the border, you'll turn that money over to me and let me take it back to Tombstone, to its rightful owners. Otherwise"—Slaughter shook his head—"you're just a bunch of Mexican bandits."

Anger darkened Romero's face as he leaned forward in the bed. "How dare you! Our cause—"

"Your cause doesn't mean a thing to the people whose savings were wiped out when you hit the bank in Tombstone," Slaughter broke in. "You talk a lot about fighting for the common people. Who in blazes did you think you were robbing when you held up that bank? Sure, some of the mine owners and other businessmen have money there, but so do the fellas who own the livery stables and the hardware stores."

Romero still glared, but he let his head sag back against the pillows behind him. "You have, what, eight men?"

"Counting myself," Slaughter said.

"And I have more than twice that many. Plus I know where the money is hidden and you do not. I would say that you should be *asking* for the money's return, Sheriff Slaughter, not demanding."

"I'm not demanding anything. Just telling you what's right. Hell, I haven't asked for those rifles back, have I? And they belong to the United States government."

"We will not give up the rifles," Romero said quietly. "Never."

"That's why I'm suggesting a reasonable compromise. Take the rifles and go back to your revolution. My men and I won't try to stop you. But leave the money for the people of Tombstone."

"And if we do not?"

"Then I reckon there'll be more fighting to do," Slaughter said.

For a long moment, they regarded each other with cool, level stares. Then Romero sighed and nodded.

"The money is under the floorboards in the office of my sister's cantina. You'll have to move the desk and pry them up. In the morning, you should take it and go, before I change my mind."

"I'm not sure I can convince my wife to leave before you're well enough to travel yourself."

"Ask her to talk to me. I will tell her she must go."

Slaughter grunted. He knew from experience that telling Viola she had to do something was often the worst mistake a person could make. But maybe Romero could be more persuasive than he was.

"I'll tell her. I don't know how much good it'll do." Slaughter stood up. "In the meantime, you should get as much rest as you can. I'm no doctor, but I think that'll do you more good than anything else."

"I agree." As Slaughter turned to leave the room, Romero went on. "Sheriff . . . whether we agree on everything or not, I appreciate what you have done for me and my men. Without your help we might have fallen prey to Donelson's schemes."

"You know the old saying about the enemy of my enemy . . . " Slaughter left the room and closed the door behind him.

He found Viola in the cantina, changing the dressing on Gabriel's wound. The big outlaw was awake. He turned his head so he could grin at Slaughter. "Your wife, she is a saint, señor! A saint! A true angel of mercy!"

Slaughter returned the grin. "She was merciful enough to marry a rough-edged old codger like me, that's true."

Viola laughed. "You're not really that old, John. But I'll admit that you're pretty rough around the edges." She pulled the sheet up over Gabriel. "There. You ought to be all right until morning."

"*Gracias*, señorita. I mean, señora. When we met I believed you to be unmarried. It takes some getting used to." Gabriel glanced at Slaughter again. "You are a lucky man, Sheriff."

"You're not telling me anything I don't already know, *amigo*," Slaughter assured him.

He looked across the hall at the door to Mercedes' office, which was closed. The knowledge that the loot from the raid on Tombstone was on the other side of that door made him want to go in there, pull up the floor, and recover it.

There would be time enough for that in the morning, he told himself.

He took Viola's hand. "You've been running yourself ragged all day, my dear. You need some rest."

She sighed. "I suppose I am a little tired. I checked on Chaco and Mercedes before I came over here, and now that Gabriel is all right, too . . ."

"Go on, señora," the big outlaw urged her. "Get some rest, as your husband says."

"All right. But I'll make sure someone is keeping an eye on you during the night. If you need me, send a man to fetch me."

"This I will do," Gabriel promised.

Slaughter led Viola back into the cantina's main room. He paused. "I could use a drink. How about you?"

"Well . . . maybe a little one."

Slaughter went behind the bar, found a bottle of wine, and poured it into glasses. "I don't think Mercedes will mind us helping ourselves."

"Probably not." Viola took the glass he handed her and raised it slightly. "To going home."

"To going home," Slaughter agreed.

They clinked the glasses together.

Chapter 33

The night passed quietly, as Slaughter hoped it would.

Up early the next morning, as was his habit, he checked with the guards currently on duty. They confirmed that there had been no sign of trouble.

Even before breakfast, Viola had gone to check on her patients.

Slaughter, on his way back to the hotel, met her as she came out of the cantina. "How's Hernandez?"

"Stronger this morning," she reported with a smile. "He told me he has the constitution of a bull. Mercedes told me the same thing, although she called him an ox instead of a bull."

Slaughter chuckled. "He's almost as big as one of those creatures, no matter what you call it." He linked arms with her. "Come along, my dear, we'll get something to eat in the hotel dining room."

As they walked along the street, Viola said, "I had a

long talk with Chaco, John. He tells me you're going to let him keep those rifles."

"It's not that I particularly *want* to let him have them," Slaughter said with a frown. "But as he pointed out, his forces outnumber what's left of my posse by more than two to one. Anyway, it's not my responsibility to recover the army's guns. I persuaded him to let us take the bank money and the rest of the loot from the raid back to Tombstone so it can be returned to its rightful owners. As far as I'm concerned, that takes care of everything I'm duty-bound to do."

"You're recovering the money, but letting the robbers get away."

"Isn't that what you'd want me to do? I thought you were sympathetic to Romero's cause."

"I am. But he rode into my husband's town and broke the law. I don't like that."

Slaughter chuckled again. "I appreciate the sentiment, my dear, but I'm willing to make an exception if it means getting you and the men safely home again."

"And you, too," Viola said softly. "I agree. You've done enough, John."

The cook at the hotel had coffee ready, along with flapjacks, fried eggs, and thick slices of ham. Slaughter enjoyed the meal and felt better after he'd eaten.

That feeling was short-lived. Chester Carlton, still wearing the bloodstained bandage around his head, hurried into the hotel dining room with a worried look on his florid face. "Mr. Gentry sent me to find you, Sheriff. He said there's something you need to see."

Slaughter set his napkin aside and reached for his hat. Irritated, he asked, "What in the world is it now?"

"I don't know," Carlton said as he shook his head. "But Mr. Gentry seemed worried."

Slaughter leaned over and pressed his lips to the top of Viola's head. "Stay here until I find out what's going on, my dear," he murmured.

"All right, but don't forget that I can handle a gun, too."

Slaughter wasn't likely to forget that.

He followed Carlton out of the hotel and along the way asked, "How are you feeling this morning, Chester?"

"Not too bad, considering I got shot in the head yesterday," the drummer replied with a smile. "This old noggin of mine hurt a little this morning, but I suppose that's to be expected."

"Well, I haven't been shot in the head myself, but that sounds reasonable enough."

"I hope whatever this new trouble is, it doesn't turn out to be too bad. I don't know about you, Sheriff, but I've had just about enough excitement to last me for a while."

"What exactly is it that you sell, Chester?" Slaughter asked. "I don't think you ever said."

"I'm in ladies' undergarments."

"Oh." Slaughter could have said more, but he didn't.

Several of Romero's men were gathered near the old mission, and a definite feeling of tension hung in the air. Gentry, Harmon, Yardley, and Tadrack were standing in front of the church, too. All of them wore worried frowns.

"What is it?" Slaughter asked as he and Carlton came up to them.

"Take a look out yonder, Sheriff." Gentry inclined his head toward the south.

Slaughter looked past the mission and saw what had caused such consternation among the men. A low cloud of dust hung in the air. It was more of a yellow haze than an actual cloud, but it was definitely there.

"Riders coming," Slaughter said grimly.

"A lot of them, from the looks of it," Gentry said. "But they ain't comin' fast, elsewise their horses would be kickin' up a lot more dust than that."

"Who do you think it could be?" Tadrack asked. "Donelson and his men coming back?"

Slaughter shook his head. "I'd say the bunch is too big for that. Must be fifty or sixty men headed this way, from the looks of that dust."

"Bronco Apaches, maybe?" Harmon suggested.

"Not likely. They'd slip up on us in small groups. We'd never know they were around until they were ready to jump us." Slaughter frowned in thought. "No, whoever it is doesn't care if we know they're coming, but they're not getting in any hurry about it. They must be pretty confident."

That fact worried Slaughter. The strangers must think they could just waltz into La Reata and do anything they wanted without anybody putting up a fight. Or they were so sure they could crush their opposition that they weren't worried about a battle.

Carlton piped up. "Maybe it's the cavalry. They could have come down here looking for those deserters."

"Maybe," Slaughter said, although he didn't believe that for a second. "Not very likely they'd be coming from that direction, though. We're not very far from the border."

"Maybe it's the Mexican army," Tadrack said. "If Romero wants to start a revolution, they might've found out about it and come to stop him. They might not care that La Reata's on American soil."

That actually made more sense than any of the other theories suggested so far, Slaughter thought. "Whoever it is, keep an eye on them. I'm going to talk to Romero."

He strode back to the hotel, and found Viola waiting in the lobby.

"What is it?" she asked. "What did Mr. Gentry want?"

Like most happily married men, Slaughter didn't believe in lying to his wife—unless there was a really good reason to do so, of course—or in keeping the truth from her. "There's a large group of riders headed in this direction from the south."

"Donelson?"

"I don't know. I want to get Romero's thoughts on who else it might be."

"I'll come with you," she volunteered.

Slaughter didn't see any reason to argue with her. He nodded. "Come on."

They went up the stairs and along the hall to Romero's

room. He was still propped up, but had dozed off. He woke up, seemed disoriented for a second, but then he steadied. "I can tell something is wrong, Sheriff. What is it?"

Slaughter told him about the dust indicating a large group of riders approaching the village.

"One of my men suggested it might be the Mexican army come to chase you down. Is there any chance of that? Could President Díaz know that you're plotting a revolution against him and sent *Federales* to nip it in the bud?"

"Impossible," Chaco replied. "Word couldn't have reached him in Mexico City so soon. We've just started recruiting men from the villages in northern Sonora. Unless . . . I suppose Díaz could have spies this far north . . . but it doesn't seem very likely to me, Sheriff."

"Do you have any other explanation, then?"

"No . . . but I have a pair of field glasses in my saddlebags. They'll be in the stable with my saddle. If you'll take them and climb into the church bell tower, you might be able to see who our visitors are before they get here."

Slaughter nodded. He should have thought of that himself.

He turned to leave, but Romero went on, "Sheriff, I'd like to have a gun."

"You're in no condition to fight, Romero," Viola said.

Slaughter nodded. "My wife is right."

"Yes, but if there is more trouble on the way . . . if

enemies reach this room in search of my life . . . it would pain me more than any physical wound ever could to leave this world without putting up a fight."

When Romero put it like that, Slaughter could understand. He would feel the same way if he were in Romero's position. "I'll have somebody bring you a six-shooter and some extra shells," he promised.

"*Gracias*, Sheriff."

Slaughter halfway expected Viola to stay with Romero, but she followed him out of the room. He wasn't jealous of the bandit, exactly, but the rapport Viola had developed with the man bothered him somewhat. It struck him as unusual, especially considering the fact that Romero had kidnapped her.

Every older man married to a younger wife probably had feelings like that from time to time, he told himself. Viola had never seemed dissatisfied with their marriage, not even for a minute, but it was difficult to forget completely the difference in their ages.

For the moment, however, he had to forget everything except the possible danger closing in on La Reata. The previous evening, Slaughter had hunted up his Henry, which had been taken from him when he was captured, and stashed it behind the desk in the hotel. He reclaimed it and stalked out of the building with Viola at his side.

"Where do you think you're going now?" he asked her without slowing down.

"With you."

It was a simple answer, but it made him feel a little better.

He waved one of Romero's men over. The bandit frowned suspiciously, but nodded in agreement when Slaughter asked for help in finding the field glasses among Romero's gear. That didn't take long. As they walked out of the livery stable, he looked at the advancing dust again. It was closer, but the riders were still apparently moving at a deliberate pace.

Joseph Cleaver and Diego Herrara had joined the other members of the posse at the mission, so Slaughter's entire force was together. He held up the field glasses and told them, "I'm going to climb up into the bell tower and see if I can get a look at whoever's coming."

Viola went into the church with him. Slaughter told her, "You don't have to go up there with me."

"My eyesight is a little better than yours, John."

He frowned. "What makes you think that?"

"I'm younger, for one thing."

"There's nothing wrong with my eyes."

"Maybe not, but I can still see better than you."

Once again Slaughter realized that arguing was pointless. He opened a narrow door below the bell tower and found a ladder behind it. "All right, if you're that determined, up you go."

His thoughts were on the mysterious force riding toward La Reata, but from this angle he wouldn't have been human if he hadn't noticed the way the trousers

Viola was wearing hugged her bottom as she climbed the ladder. That was a good thing, he told himself. It showed that he was still alive, that the blood was still coursing through his veins.

He turned his attention away from his wife's bottom and back to the problem at hand as he climbed after her, taking the rifle with him.

The bell tower was open on all four sides, with a thick beam at each corner supporting the tiled roof. A ledge ran around the inside so that the sides of the tower formed a waist-high wall. The big bell hung in the center, also supported by thick beams. They had an excellent view in all directions.

At the moment, the only one Slaughter cared about was south. He handed the Henry to Viola and used both hands to raise the glasses to his eyes and steady them. The landscape seemed to leap toward him through the lenses. After a moment, he located the riders and stiffened as he recognized the gray uniforms they wore. Those were Mexican soldiers, all right . . . and technically they were invading the United States since they were north of the border.

Slaughter tracked the glasses toward the front of the column, lowering them slightly in order to do so. He wanted to see who was leading the invasion.

A couple riders were out in front of the others. One was a swarthy man with a hawk nose and a thick black mustache. He wore a lot fancier version of the Mexican army uniform with a bright red sash angling across his barrel chest and a hat with a red plume on his head. Anybody with a uniform that flashy had to be a general, Slaughter thought.

But it was the sight of the man riding beside the officer that made Slaughter grate a heartfelt curse.

"Who is it, John?" Viola asked tensely.

"The last low-down varmint I wanted to see again so soon. Captain Brice Donelson."

Chapter 34

"That sounds like General Alphonso Montoya," Romero said a short time later. Slaughter had described to him the man approaching La Reata with Donelson. "A vain, brutal man. He has hauled many men in Sonora in front of a firing squad for little or no excuse. The cruelty of officers such as Montoya is a large part of the reason we want to overthrow Díaz." Romero paused. "There have been rumors that Montoya would like to see *El Presidente* removed from power as well. That would make the path clearer for Montoya's own ambitions."

"That explains it, then," Slaughter said as his keen brain put together the final pieces of the puzzle.

"Explains what?"

"Donelson's plan. He was going to sell the rifles to you, then double-cross you, murder you and your men, take the rifles back, and turn around and sell them to this General Montoya. If Montoya wants to put together a little revolution of his own, he can use a supply train full of brand-new Springfields, can't he?"

Grim-faced, Romero nodded. "With those rifles, Montoya could wipe out many of his enemies."

"Donelson must have had a rendezvous arranged with him south of the border where he would turn over the guns," Slaughter mused. "When everything fell apart here, he met Montoya anyway and told him where he could find the Springfields. Now Montoya's on his way to get them."

Romero looked like he wanted to jump out of the bed, but his injured body wouldn't let him. "We must stop him. We must not allow a devil like Montoya to get his hands on those rifles."

"I don't like that idea, either. And it galls me that he thinks he can just ride across the border into my country and take whatever he wants."

"That is Montoya's way. He does what he wants and kills whoever is in his way. No one has ever been able to stop him."

"Maybe today is the day that changes."

Romero frowned. "A bold statement, but how? You said Montoya has sixty men. That's many more than you and I can muster, even if we combine our forces."

"How many people live in La Reata?" Slaughter asked quietly. "I'll bet we can arm every able-bodied man with a dozen Springfields and as much ammunition as he could fire in a day."

That idea made Romero lean forward with a look of interest on his lean face. "Many of the people here have relatives scattered throughout Sonora. Montoya's cruelty is bound to have touched nearly everyone. The men will fight. I know they will. Some of the women will, too."

"I'm going to bring a couple of your men up here," Slaughter said. "You can give your orders to pass them along to the others."

"What I will tell them is to follow *your* orders, Sheriff."

Slaughter frowned. "Will they do that?"

"They will if I tell them to. An army needs a commander in order to function. Right now, my men and the people of La Reata are your army, Sheriff."

Slaughter nodded solemnly. "I'll try to live up to that faith."

"One more thing," Romero said as Slaughter turned to leave. "Where is Señora Slaughter?"

"She's up in the church bell tower with your field glasses, keeping an eye on Donelson and Montoya." Slaughter smiled. "I left my Henry up there with her, too, in case she needs to pick off any varmints."

"Your wife, she is quite a woman."

"Not telling me anything I don't already know, *amigo*."

He also knew there was no time to waste. For the next fifteen minutes, he hurried here and there in the village, giving orders and explaining what everyone was supposed to do. Romero's men seemed reluctant to cooperate, but the two lieutenants Romero had spoken to in his hotel room lashed the men with words and ensured that they would do what Slaughter told them to do. The main thing was to spread throughout the village and pass the word that any man willing to fight Montoya's invaders should go to the church and arm himself with several rifles and as much ammunition as he could carry.

Then the defenders of La Reata were to find good places from which to fight.

Slaughter was walking in front of the church when Viola leaned out from the bell tower and called, "John, several riders have broken off from the others! They're coming toward town!"

A delegation to deliver Montoya's demands, Slaughter thought. He looked up at his wife. "Keep your head down up there!"

"How can I keep my head down and shoot at the same time?"

That was an entirely logical question. Slaughter didn't have an answer for it, so he just laughed, waved at her, and then called, "Mose!"

Tadrack trotted over to him. "What is it, Sheriff?"

"Some of those fellows are coming in, and I'm going out to meet them and talk to them. How about coming with me?"

Tadrack looked surprised. "Why me?"

"I want a steady man beside me. Since the booze burned itself out of you, you've been pretty steady. Take a look at your hand now."

Tadrack did so, lifting his right hand and gazing at it

for a few seconds. It didn't tremble at all. "Well, what do you know about that?" he said softly.

"You're going to have a problem when you get back to Tombstone. Somehow I don't think you're going to be content to be a saloon swamper anymore."

"Reckon I'll have to live through whatever happens today before I need to worry about that," Tadrack said with a smile.

"That's a good point. Come on."

In the stable, they saddled up quickly. Riding past the church a few minutes later, they saw that the three riders who'd been approaching the village had stopped about five hundred yards to the south. The rest of Montoya's force was a quarter mile behind them.

Slaughter and Tadrack rode toward the men at a deliberate pace. Slaughter wanted to seem calm and steady, even though inside he was anything but.

As the gap between them closed, he saw that one of the men wore blue, while the other two were clad in gray uniforms. When he came close enough to recognize Donelson, he wasn't surprised. The two men with the deserter were officers, but their uniforms weren't as gaudy as Montoya's. The general had stayed back with his men where it was safe.

Slaughter reined in when he was thirty feet from Donelson and the two Mexicans. He leaned forward a little in the saddle and called, "I didn't expect to see you again, Donelson. I thought you'd keep running with your tail between your legs like the cowardly dog you are."

"You can insult me all you want, Sheriff. All I care about is those guns. Load them back onto the wagons, send them out here, and nobody else has to die. You can all go on your way peacefully. No grudges."

"Damned right I hold a grudge," Slaughter snapped. "You betrayed your country, mister. You were responsible for the deaths of some good men."

"A tinhorn gambler and an embezzler?" Donelson laughed. "Please, Sheriff. No one in Tombstone will miss either of those two."

"What about the men who died in La Reata?"

"Some of my men died there, too." Donelson waved a hand impatiently. "Anyway, there's no point in arguing about this. My friends want those guns, and they're going to get them, one way or another. Just turn them over, so that no more blood has to be spilled."

"Do you really think General Montoya is going to just turn around and ride away? He's invaded the United States this morning, Donelson. Unless he's willing to cause an international incident and draw the attention of President Díaz, he can't afford to leave any witnesses behind. I'll bet he's not ready for Díaz to know that he's plotting a revolution just yet."

That had just occurred to Slaughter, but as he spoke the words he knew the truth in them. It would be better all around for Montoya's plans if he wiped La Reata and all its inhabitants off the face of the earth.

"You're wrong," Donelson said. "The general gave me his word."

Slaughter could tell that Donelson realized the truth, too. It was shaping up to be a massacre.

It wouldn't do any good to cooperate. The villagers might as well fight back, Slaughter thought. Their lives were on the line either way.

"The general wants those guns." Donelson's voice was bleak with acceptance.

"Let him come and get 'em."

Chapter 35

For a second, Slaughter thought Donelson was going to yank out the pistol on his hip and start blazing away.

But then the renegade captain snapped, "You'll regret this, Slaughter," and hauled his horse around to ride back toward Montoya's force.

The two Mexican officers, who had sat on their horses impassively without saying a thing during the entire exchange, turned their mounts and followed him.

"Come on, Mose," Slaughter said as he wheeled his horse. "We'd better get back to town. We don't know how long this truce is going to last."

Not long, they discovered a moment later when the Mexicans charged, yelling and shooting.

Slaughter and Tadrack were still well short of the village when the attack began. They leaned forward and urged their horses into a desperate gallop.

"This isn't fair!" Tadrack shouted over the drumming hoofbeats. "They should've let us get back to La Reata!"

"I don't think Montoya cares about fair!" Slaughter replied. "As soon as he could tell we weren't going to cooperate, he was ready to start the ball."

"Well, you did tell him to come and get 'em!"

When Slaughter glanced over at his companion, he saw that Tadrack was grinning.

He knew the comment he had made earlier was correct. If they survived, Tadrack would never be content to go back to being a boozed-up saloon swamper.

But their survival was still very much in doubt.

Slaughter looked back over his shoulder and saw spurts of dirt and gravel being kicked up by the bullets that struck the ground ten or fifteen yards behind them. Luckily, the horses they had ridden out were fresh after a night's rest and running well.

Shots began to ring out from the village. Powder smoke spurted from windows in some of the buildings. Muzzle flashes came from the bell tower in the mission. A smile plucked at his mouth. Viola was taking cards in the game, and that didn't surprise him at all.

The covering fire slowed Montoya's men slightly, enough to give Slaughter and Tadrack time to gallop around the church and put the sturdy building between them and the attackers. They didn't slow down until they reached the livery stable and raced inside where the horses would be relatively safe.

Slaughter's booted feet hit the ground almost before his mount stopped moving. Tadrack was right behind him. A couple teenage boys, grandsons of the liveryman who had been shot down the day before, were waiting to take charge of the horses. Slaughter and Tadrack left the stable and ran back to the church.

A middle-aged man, also a citizen of La Reata, met them with loaded Springfields. "We have more ready, señores. Those of us who are not good shots can still load rifles."

Slaughter nodded. "That's a very important job. Thank you, my friend."

He and Tadrack hurried to the rear of the church and entered the graveyard behind it. They knelt behind a couple tombstones to use the markers as cover. Some of the shots from the attackers were already reaching the mission. Bullets thudded into the rear wall while others ricocheted off the tombstones.

Even though it seemed rather disrespectful, Slaughter rested the Springfield's barrel on top of the grave marker behind which he knelt and looked for the flashy uniform with the red sash. When he didn't locate Montoya right away, he drew a bead on the charging Mexican soldier waving a sword over his head, figuring him for an officer.

Slaughter pulled the trigger. The Springfield cracked and kicked against his shoulder. The Mexican threw his arms in the air and the sword went flying. The officer toppled off his horse and vanished under the trampling hooves of the other mounts around him.

Tadrack's rifle blasted, too, and another rider in the vanguard of the charge flew out of the saddle.

"Here, *señores*!"

Slaughter turned to see the man who had handed

them the Springfields. He had carried four more loaded rifles to them, and he had brought a box of ammunition as well.

"Let's stagger our shots, Mose," Slaughter told Tadrack, "and give our friend here time to reload for us."

"Sounds good, Sheriff," Tadrack agreed.

For the next few minutes, the two men kept up a steady, withering fire. Combined with Viola's deadly accurate aim from the bell tower and the shots from the village's other defenders, it all took a toll on Montoya's men and blunted their charge. The soldiers began to haul back on their reins. The horses started to mill around and kick up dust.

A moment later, the attackers retreated, spurred on their way by more gunfire from La Reata.

Slaughter stood up and watched the riders recede into the distance. They left a dozen men and several horses sprawled on the sandy ground behind them.

"I suppose it's too much to hope that they'll turn around and go home now," Tadrack said.

"We dealt them some significant damage, but I doubt if Montoya cares how many men he loses as long as he gets the rifles in the end. He'll be back." Slaughter nodded. "And we'll be ready for him."

"Peasants!" General Montoya raged at his officers who had survived the opening skirmish. They stood around him with enlisted men holding their horses for them. "You have allowed yourselves to be routed by peasants!"

"They are well-armed peasants, General," one of the men ventured to say.

"Armed with *my* rifles!" Montoya bellowed.

Donelson jumped in. "Slaughter's to blame for this. Romero is badly wounded or dead, so Slaughter's the only one they have to lead them. He's stubborn, and he's lucky. He's demonstrated that he has the ability to slip out of situations that ought to prove fatal to him."

"Then he must be dealt with," Montoya snapped.

"We already tried that—"

"No, I mean he must be killed! You, Captain Donelson, take a small group of men, get into La Reata, and kill this man Slaughter."

Donelson knew he was edging into dangerous territory, but he asked, "How are we supposed to get into the village? I'm sure Slaughter has posted sentries all around the place, and it's broad daylight. I suppose we could wait for night—"

"I am through waiting!" the general interrupted once again. "Those who oppose me will be crushed at a time of my choosing!" With a visible effort, he controlled his rage. "There will be a distraction, another frontal assault on the village. While that is going on, all eyes will be on the fighting. That is when you and the men you take with you will slip into the village, Captain. Kill Slaughter and take as many hostages as you can. Women and children will be best. We will force those fools to see that they must cooperate with us."

"All right, General," Donelson said with a nod. He wasn't sure that killing Slaughter and taking some hostages would accomplish what Montoya wanted . . . but it was true that Slaughter seemed to be the only natural leader among the defenders of La Reata.

Unless it was that wife of his, Donelson mused. The fiery Viola Slaughter might be able to rally the men to keep fighting. It would be a good idea to make sure she was one of the hostages, if at all possible, he decided.

Montoya calmed down. "When you have picked your men, Captain, let me know. I'll give you half an hour to circle the village out of sight and get into position to the north. Then we will attack again with all the sound and fury we can muster, giving you your chance to infiltrate. Is that clear?"

"Perfectly, General. I'm going to take some of my own men with me, if that's all right."

Montoya waved a hand. "Take whoever you like. Just accomplish the task I have given you." The hawk-like face turned hard as flint. "But if you fail, you should flee back to whatever prison awaits you in the north rather than returning to me. I do not tolerate failure."

"We won't fail, General. I give you my word on that." Donelson meant it. He was sick and tired of having his plans ruined. He was going to rid himself of the problem of John Slaughter, or he was going to die in La Reata. One of them would not live to see the sun go down.

Chapter 36

Slaughter figured Montoya wouldn't attack again right away. After encountering so much unexpected resistance, the general would probably want to lick his wounds for a little while before launching another assault.

That gave Slaughter a chance to check the defenses in La Reata. He was pleased to discover that they had suffered no casualties in the first skirmish. A lot of shots had been fired by Montoya's soldiers, but the thick adobe walls of the buildings had stopped them all.

Satisfied so far, he climbed the ladder to the bell tower and found Viola reloading the Henry.

"I need some more ammunition, John. And I think you should send a couple men up here with repeaters. This is a perfect spot to pick off those—" She stopped what she was saying as she finished thumbing cartridges through the rifle's loading gate. "Well, I suppose I should be ladylike and not use bad language."

Slaughter laughed and pressed a kiss to her forehead. "My dear, you're the only woman I know who can dress like a Mexican bandit, shoot a Henry rifle better than most men, and still worry about being a lady. I'd say you're the most remarkable lady in the entire territory!"

She worked the Henry's lever to throw a fresh shell into the firing chamber and smiled at him. "You're such a flatterer, John Slaughter."

He didn't care if they were in plain view of the entire village. He put a hand under her chin, tilted her head back a little, and gave his wife a lusty kiss.

No matter what else happened in the future, Slaughter knew the best thing he had ever done or ever would do was marrying Viola Howell.

Donelson wished he had Lonnie Winters with him. The Southerner was the best pure killer the captain had ever encountered. He was pretty sure that Winters was dead, though. Otherwise, the former corporal would have already shown up.

It was a shame, but Donelson would just have to make do with what he had—Armstrong, Jones, and three other troopers—the best of the bunch left from those who had deserted with him.

The six men lay sprawled in a slight depression about a hundred yards from the northern outskirts of La Reata. They had ridden in a wide circle around the town, not wasting any time, but not galloping, either. To have done so would have kicked up too much dust and alerted Slaughter or someone else that something was going on.

When they'd reached a certain point, they'd dismounted and approached the village on foot, using the scrubby brush that dotted the plains for cover, until finally, they were close enough that they dropped to their bellies and continued on that way.

Donelson pulled his watch from his pocket and opened it. Half an hour had passed since they left Montoya's forces. He snapped the turnip closed and slipped it back into his pocket. Any minute, Montoya ought to be starting the attack that would serve as a distraction.

Sure enough, guns began to roar in the distance. A moment later, the village's defenders began returning the fire.

Donelson would have liked to have gotten a little closer to begin the final dash he and his men had to make, but the depression was the last bit of cover. He put a hand on the ground and got ready to push himself to his feet. "If anybody tries to stop us, go ahead and kill them. Good luck, boys. Let's go!"

The six deserters charged out of the depression and raced toward La Reata as fast as they could.

Slaughter figured Romero would like to know how things were going, so after he climbed down from the bell tower and left the church, he headed for the hotel.

He was surprised to find Mercedes sitting in the room with her brother. She had a bulky bandage on her left shoulder and that arm was in a black silk sling, but she had gotten some of her color back and seemed to feel fairly strong.

Romero looked like he wanted to be in the thick of the fighting. "What happened, Sheriff? Is Montoya gone?"

"No, he tried an attack but we made his men turn and run. He pulled back a mite, but I'm sure he'll try again." Slaughter paused, then added, "Donelson was with Montoya's men earlier."

Mercedes cursed bitterly. "Will that man always plague us?"

"Not much longer," Slaughter told her. "I've got a hunch that today is the showdown. One way or another, it'll all be over soon."

"We either triumph . . . or die," Romero said.

Slaughter shrugged. "In the end that's usually what it comes down to. We have plenty of guns and ammunition, though, and we hold the town. The people of La Reata are fighting well. I think Montoya can throw his soldiers against us all day without taking the village. Sooner or later they're going to get tired of being wiped out."

Romero shook his head. "They will not turn on Montoya. They all fear him too much. Most of them are no better than outlaws, criminals from the slums and jails of Mexico City. Those are the sort of mindless brutes Montoya and the other generals want in the army. They will fight to the end if Montoya orders it."

"Then we'll just have to kill them until Montoya is the only one left," Slaughter said coldly. "It's a shame, but he'll massacre everybody in La Reata if he gets the chance."

"*Es verdad*. If you will help me get up, Sheriff, I would like to do my part in defending the village—"

"No!" Mercedes exclaimed. "You are still much too weak, Chaco. You have to stay here and rest."

"A man must fight!" Romero argued.

"You've done your fighting in the past, and I've got a hunch you'll do more in the future. Your sister's right, Romero. In your condition, you'd be more of a liability than a help." Those were harsh words, Slaughter knew, but they were also true.

Romero appeared to know it, too. With a grimace, he slumped back against the pillows behind him.

Before they could say anything else, Slaughter heard guns barking again. The second attack he'd expected had come. He told Mercedes, "Stay with your brother, señorita."

"I will," she promised. "I wish I could be with Gabriel, too."

"I have men posted in the cantina. They'll look after him."

Slaughter hurried downstairs and out into the street. He heard the Henry cracking from the bell tower, along with the sound of several Springfields firing up there as well. He had sent Mose Tadrack and a couple of Romero's men who were good shots to join Viola in the tower. From up there, they could take a heavy toll on Montoya's men.

Slaughter started for the church. He would lead the defense from there.

Donelson's long legs carried him over the ground. The soles of his boots slapped against the dirt. His heart slugged heavily in his chest. He expected to feel the shock of a bullet striking him at any second as he ran toward the village with the five men right behind him.

He reached the closest building unscathed, and paused to catch his breath as he pressed his back against the adobe wall. The other men arrayed themselves along the wall beside him.

"Can't believe . . . we didn't get shot," Armstrong panted.

"Just wait," Jones said bleakly.

As soon as Donelson's pulse wasn't hammering so loudly in his head anymore, he said, "Spread out. We'll work our way down the street, three on each side. Find Slaughter, and if you can kill some of his posse or Romero's men along the way, don't hesitate."

"Won't they hear the shots and realize we're attackin' 'em from this direction?" Armstrong asked.

"With so much shooting going on everywhere else, it's not likely," Donelson said. "Armstrong, Jones, you'll be with me on the left side of the street. The rest of you take the right side."

The men nodded in understanding, then split up as Donelson had ordered. He ducked around the corner of the building and hurried along the street.

He was passing the entrance to the livery stable when a teenage boy suddenly lunged out, yelling and thrusting a pitchfork at him. The attack took Donelson by surprise, and he might have wound up with the fork's sharp tines buried in his belly if Jones hadn't snapped a shot from his rifle that smashed the boy's shoulder and spun him around.

Armstrong yelped. "That pup almost got you, Cap'n." He raised his rifle. "I'll finish him off—"

That was as far as Armstrong got. Before he could pull the trigger, a shotgun boomed and a load of buckshot smashed into the squat trooper, shredding his face and upper chest into raw meat. The blast knocked him over backward.

A second boy had emerged from the shadows inside the barn to fire that shot. He swung the scattergun's twin barrels toward Donelson and Jones to touch off the second barrel, but Jones leaped forward and knocked the shotgun up with the barrel of his empty rifle. He slashed the Springfield's stock to the side of the boy's head and dropped him in an unconscious heap.

"Leave them!" Donelson snapped. He had just spotted John Slaughter. The lawman from Tombstone had stepped out of the hotel, several more buildings along the street from the stable. He didn't even glance in their direction as he turned toward the church at the end of the street.

Donelson rushed closer, eager to seize this chance. He lifted his revolver and drew a bead on the back of the unsuspecting Slaughter.

Another few seconds and Slaughter would finally die, Donelson thought with a savage, exultant grin on his face.

Chapter 37

The roar of gunshots was torture to Gabriel. He had never been around fighting before when he wasn't in the thick of it. The two old gringos, Gentry and Harmon, who had been left in the cantina with him, insisted that he had to stay in bed and rest.

Enough was enough, he told himself. He had no desire to be in Mercedes' bed if Mercedes wasn't in it, too.

Gritting his teeth against the weakness that filled him, Gabriel got his hands under him and pushed.

He rolled onto his side and swung his legs off the bed. When he stood up, the room spun crazily around him for a moment before his head settled down. Then, with his jaw still clenched, he started stiffly toward the door. The pain in his back subsided slightly as he stepped into the cantina's main room.

Gentry and Harmon stood near the door, holding

Springfields. When they heard Gabriel's shuffling steps, they looked around in surprise.

"Dadgummit, Hernandez," Harmon said. "You ain't supposed to be outta that bed."

Gentry added, "Miz Slaughter'd prob'ly skin us alive if she knew we let you get up. Not to mention that sister o' Romero's."

"You better—"

The crack of a rifle shot interrupted Harmon. It was followed almost immediately by the boom of a shotgun somewhere not too far off. Both old men looked toward the door.

Gentry exclaimed, "What in blazes—"

A familiar figure appeared in the street just outside the cantina. Gabriel's eyes widened and his face flushed with rage as he recognized the man. All the pain inside him vanished and was replaced by anger as he lowered his head and charged like a maddened bull between Gentry and Harmon.

Donelson never saw what was coming as Gabriel fell on him like a mountain.

Slaughter heard the commotion behind him and whirled around in time to see Gabriel emerge from the cantina and crash into Donelson. The renegade officer went down under the impact, but he hung on to his gun and slashed at Gabriel's head with it. The revolver slammed into the big outlaw's skull and momentarily stunned him.

Slaughter had instinctively drawn his Colt as he turned, but he couldn't risk a shot with Gabriel and Donelson so close together. Somehow, he wasn't surprised to see Donelson in La Reata. He had sensed that the two of them would wind up facing each other again, even when it had looked like Donelson had fled and might never come back.

A rifle cracked across the street and a bullet buzzed past Slaughter's ear. He pivoted and dropped to one knee as he thrust the Colt out in front of him. More of the blue-uniformed deserters had slipped back into La Reata, and one of them was drawing a bead on him.

Slaughter fired first and sent a .45 slug punching into the man's belly. As the trooper doubled over and collapsed without firing his rifle, Slaughter shifted his aim to the one who had fired the shot at him and squeezed off another round, drilling that man as he tried to reload the Springfield in his hands.

At the same time, Gentry and Harmon burst out of the cantina and joined the fight. Gentry downed the third and final trooper on the other side of the street while Harmon traded shots with the man who had been with Donelson. The saddle maker staggered as the deserter's bullet struck his hip, but his shot had found its target and driven into the trooper's chest, killing him. The man dropped his rifle and toppled over backward with his arms outflung.

That left only Brice Donelson. He freed himself from Gabriel's grip and came up firing. Slaughter felt the wind-rip of a slug past his ear. His pearl-handled Colt roared and bucked in his hand as he triggered it. He fired all three rounds left in the cylinder.

All three rounds slammed into Donelson's chest. The impacts made the renegade captain take a step back, but he didn't go down. Stubbornly, Donelson stayed on his feet. His gun had sagged, but he struggled to lift it for another shot.

Slaughter's Colt was empty, as were the Springfields held by Gentry and Harmon. Donelson seemed to know that. He grinned as he thumbed back his revolver's hammer . . .

Blood welled from his mouth and he pitched forward on his face. He twitched once and didn't move again.

Slaughter didn't have time to feel any satisfaction at the fact that Donelson was dead at last and would never plague him again. La Reata was still under attack by Montoya's men. Slaughter pulled fresh cartridges from his pocket and started thumbing them into the Colt.

"Riders comin' from the north, Sheriff!" Gentry called to him. The liveryman had dropped to a knee beside Harmon, who had collapsed from being nicked on the left hip.

"I'm all right, Luther, dadblast it!" Harmon complained. "Get your rifle reloaded before that new bunch of trouble gets here! And reload mine while you're at it!"

Slaughter paused as he snapped the Colt's cylinder closed. He saw the dust cloud closing in on the village from the north and for a second he thought the same thing that Gentry and Harmon had, that some of Montoya's men had circled around and were attacking from that direction.

When he got a look at the two men galloping hard in the forefront of that group, he recognized them.

Stonewall Jackson Howell and Burt Alvord had made it at last, and they had several dozen fighting men from Tombstone at their back.

The charge by the Mexican soldiers had almost reached the southern edge of La Reata. Slaughter waved Stonewall and Burt on and shouted to them. "Invaders!"

That was enough to send the force from Tombstone smashing into Montoya's men with all guns blazing. The soldiers hadn't expected reinforcements to show up, and the attack crumpled almost instantly. The chaos that ensued filled the air with dust, gun smoke, and a terrible cacophony of shooting and yelling.

It was all over in minutes.

The ragtag remnants of Montoya's force fled south as fast as they could go. Slaughter knew they wouldn't be coming back. He didn't figure they would stop running until they were deep inside Mexico, even if Montoya tried to rally them.

He holstered his gun and hurried over to Gabriel's side. He had seen enough to know that the big outlaw had saved his life by tackling Donelson. He grasped Gabriel's arm and pulled. "Let me give you a hand, *amigo*."

With Slaughter's help, Gabriel climbed to his feet, swaying a little. "The fight, she is over?"

"Seems to be."

"Good. I think maybe I'm tired after all."

Gabriel started to fall, but Slaughter caught him

and braced him up. Spotting Diego Herrara and Pete Yardley, he called, "You men give me a hand here!"

Slaughter turned Gabriel over to them and told them to help him back into the cantina. He had spotted Stonewall and Burt walking their horses along the street toward him. Rifles cracked occasionally as the men from Tombstone sent hurry-up shots after the fleeing Mexicans, but other than that the shooting had stopped.

The two deputies reined in. Stonewall thumbed his hat back and grinned at his boss, who was also his brother-in-law. "Looks like we got here just in time, Sheriff."

Slaughter snorted. "Almost too late, if you ask me. Anyway, I think we would have beaten General Montoya's men without your help. It was just a matter of time."

"General Montoya?" Burt repeated. "Was that the dadgummed Mexican *army*?"

"That's right. You boys just turned back an invasion of the United States."

Stonewall let out a low whistle. "Hear that, Burt? We're heroes!"

Slaughter wasn't going to waste time arguing with the youngster, especially when Burt pointed to the body of one of the deserters who had been with Donelson and exclaimed, "Hey! I know that *hombre*."

"Who is it, Burt?" Slaughter asked.

"He's the fella who came into Tombstone yellin' about that silver strike in the Dragoons."

"Yeah, the silver strike that turned out to be a dang

bust," Stonewall added with a disgusted look. "There wasn't any silver."

Slaughter nodded slowly. It all made sense. Donelson had planned the whole thing carefully, sending a man into Tombstone dressed as a prospector to start a rush to the Dragoons. That had left the town largely undefended and made it easier for Romero and his men to rob the bank of the loot they would use to buy the stolen rifles.

It was a pretty cunning scheme, Slaughter thought, but in the end it hadn't gotten Donelson anything except a few fatal ounces of lead in his vitals.

"I'd sure like to know what's goin' on here," Stonewall went on.

"I'll tell you all about it later," Slaughter said. "Right now I need to find your sister and make sure she's all right."

He hurried toward the mission, but he hadn't gotten there yet when the double doors opened and Viola rushed out. She ran to meet Slaughter, who swept her into his arms.

"You're all right?" he whispered as he held her and brushed his cheek against her hair.

"Never better, now that I know you're all right."

That was true for both of them, Slaughter thought. They made quite a team.

That evening the cantina was full and the merriment was great. La Reata had been saved.

The joy was tempered by the fact that several more of

Romero's men had lost their lives in the fighting. Out of the force he had taken to Tombstone, only he, Gabriel, and three other men remained alive.

Romero had insisted that he was strong enough to get up and come to the cantina to join the gathering. After considerable argument, Viola and Mercedes finally had agreed, and some of the men Stonewall and Burt had brought with them from Tombstone had carried the bandit leader to the cantina on the same stretcher that had been used to transport him earlier. Once there, he had been set up in an armchair with pillows around him.

Gabriel felt much better. "I'm bouncing back like the big strong bull that I am," he claimed in a booming voice.

Mercedes, sitting beside him with her good hand on his arm, said quietly, "I'll make sure of it".

Romero looked around the big table where they all sat—Slaughter, Viola, Stonewall, Burt, Mose Tadrack, Gabriel, and Mercedes—and said gloomily, "My revolution is over before it ever began. You might as well take those rifles back with you after all, Sheriff. Five men cannot hope to overthrow a beast like Díaz."

"Five men and one woman," Mercedes said. "I'm selling the cantina and going back to Mexico with you and Gabriel, Chaco. I never should have left."

"You don't have to do that," her brother told her.

"I think I do." She patted Gabriel's arm. "Someone has to look out for this reckless animal."

Slaughter said solemnly, "I'll take the rifles to the

army, all right . . . all the ones I was able to recover, anyway."

"What do you mean by that?" Romero asked.

"Seems to me like one wagonload must have gone astray somewhere. There was no sign of them here in La Reata."

Viola squeezed his arm, and he knew by her reaction that he had made the right decision.

"With those rifles," Romero mused, "a man might be able to drum up some interest in removing a dictator from power."

"Stranger things have happened," Slaughter said. "All the money is going back to Tombstone with me, though."

Romero shrugged and nodded while Gabriel made a face. Clearly, he wasn't fond of the idea of giving up all that loot. But Slaughter didn't expect him to cause any trouble over it.

Stonewall said, "You know, we found Jack Doyle's body on the way down here, Sheriff."

"Gave him a decent burial," Burt added.

"I appreciate that," Slaughter said.

Stonewall went on. "That wasn't much of a posse you brought down here. A bunch of old men and storekeepers and—no offense, Tadrack—a saloon swamper."

"Oh, I don't know." Slaughter leaned back in his chair. "I think we did all right for ourselves. Don't you agree, Deputy Tadrack?"

Stonewall looked surprised.

A grin broke out across Tadrack's face. "You mean that, Sheriff?"

"I do," Slaughter declared. "I told you you'd need a new job when you got back to Tombstone. You've got one, if you want it."

"I'll take it. And I'm much obliged to you."

Stonewall said, "Well, hey, I . . . I didn't mean nothin' by what I said—"

Viola laughed and told her brother, "Just let it go, Stonewall. Who knows, Mose might wind up being sheriff one of these days, if I can ever convince John to give up being a lawman and come back to the ranch permanently."

Slaughter smiled. "Not for a while yet, my dear. Not for a while."

J. A. Johnstone on William W. Johnstone
"When the Truth Becomes Legend"

William W. Johnstone was born in southern Missouri, the youngest of four children. He was raised with strong moral and family values by his minister father, and tutored by his schoolteacher mother. Despite this, he quit school at age fifteen.

"I have the highest respect for education," he says, "but such is the folly of youth, and wanting to see the world beyond the four walls and the blackboard."

True to this vow, Bill attempted to enlist in the French Foreign Legion ("I saw Gary Cooper in *Beau Geste* when I was a kid and I thought the French Foreign Legion would be fun") but was rejected, thankfully, for being underage. Instead, he joined a traveling carnival and did all kinds of odd jobs. It was listening to the veteran carny folk, some of whom had been on the circuit since the late 1800s, telling amazing tales about their experiences, that planted the storytelling seed in Bill's imagination.

"They were mostly honest people, despite the bad reputation traveling carny shows had back then," Bill remembers. "Of course, there were exceptions. There was one guy named Picky, who got that name because he was a master pickpocket. He could steal a man's socks right off his feet without him knowing. Believe me, Picky got us chased out of more than a few towns."

After a few months of this grueling existence, Bill returned home and finished high school. Next came stints as a deputy sheriff in the Tallulah, Louisiana, Sheriff's Department, followed by a hitch in the U.S. Army. Then he began a career in radio broadcasting at KTLD in Tallulah, which would last sixteen years. It was there that he fine-tuned his storytelling skills. He turned to writing in 1970, but it wouldn't be until 1979 that his first novel, *The Devil's Kiss*, was published. Thus began the full-time writing career of William W. Johnstone. He wrote horror (*The Uninvited*), thrillers (*The Last of the Dog Team*), even a romance novel or two. Then, in February 1983, *Out of the Ashes* was published. Searching for his missing family in a post-apocalyptic America, rebel mercenary and patriot Ben Raines is united with the civilians of the Resistance forces and moves to the forefront of a revolution for the nation's future.

Out of the Ashes was a smash. The series would continue for the next twenty years, winning Bill three generations of fans all over the world. The series was often imitated but never duplicated. "We all tried to copy the Ashes series," said one publishing executive, "but Bill's uncanny ability, both then and now, to predict in which direction the political winds were blowing brought a certain immediacy to the table no one else could capture." The Ashes series would end its run with more than thirty-four books and twenty million copies in print, making it one of the most successful men's action series in American book publishing. (*The Ashes* series also, Bill notes with a touch of pride, got him on the FBI's Watch List for its less than flattering portrayal of spineless politicians and the growing power of big government over our lives, among other things. In that respect, I often find myself saying, "Bill was years ahead of his time.")

Always steps ahead of the political curve, Bill's recent thrillers, written with myself, include *Vengeance Is Mine, Invasion USA, Border War, Jackknife, Remember the Alamo, Home Invasion, Phoenix Rising, The Blood of Patriots, The Bleeding Edge*, and the upcoming *Suicide Mission.*

It is with the western, though, that Bill found his greatest success. His westerns propelled him onto both the *USA Today* and the *New York Times* bestseller lists.

Bill's western series include *The Mountain Man, Matt Jensen, the Last Mountain Man, Preacher, The Family Jensen, Luke Jensen, Bounty Hunter, Eagles, MacCallister* (an Eagles spin-off), *Sidewinders, The Brothers O'Brien, Sixkiller, Blood Bond, The Last Gunfighter,* and the upcoming new series *Flintlock* and *The Trail West.* May 2013 saw the hardcover western *Butch Cassidy, The Lost Years.*

"The Western," Bill says, "is one of the few true art forms that is one hundred percent American. I liken the Western as America's version of England's Arthurian legends, like the Knights of the Round Table, or Robin Hood and his Merry Men. Starting with the 1902 publication of *The Virginian* by Owen Wister, and followed by the greats like Zane Grey, Max Brand, Ernest Haycox, and of course Louis L'Amour, the Western has helped to shape the cultural landscape of America.

"I'm no goggle-eyed college academic, so when my fans ask me why the Western is as popular now as it was a century ago, I don't offer a 200-page thesis. Instead, I can only offer this: The Western is honest. In this great country, which is suffering under the yoke of political correctness, the Western harks back to an era when justice was sure and swift. Steal a man's horse, rustle his cattle, rob a bank, a stagecoach, or a train, you were hunted down and fitted with a hangman's noose. One size fit all.

"Sure, we westerners are prone to a little embellishment and exaggeration and, I admit it, occasionally play a little fast and loose with the facts. But we do so for a very good reason—to enhance the enjoyment of readers.

"It was Owen Wister, in *The Virginian* who first coined the phrase *'When you call me that, smile.'* Legend has it that Wister actually heard those words spoken by a deputy sheriff in Medicine Bow, Wyoming, when another poker player called him a son of a bitch.

"Did it really happen, or is it one of those myths that have passed down from one generation to the next?

I honestly don't know. But there's a line in one of my favorite Westerns of all time, *The Man Who Shot Liberty Valance*, where the newspaper editor tells the young reporter, 'When the truth becomes legend, print the legend.'

"These are the words I live by."

Turn the Page for an Exciting Preview!

THE GREATEST WESTERN WRITER OF THE 21ST CENTURY

An epic saga of the O'Briens, father Shamus and his sons Samuel, Patrick, Shawn, and Jacob, homesteaders fighting to survive in the untamed western wilderness . . . A USA Today bestselling author whose novels ring with authenticity and power . . . A thrilling adventure across the border of Mexico—up against an enemy more powerful and deadly than any the O'Briens could ever envision . . .

A TIME TO SLAUGHTER

New Mexico Territory is no stranger to bad men. But south of the border, on the wild Mexican coastline, is another kind of wicked—a murderous Arab with a ship full of stolen women to be sold as sex slaves in the four corners of the world. Among them is a missing local schoolteacher Shawn O'Brien has been searching for—a woman with a past she's kept carefully hidden. Shawn, along with a half-mad bear hunter and a professional hangman fight their way to the coast for a blood-soaked battle between the slavers and U.S. Navy men who are almost eager to die in battle in service to their leader. When the action runs aground, O'Brien gets his chance to face down an Arab sheik who profits from human misery . . . and makes a sport of slaughter . . .

THE BROTHERS O'BRIEN
A TIME TO SLAUGHTER

by William W. Johnstone
with J. A. Johnstone

Coming in May 2014 wherever Pinnacle Books are sold.

Chapter 1

Black was the sky and bitter the wind, but Silas Creeds felt no chill, for the wind was not colder than he and the sky no blacker than his killer's heart. Truth to tell, he was highly amused. In the dead and dreary winter of 1888, he was not in the New Mexico Territory to kill a man, but to return a runaway woman to her rightful owner.

This was a first for him, and the cause of his mirth.

From a rise studded with pines, he looked down on the Dromore ranch. Pyramids of windblown snow lay at the bases of each trunk as though the trees had dropped their drawers in preparation for a scamper down the hill. His thoughts turned to the job at hand. How does a man born to the gun treat another man's trophy woman?

Well, he could truss her up and throw her behind his saddle, Creeds decided. Or he could loop a noose around her neck and drag her after his horse.

Neither method struck him as satisfactory. He shook his head, a smile playing around the corners of his thin scar of a mouth. It required some serious thought. Why did Zebulon Moss want the treacherous little whore back anyhow? It would've been a lot simpler to put a bullet into her and have done. Serve her right.

Creeds sighed. Ah well, Zeb knew his own mind and he set store by the little baggage, so there was an end to it.

A lone rider hazing a Hereford bull toward a cattle pen near the big plantation house took his attention. The puncher showed a shaggy wing of gray hair under his hat, but the turned-up collar of his sheepskin hid his face.

Creeds grinned and slid the Winchester from the boot under his left knee. He drew a bead on the rider and had him dead to rights. A head shot, easy at that distance. "Pow!" Creeds said quietly.

The puncher rode on and Creeds shoved the rifle back into the leather. There was to be no killing on this trip. "Just bring my woman back," Zeb had said. He was paying the money, so he got to choose the tune.

Creeds scanned the ranch again.

A big plantation house with four pillars out front, white-painted fences and corrals, a bunkhouse for seasonal punchers and the single hands, a commissary, and a row of eight neatly built cabins for the married men.

Creeds nodded. No doubt about it, those were civilized

folks down there, and that meant they'd be fat and sassy and easy to kill.

Set apart a ways from the other buildings was a timber structure with a V-shaped shingle roof and a low bell tower. Smoke from its iron chimney tied bows in the wind and even from where he sat his horse Creeds heard the noisy laughter of children. The building was painted red and that amused him greatly. "Well, well, well, ol' Zeb's information was correct . . . Trixie Lee is out in the boonies, teaching snot-nosed brats in a little red schoolhouse."

That was a far cry from working the tinpans and cowboys up Santa Fe way. And an even farther cry from being Zebulon Moss's kept woman, bought and paid for.

Creeds shook his head. He had to smile. Damn, this was getting better and better. A real challenge.

He was a tall, scrawny man, dressed in the ankle-length black coat he wore summer and winter. On his head, he sported a battered silk top hat he thought became him, and a long woolen muffler in the red Royal Stuart tartan was wound twice around his turkey neck. He'd taken the scarf off a tinpan he'd shot a spell back, but he couldn't remember the exact circumstances of that killing. After a while they had a way of all running together.

Apart from the rifle under his knee, Creeds showed no other weapons. But the pockets of his coat were lined with buckskin and in each nestled a Colt double-action Lightning revolver in .38 caliber. A careful man, he'd bobbed the hammers of both guns so his draw would not be impeded.

Creeds had killed seventeen men. One he did remember was good ol' Charlie Peppers, who was reckoned by them who knew to be the fastest man with a gun south of the Picketwire.

After the fight, Creeds had taken Charlie's title and his left ear as a trophy. He'd also bedded his woman, but that ended badly when he'd had to shoot her after she came at him with a knife in her hand, crying rape.

All in all, Creeds considered himself the West's premier gunfighter, and no one cared to argue the point with him.

Silas Creeds was trespassing on Dromore range and knew men had been shot for less, but it didn't trouble him in the least. He was confident of his gun skills, and such fears were for lesser men. He rode past the big house, skirted the corral where the Hereford bull was penned up, then crossed fifty yards of open ground to the red schoolhouse.

He drew rein and studied the front of the building, a flurry of snow spinning around him. Because of the iron-gray sky the windows on either side of the door were opaque and stared back at him like lifeless eyes. Inside the kids were quiet, probably studying their ciphers, he guessed. Or was Trixie telling them about the good old days in Santa Fe?

After a while he stood in the stirrups and yelled, "Trixie Lee! Come out!"

The children's voices raised in an excited babble and Trixie hushed them into silence.

"Trixie Lee!" Creeds yelled. "Get out here! I won't tell you a second time."

The door opened a crack and the woman's voice called out, "What do you want, Creeds?"

"Me, I want nothing, Trixie. But good ol' Zeb wants his woman back in his bed. He says he's hurting for you real bad, if you get my meaning."

"I'm not going back," Trixie called out. "I'm not going anywhere with you, Creeds."

Creeds relaxed in the saddle and smiled. "Trixie, Zeb paid two hundred dollars for you, fair and square as ever was. You're his property. Now get the hell out here or I'll come in after you."

"You heard the lady. She's not going anywhere with you."

The gunman's head turned like a striking snake toward the handsome young man who lounged against the corner of the building. The man's sheepskin was open and he wore a belted Colt.

Creeds' yellow, reptilian eyes glowed. "Who the hell are you?"

"Me? I'm the man who's throwing you off this property."

"Give me a name." Under Creeds' sparse mustache,

his thin lips were peeled back from his teeth. "Damn it, boy. I never did cotton to gunning a nameless man."

"Name's Shawn O'Brien. I'm co-owner of this ranch, and you're on it, Creeds, which is causing me no little distress."

"So you've heard of me, O'Brien?"

"Some talk."

"What did you hear?"

"That you're a tinhorn killer who'll cut any man, woman, or child in half with a shotgun for fifty dollars."

"Hard words, O'Brien. And payment for such words don't come cheap." A wrong-handed man, Creeds slipped his left hand into the pocket of his coat.

But suddenly he was looking into the muzzle of Shawn's Colt.

"Mister," Shawn said, "when you bring that mitt out, either have a prayer book in it or nothing at all."

As slow as molasses, Creeds' long-fingered hand spidered out of his pocket. "All right. You got the drop on me, O'Brien."

"Seems like."

"I want to talk with Trixie."

"You've already done that, and she's not interested in anything you have to say."

Creeds, irritated that he'd been shaded on the drop by a hick with cow crap on his boots, turned away from Shawn and yelled with a vicious edge to his voice, "Trixie! Get the hell out here!"

The triple click of Shawn's cocked Colt was an exclamation point of sound in the snow-spun morning. "Mister, I warned you—"

But he bit off his remaining words when the school-house door opened and Trixie Lee stepped outside.

Creeds grinned. "Good to see you again, Trixie. Now get up on the back of this here hoss. We got some travelin' to do."

The girl shook her head. "I told you I'm not going anywhere with you, Silas."

"And I told you that Zeb wants you back."

"Zeb doesn't want me." Her fingers touched the deep scar that ran from the corner of her left eye to her mouth. "He just can't handle the thought that a woman would even think about running out on him."

"That doesn't signify with me, Trixie. But Zeb paid two hundred dollars for you, more than your puncher friend here makes in a year. The way I see it, he ain't getting his money's worth what with you lighting a shuck for a schoolhouse on a hick ranch an' all."

"I'll pay him back. Tell him that. It may take me a couple years, but I'll repay every last cent of his money."

Creeds shook his head. "He wants his woman, not the money."

"Then he can go to hell," Trixie spat out. "And tell him to take you with him."

"You heard the lady," Shawn said, stepping away from the corner of the building. "Now fork that bronc on out of here and don't even think about coming back."

Creeds smiled and glanced at the sky. Lifting his top hat, he revealed a bald head covered with a red bandana.

"Oh, I'll be back, cowboy, count on it. No man gets the drop on Silas Creeds and lives to boast of it."

Holding the hat with his right hand inside it, he brushed off a few flakes of snow from the crown.

A moment later, a bullet slammed into the hat.

Chapter 2

The bullet hit the holstered derringer under the crown, and rammed the sneaky gun with venomous force into Creeds' hand. The man yelped, let the top hat drop, and shook his stinging fingers.

"I seen that tinhorn trick for the first time twenty years ago. It didn't fool me then and didn't fool me now." Grim old Luther Ironside, the Dromore *segundo*, walked from the corner of the schoolhouse behind a smoking Colt. "You heard Mr. O'Brien, Creeds. Now git off his damned property."

Creeds was livid, raging beyond anger. The gunman's face twisted into a demonic mask of hate as he stepped along the ragged edge of insanity. He was enraged enough to draw.

"Try it, Creeds." Ironside's voice was low and dangerous. "See what happens." Snow flurried around him and his gray hair tossed in the wind. He looked like an Old Testament prophet come to justice.

Creeds was game, but he backed off like a snail into its shell when he saw Ironside adopt the classic gun-fighter pose, right arm extended, the revolver steady in his fist, left foot forming a T behind the heel of the right, deciding he didn't want any part of the tall old man. Not that day. "Mister, I'll be back and I'll kill you."

Ironside nodded. "Yeah, you do that, sonny. But wait until them fingers o' your'n have straightened out some. A blowed-up sneaky gun stings like the dickens."

Creeds swung back to Trixie. "Last chance."

The girl shook her head, turned on her heel, and rushed back into the schoolhouse.

"I'm going, O'Brien," Creeds said. "But I'll be back and I'll bring down the fires of hell on this place."

Shawn picked up the man's hat and handed it to him. "You'll need that. Keep your head warm."

The gunman cursed, then swung his horse away and was soon swallowed by cartwheeling snow, winter dark-ness, and distance. His threat hung in the air and made the morning foul.

"We should've killed that feller, Shawn," Ironside said. "I figger I taught you better than that."

"I thought about it. But it didn't seem to call for a shooting."

"Damn it, he had a sneaky gun,"

"Yes, he did at that. Why didn't you kill him, Luther?"

Ironside was silent for a moment, but couldn't find

an answer. Finally, he said, "Well, your brother Jacob would've gunned him right off."

"Probably."

"No probably. Jake would've gunned him fer sure."

"Yes . . . he . . . would . . ."

Ironside snorted like an angry bull. "Hell, Shawn, you're not listening to me."

"I'm thinking, Luther."

"Thinking, huh? Well study on this— if you've got the drop on a man, never let him take his hat off. I teached you that a long time ago."

Shawn smiled. "I guess I must've slept through that lesson."

"I guess you did, an' it near got your fool head blowed off."

"But you were around to save me, Luther, as always."

"Damn right I was, as always."

Shawn quickly stepped close to the old man, taking him by surprise, then laid a smacking kiss on Ironside's unshaven cheek. "You're my hero, Luther." He grinned.

Ironside rubbed his cheek as though he'd just been stung by a hornet. "Damn it, boy, don't ever do that again."

Shawn laughed and walked toward the schoolhouse.

Ironside watched him until he opened the door and stepped inside. Only then did Ironside smile. God knows, he'd tanned their hides often enough doing it, but he'd taught his O'Brien boys right. No doubt about that.

* * *

When Shawn stepped into the school, the black eyes of a dozen kids turned to him. All were the children of the Dromore vaqueros, and their education was one of his father's pet projects.

His spurs chiming in the sudden hush, Shawn walked to the front of the class. He smiled at the teacher he knew only as Julia. "We have to talk."

The woman nodded, realizing that the morning's events had changed everything. She turned to her class. "Children, the snow is getting heavier. I'm letting school out early today."

The kids had learned enough English to understand the gist of that. They cheered before stampeding out the door in a wild tangle, perhaps fearful that Miss Julia might change her mind.

After the children left, Julia said, "I guess I've got some explaining to do."

Shawn nodded. "Trixie Lee to Miss Julia Davenport is quite a leap. It confuses a man."

"Julia Davenport is my real name. I was Trixie Lee when I worked in Zebulon Moss's saloon in Santa Fe. He gave me that name and I've always hated it."

"All right. Tell me about it," Shawn said, his chin set.

But Julia saw no accusation or judgment in his eyes. Rather she saw a reined patience, a man waiting for what was to come. She wiped off the chalked blackboard with a yellow duster, giving herself time to collect her thoughts and leaving circular white smears that matched the color of her face.

Shawn came from a direction she didn't expect. "Did Moss give you the scar on your face?"

Julia turned then shook her head. "No, no, he didn't."

Shawn waited. The only sound in the room was the whisper of the north wind around the eaves and, far off, the voices of the children.

"My mother did that with a carving knife," Julia explained. "It was part of a carving set that had been a wedding present to her and Pa."

"What happened?"

"She went crazy. Mad, I guess you'd say. Pa failed at everything he'd tried in life, including the poems he wrote that nobody ever published. Farming on the Kansas plains was his last chance to make good. Have you ever been in Kansas?"

Shawn shook his head.

"It's a flat, lonely place, grass as far as the eye can see and not a tree in sight. Well, Ma stuck it out for five years—five years of drought, prairie fire, torrential rains, blizzards, whirlwinds, locusts, rattlesnakes, and gray wolves, to say nothing of horse thieves and begging, destitute Indians." Julia smiled. "What is it they say? 'In God we trusted, in Kansas we busted.' That's how it was with us, and with our poverty came not only hunger but the death of hope."

"When you talk about Kansas, you shut your eyes," Shawn said.

"I'm seeing it again, just like it was, so lonely and bleak."

"And it finally drove your ma mad?"

"Yes. I guess it was the loneliness that drove her mad, that and the constant prairie wind. The wind blows day and night and it never stops, not for a moment. Then one day, she went outside the cabin and screamed and screamed and we thought her screams would never end. Finally Pa took her inside and she was quiet for a few days. I mean she didn't speak or eat; she just stared and stared at nothing. Then, on the Sabbath, after Pa had read from the Bible, Ma got the carving knife and stabbed my little sister Bethany through the heart. She slashed at me and gave me the scar on my face, then she cut her own throat."

Julia blinked, seeing pictures she didn't want to see. "There was blood everywhere. The cabin was full of blood, red, scarlet blood on the floor, on the walls, all over Pa, all over me. Then Pa roared as though he was in pain and he held Ma and my sister to him for a day and a night and then another day. We buried the bodies away from the house, but shallow because the ground was hard with frost. The coyotes came and took them and we never found anything of Ma or Bethany again."

"I'm sorry," Shawn said, knowing how inadequate that sounded.

Julia took a breath and continued. "After that we moved to Dodge, where Pa thought he might prosper in the dry goods business, but he died of nothing more serious than a summer cold within a year."

Shawn stepped to a side window and looked outside. Sky and earth were the same shade of dark purple, and snow cartwheeled through the sullen day, driven by a wind cold as a stepmother's breath. Julia had lit the oil lamp on her desk, but its dull orange glow did little to banish the gloom shadowing the schoolhouse.

"So you were left alone in the world," Shawn said. "You were just a child, I guess."

"I lived as best I could for a while, then I jumped a deadheading freight to Wichita. I couldn't find a job, so I worked the line for the next three years for a four-hundred-pound gal I knew only as Big Bertha. That's where Zeb Moss found me. I'd just reached my seventeenth birthday."

"And he gave you a new name," Shawn said.

"And a job. He paid Bertha two hundred dollars for me and made me a hostess in his saloon in Santa Fe. He said with my scarred face I'd have freak value to customers who valued such things."

"So after a while you ran away and came here?"

"Not for a couple years. I became Zeb's kept woman and he never let me out of his sight. Then I read an advertisement in the newspaper about a teaching job and answered it. I made my break from Zeb when Colonel O'Brien wrote, telling me the job was mine."

"You sent references to the colonel," Shawn said. "Pa said you were obviously a genteel young lady of good breeding and that you'd worked as a tutor back East."

Julia smiled slightly. "Say what's on your mind, Shawn. Tell me I'm not a genteel young lady at all. I'm just a cheap whore and now my pimp wants me back."

Chapter 3

Julia Davenport's words stung Shawn O'Brien like wasps, yet he had to push her and discover why the colonel could make such a mistake. "Your references were impeccable. You sent three letters of recommendation from good Boston families that fooled even Pa, and he's not a man easily hoodwinked."

Julia looked like a woman in pain. "The letters were forged by a Caddo Indian by the name of Billy One Wing. He's got only one arm, but he's the best counterfeiter in the business. He gets a lot of work from Zeb, and I gave him mine. I trusted Billy because he doesn't like white men and knows when to keep his mouth shut."

Shawn nodded. "He must be good to have fooled the colonel."

"Billy One Wing could fool anybody." Julia took her cloak from the peg on the wall and threw it around her shoulders. She doused the oil lamp, then said, "Well, shall we go see the colonel?"

"You're a good teacher, Julia. Everybody agrees on that."

"My ma taught me to read and cipher. The rest I know comes from books."

"I'll talk to the colonel first," Shawn said. "Prepare the way."

"What difference does it make? You know he'll fire me and throw me out of Dromore."

"If he does, what will you do?"

"I don't know. Run somewhere else, I guess. Just keep on running until Zeb Moss tires of chasing me."

Shawn thought for a moment, and then said, "Everything blew up this morning, Julia. Under different circumstances I would've said nothing to the colonel about your past, but suddenly you're a danger to Dromore. You heard Silas Creeds. He means to do us harm if he can."

"I understand, Shawn. You must do what you have to do. I'll survive."

"I'll talk to him," Shawn offered again. "When we go back to the house, just go to your room and wait."

"For what?"

"For whatever the colonel decides."

"Is he down on whores?"

"He's down on anything or anyone that's a threat to Dromore."

"And that includes me?"

"Yes. I'm afraid it does,"

Julia nodded. "Then I'll do as you say."

She and Shawn walked to the door, but Julia stopped and looked up at the tall O'Brien brother. "Knowing what you've learned about me, could you love a woman like me, Shawn?"

Shawn smiled. "What kind of question is that to ask a man?"

"It's simple enough. Could you love a woman like me?"

"I don't know."

"Is it the scar? In your eyes am I the troll that lives under the bridge?"

"No, you're a beautiful woman, Julia. I think that scar adds to your attractiveness, not detracts from it."

Julia absorbed that. "The reason I asked is I want a man to love me one day."

"One day a man will, depend on it."

"But not you?"

"I've still got growing to do, Julia. Maybe a few years from now I could, but not right now."

"An honest answer."

"It's how I feel."

"Will you give me your arm when we walk to the house?"

"I'd be honored," Shawn said.

"So she's a whore," Luther Ironside said to the others gathered in the parlor of Dromore. "Damn me, but I knew it all along. I can just tell, you understand?"

Colonel Shamus O'Brien winced. "Luther, you think every woman is a whore until she proves otherwise, usually to your disappointment."

"Shawn, how seriously do you take Silas Creeds' threats?" Samuel, Shawn's oldest brother, looked at him in earnest.

"He's a killer, Sam," Shawn said. "I take anything he says seriously and so should you."

"Damn, I should've plugged him when I had the chance," Ironside whined.

"If it's not him, it will be somebody else," Shawn said. "Zebulon Moss wants his woman back and he'll kill to get her."

"Why?" Samuel asked. "I mean, she's a pretty woman, even with the scar an' all, but if what I've heard about Moss is correct, he's rich enough to get any woman he wants."

"How do you know, Sam?" Patrick, Shawn's brother, asked.

"You mean about Moss?"

"Yeah. How do you know he's rich?"

"He owns half of Santa Fe. I heard that the last time I was up that way, and there are some who reckon ol' Zeb got his start in the bank-robbing profession. Of course they don't say it out loud. Silas Creeds is just one of the thugs he hired to keep his business interests running smoothly."

"You mean his saloons?" Shamus asked.

"Saloons, opium, prostitution, the protection racket, you name it. Zeb's got a dirty finger in a lot of pies."

"Enough about Moss," Shawn said. "We're supposed to be talking about Julia Davenport."

"Hell, get rid of her, I say," Ironside said. "We don't want a whore teaching our kids. God knows what she'll tell them."

"Luther," Shamus said, "may I remind you that when you served in my regiment in the war you ran a few rackets of your own, including, but not limited to, selling rotgut whiskey to the new recruits and acquiring fancy women for their officers. And if memory serves me correctly, you and the quartermaster regularly traded coffee and flour to the Rebs for cigars, chewing tobacco, and Confederate scrip and made a tidy profit doing it."

Ironside opened his mouth to speak, but the colonel held up a silencing hand. "As for teaching, you taught my sons about whoring, drinking, cussing, gunfighting, and riding fast horses. Readings from Holy Scripture were notably absent from your curriculum, as was righteous instruction on the path to eternal redemption."

Satisfied that he'd stated his case in an exemplary fashion, Shamus sat back in his wheelchair. "Now, Luther, no more about who should teach who, please. You are hardly qualified to have any opinions on the matter."

Patrick grinned. "I bet you're sorry you spoke, Luther."

Ironside growled something under his breath and Shamus said, "What? What was that?"

"Nothing," Ironside said. "I didn't give my opinion on nothing."

"And I should hope not," Shamus said. "The very idea."

"Do you gentlemen mind if I say something?" Samuel's wife Lorena interrupted.

"Please do," Shamus said, scowling at Ironside. "It will be a pleasant change to hear someone talk common sense for a change."

"We hired a teacher, not a past," Lorena pointed out. "As it happens, Julia is an excellent teacher and the children love her. What more can we ask of her?"

"Hear, hear," Patrick said.

"I don't think it's for men, including you, Luther, to sit in judgment on her. It was men who used and abused Julia in the past and if you send her packing, you'll be continuing that abuse, all of you."

"Hear, hear," Patrick said again.

Shamus looked at him. "Patrick, don't say that again." To Lorena he said, "There is a possibility that she could—"

"Probability," Shawn interrupted.

"Bring danger to Dromore. How do you address that, Lorena?"

"Colonel, you've never shied away from danger before."

"True, but Miss Davenport is not kin. She's a stranger to us. But she's an employee of this ranch and deserves a fair hearing. She's our schoolteacher and an important part of Dromore, no doubt about that." Shamus turned to his sons. "Patrick, Samuel, and Shawn, your opinions, please."

"What about me?" Ironside said.

"You've already made your feelings known, Luther," Shamus said.

"But I've changed my mind, Colonel. What Lorena said about us being no better than the men who abused her in the past kinda rang true with me."

"A most singular change of mind indeed, Luther," Lorena said. "But of the greatest moment." She looked around the study. "Well, what do the brothers O'Brien think?"

Shawn cast his vote. "I'm for keeping her right here at Dromore."

"I agree." Patrick nodded.

"That sets fine with me," Samuel agreed.

"Colonel?" Lorena looked to her father-in-law.

"I'll think on this and give you my answer in the morning," Shamus said. "I will pray to Our Lady of Good Counsel and beg her advice on this matter."

"Good. She's a woman." Lorena smiled.

"And the virgin mother of God," Shamus said.